Inked: Rise of a Sorceress by JV Delaney
Published by JV Delaney

1ˢᵗ Edition 2020, paperback.

ISBN: 978-1-925999-53-2 (print)
       978-1-925999-54-9 (epub)
       978-1-925999-55-6 (mobi)

Publishing services by: PublishMyBook.Online

Inked
Rise of a Sorceress

BOOK TWO

JV DELANEY

Chapter One

I have left behind the creatures I admire and adore to live in the harsh Outback. It's the punishment I've given myself for Drake's death.

It has been four long boring months since I left Elyograg Castle and I wonder how Raven is and if she has had the baby. I wish she had a phone, as my telepathy isn't strong enough to reach her.

My heart skips several beats when my thoughts drift to Lazarus. When memories of leaving him control my dreams, I wake up distressed and breathless and gasping for air.

As much as my heart and soul cries for him, leaving will keep him and the elite creatures safe. It takes all my strength to push the memory of them away.

I have travelled in an unknown direction, stopping in small country towns where the locals are friendly, but sometimes too friendly. They want to know everything about my past and what I am doing now. I tell them enough to satisfy their curiosity.

An elderly couple has kept me in work on their cattle station for the past four weeks. I help drive their cattle from out in the middle of nowhere to the main homestead. The temperatures reach a blistering heat and the work is exhausting with little or no reward, but I feel at peace rocking side to side on my horse as we drive the cattle over millions of acres of bushland. My food and board are covered, with an extra two hundred dollars handed to me each week. It's a lonely life and not one I had envisioned when

I'd started out at the beginning of the year.

They have several Aboriginal staff that politely nod and keep to themselves. They seem wary of me. It's as though their gods have told them who and what I am, or maybe they can smell the blood on my hands. We work side by side without speaking, which suits me just fine.

Today's no different. Blue Boy walks at a slow comfortable pace behind the cattle. I remove my Akubra hat, reach for my bottle of water, then splash it over my face. I take a mouthful, swish it around, then spit it out. The amount of dust I eat walking behind this mob is disgusting.

Up ahead, a lone steer heads off on an old track. 'I'll get it!' I yell and, to my surprise, I get a grunt as an acknowledgement from one of the men.

I jump Blue Boy into a canter and head to the far side of the steer. I need to cut him off but keep behind his shoulder so he doesn't stop and turn back on me.

The steer shies away from something. It's my handsome wedge-tailed eagle. The steer soon loses interest and drops its head to eat the dried grass, giving me time to chat.

'Hello, big fella!' I say, stopping my horse beside it. I'm always happy when I get my weekly visit. It gives me a chance to talk where someone cares enough to listen.

'You won't believe it, but I just got my first grunt from one of the men! Things are starting to look good.'

The large eagle is perched on top of a small tree, its weight making the branch bend.

'I wish I understood the connection you have with me. Don't get me wrong, I'm not complaining, I'd be lonely if I didn't have you.'

It turns its head side to side, always looking out for anything coming our way.

'You don't need to worry, we are alone. And I don't need to

use any of my senses; the stockmen never wait for me. They're still scared of me.'

The eagle squawks and rustles its feathers.

'I miss Lazarus. It's hard to keep my mind occupied whilst droving. It always drifts back to him. And then I start to wonder if Raven has had her child and who it looks like.' I sigh, as images flash before me of the ones I've left behind.

'If there's any chance you're an elite creature, now would be a good time to reveal it.'

The eagle stops twisting its head and looks directly at me. I hold my breath in anticipation of it changing form. It spreads its large wings wide open and flaps them a few times before folding them in. I don't want to offend it, so I decide not to question it further, as its company is appreciated and some days, needed.

The lone steer realises the rest of the mob has moved on and calls out.

'That's my cue to get back to work. Fly safe, my friend, and I'll see you next week.' I'm amazed that it waits until I finish my whiny tale before squawking and flying away.

When I reach the yards, the Aboriginal men have corralled the cattle and have started to castrate, tag and drench them.

'This one tried to get away,' I chuckle, as I push the stray into the corral. I'm not surprised when they ignore me.

I look at them one at a time. I don't and have never existed to these men. 'I'll tend to your horses.' I wait for some small reply; a wave of a hand, a sniff, a grunt, anything. But nothing.

'That would be great! Thanks, Jasmine. Oh, you're very welcome,' I say loud enough for them to hear. I head over to attend to their horses. 'I'm feeling the love, boys.'

It's Friday night and, for the last month, the men and I have headed into town to the local pub for dinner. It's always a quiet car drive. If one of them accidentally speaks, it's spoken in their dialect so I can't understand. None of them ever holds eye contact with me; their heads look out the truck window. As soon as we arrive at the pub they head straight into the bar and leave me standing outside alone.

I head into the dining room to over-drink and eat a half-decent meal. I have drunk more alcohol in the last four months than I have in my entire life. It numbs the pain when I remember Grandfather, Drake and Lazarus. Alcohol is a band-aid for my broken heart.

I order the same boring meal each time—Chicken Parmigiana. I keep my eyes low because I don't want to talk to anyone, even though the local stockmen and women come here for their social catch up. There are stables and yards out back where locals and travellers can leave their horses or trucks overnight.

Tonight's no different from any other. The timber-lined dining room has a dozen locals who have pulled chairs and tables together to socialise. I've chosen a small table away from everyone and close to an open window. I'm waiting for the cooler night air to come and dry the sweat from my body.

My meal is placed in front of me together with my fourth glass of Jack. I'm exhausted and, with the added drug of alcohol, I'm trying to keep my head from falling into my plate of food. I've turned my back on my powers except for my silencing spell. I use it to block out the loud and cheerful voices around me, altering it to a more of a rumbling hum.

While concentrating on holding my eating tools and guiding them through my chicken, I hear a voice as clear as day.

'Hello, beautiful,' the voice echoes. I swing my head up and see a tall young man standing in front of me. *'You can*

hear me, can't you?' His lips stay perfectly still.

I panic; I don't want him to know I can hear him. I drop my face, placing it several inches from my plate and continue to eat.

'Can I join you?' he asks in a normal loud voice.

'No!'

'Come on, Jasmine. Where is your Melbournian hospitality?'

My head shoots up, my jaw dropping wide open. Who is he and how does he know my name?

I let my eyes roll over him, taking in his features. He has long brown hair; the healthiest hair I have seen on a man. It even shines under the gloomy pub lights. His eyes are blue, similar to Raven's and mine, but lighter than a gargoyle's.

'I don't know you. Leave me alone or I will ask the bouncer to remove you.' I drop my head to stare at my food.

'We are in the middle of nowhere. There's no bouncer here.' He pulls out a chair and sits. 'I know your cousin, Sky.'

I ignore him and continue to eat my meal.

'Would you like another drink?'

'Sure, as long as I don't have to pay for it.' He stands and heads for the bar. I watch out of the corner of my eye as he orders himself a beer then hesitates when ordering my drink.

'Is it Jack Daniels and Coke, Jasmine?' He echoes and, without thinking, I nod my head. Shit! How stupid am I? I silently hit myself in the back of the head.

He smiles and nods back. *'Now, that wasn't so hard, was it?'*

I contemplate running for the door but I don't have my truck. I could run into the bar where my workmates are but they're already sceptical about me and would leave me for the devil to take.

He returns quicker than expected. He places my drink in front of me and I scull the remaining Jack from my original glass. 'Thanks.'

'You are very welcome.'

'Use your voice or leave. I won't use my telepathic power for no reason.'

'I didn't mean to offend you,' he says. 'I sensed you when I walked in and felt a connection to Sky.'

'I'm at a disadvantage, as you know my name and I don't know yours.'

'How rude of me. I am Ronan.'

'Just Ronan?'

'You know very well the elite creatures in our line of work never divulge surnames.'

'How do you know Sky?'

'I knew her when she first left home but unfortunately, I have lost contact with her.'

'That doesn't answer my question. I will ask once more before leaving you to sit here by yourself. How do you know Sky?'

'We were best mates and lived together for a long time. She wanted to travel and seek out a clan of gargoyles and dragons that her grandfather used to work with. I stayed with several other sorcerers to learn as much as I can. I have been travelling for the last two years trying to find her.'

'Were you two dating?'

'We were just good mates. Apparently, she had just got out of a relationship with a dragon when I met her.'

'Ah, Falcon. That was many years ago.'

'So you have been in contact with her recently? I'm having trouble tracking her.'

I ignore his question and ask another of my own. 'When you walked over, you said you sensed me. How?'

'When a sorcerer kills a dragon, you inherit its sense of sensitive hearing and heightened sense of smell. A heartbeat sounds like a drum kit next to my ear. I presume you have never killed a dragon.'

'I don't go around killing things. Plus, I have never seen a dragon,' I shrug my shoulders. I killed Attor and my senses are the same, so he must be lying. I have an uneasy feeling about this stranger. 'Why did you kill the dragon?'

'It was either him or me.'

'I find that hard to believe. I've heard they're good at heart and non-threatening.'

'It depends if they want something you've got.' He smirks, picking his drink up and taking a sip.

'What is it you have that is so special?' I raise my eyebrows, intrigued.

'Are you that naïve? They pretend to be your best friend, your lover and your mate for life, but all they want is your sorcery. There's a war happening in London and it is soon to spread to Australia. After the European dragons eradicate the gargoyles over there and keep only those loyal to them, they will come here.

'Australia has such vast lands where they will be able to breed and train without being seen by the human eye. After creating an army, they will attack any creature that doesn't bow to them. We, my dear Jasmine, are tools in their evil plan.'

'I'm nobody's tool!'

'When was the last time you saw Sky? Or has she changed her name?'

'Her name is still Sky and I haven't seen her since she left home.'

'Jasmine, we can do this the hard way or the easy way,' he says in a low angry tone.

'What do you want with her?'

'She needs to join me in the hunt for dragons. We need to kill and gain the power of the strongest dragons in Australia before the others come and beat us to it. Then, with the remaining dragons, we will control or kill the gargoyles that rebel against us.'

'You deluded control freak!'

'It's you who's deluded. Why should we stand back and let foreigners rule our land? Who's to say we can't rule it? It's our country and our creatures.'

'For one, the creatures are not ours. Two, no one should rule the creatures in Australia. They are free just as you and I are.'

'Is that why the creatures hide from humans? Because they're free?'

'They hide because the human race is greedy. They'll use them for entertainment, lock them up in cages or dissect them to satisfy their own curiosity. The creatures would never be free amongst the humans.'

'With me as their ruler, they will. With Sky beside me and you and the gargoyles under my command, we will take on the foreigners before taking on the rest of Australia.'

'Again, you're very much deluded if you think Sky or I would help you kill a creature. Plus, I'm sure the gargoyles will fight back if their lives are under threat.'

'They won't attack first, which gives us sorcerers the upper hand. They are useless!'

'Gargoyles will fight if their family castle is about to be overrun. They're not fairies; they're strong creatures that can rip you to shreds. Personally, I wouldn't tick one off.'

'Sounds as though you know more than you're saying.' He leans over and grabs hold of my arm. 'If we breed the gargoyles without giving them a soul from the vault we can train them to fight on our command. A soulless gargoyle is a strong weapon.'

He shuffles his chair closer to me, his grip becoming firmer. 'How advanced is your sorcery?'

'Telepathic waves are all I have. I don't acknowledge or want to be a part of that world so I've closed it down.'

'Well, sweet Jasmine, I'm not giving you a choice. You will

reveal where your beloved cousin is or I will force it from you. I can and will make you will tap into your sorcery the hard way.' He snarls and digs his fingers into my arm.

'What the hell? Let go of my arm. You're hurting me!'

'Yell all you want, most of the men here are either drunk or sense that I am something they don't want to cross. Superstition scares most of the Aboriginals away.' He laughs. 'So what is it going to be?'

'Let me go!' I stand up and rip my arm from his grasp. I race into the public bar. The men look up but then drop their eyes to their beers. I turn around to find Ronan towering over me. He places his large hand on my shoulder.

'I told you they don't want to cross me and nor should you,' he whispers close to my ear. 'See? I'm already a ruler.'

'I don't know where she is and if I did I still wouldn't tell you. I don't see how I can help you in any way. I refuse to kill anything, especially a dragon!' I shrug his hand from my shoulder.

He lifts his head as if he smells something, similar to what a dog would do. 'Fire. I can hear fire and smell smoke.'

I listen but I can't hear anything. 'I can hear…'

'Come with me now!' He latches onto my arm and drags me out of the pub towards the barn. As we round the corner of the pub I can hear the heart-wrenching sound of screaming horses. He's right. The barn is on fire.

'There are horses in the stables!' I run as fast as my legs can carry me.

Ronan is beside me as we arrive at the inferno that covers the barn's entrance. He opens his hands and I see the swirling anorics forming in his open palms.

'Your anorics are black. You're drawing from negative energy!'

'It's the only way to win. I tried to tell Sky the same thing but she wouldn't listen and ran from me. I'll teach you how to draw on this dark side and together we will eradicate any creature that crosses our path.'

Ronan turns his concentration back to the flames in front of us. 'I will shoot a hole in the side of the barn and hope I don't hit my horse.' He lifts his hands higher and is about to launch his anorics.

'Don't, you'll hit them! I'll run through and release the horses.' I don't wait for his reply and, without hesitating, run into the flames, praying I won't get burnt again.

I hit the wall of fire with my eyes closed and keep running until my skin stops stinging. I pray I'm through the flames when I slowly open my eyes. The heat is intense and I can smell my singed hair. Or is it the horses' hair?

The smoke is thick, making it difficult to breathe. Removing my t-shirt, I place it over my mouth and nose. It helps. I run past three stables which have several horses screaming in fear, unhitching their latches as I go.

The last three stable doors have caught on fire and I race to unlock them. My hands are burning and I cough, trying to find clean air for my lungs. I squint, trying to see through the thick smoke as I unhitch the last door.

Three horses are still inside the stable with me. They're panicking and confused, not knowing which direction they should run. I'm unable to inhale a lungful of clean air to yell so I wave my burnt hand behind the rumps of the horses. Pressing my t-shirt hard up against my face, I slap one horse on his rump and he takes off, with another shooting out the back of the barn.

The last horse is staring down at me, wide-eyed, galloping on the spot in pure fear. I drop my t-shirt and, using both hands, force him to face the direction I want him to go. I race behind him and slap his large rump. He lets out a frightened kick with both back legs, barrelling me in the stomach, which forces me to the barn floor. I see his rump as he runs out the rear of the barn.

I try to stand but his kick has winded me and my body disobeys any order I give it. I try to calm my panicked and lost breath, but any air I gain is filled with smoke. Defeated, I drop my head back, lying flat, looking up at the inferno above me. The roof is a firestorm and I fear this may be my end.

I cough, gasping for clean air, feeling my lungs burn as I inhale the intense heat. Parts of the roof are falling and caving in with fierce blazing debris landing beside me. I try again to move but my body is a lead weight.

Closing my eyes, I picture Lazarus in his handsome human form then I see him in his magnificent red dragon form. I blink several times, trying to lubricate my eyes. The walls are lacquered with flames with the roof breaking apart and falling toward me. This is my last chance to survive. I need to roll over and crawl out of this burning barn.

My throat is on fire as I draw a deep breath, summoning up all the strength I have. But as I'm about to roll over my legs are pinned back down by blistering debris. 'Ah! Help me! Help!'

The smell of burning hair and flesh fills my nostrils. The pain has surpassed my threshold making it difficult to stay conscious.

I can't open my eyes—the heat is too intense.

This is my end. I see no escape. This is my punishment for the deaths of my loved ones.

My body no longer registers the pain and goes limp with defeat. I pray my death will be fast and that Lazarus will forgive me for never returning.

CHAPTER TWO

ALTHOUGH MY SKIN burns, I have a cool calmness flood me when I see Lazarus' emerald green eyes staring down at me.

Then everything goes black. Is this my death? Where's my angel to take me to heaven? It's said you're supposed to get chauffeured to heaven by an angel. What a load of hogwash! Dying is such a disappointment.

I pinch my leg—I'm still alive. I can hear the blazing barn roar and feel the heat but by some miracle, I'm sheltered.

I move my hand up and feel what is encasing me. It's something I will never forget—the lumpy scales of a dragon. Is a dragon taking me to heaven or is this…?

'Lazarus?' I force my murmured words through gasping breaths of air. I hear a low rumble and recognise it instantly. 'I love you.' I cough, gagging on the words, which may be my last.

'You need to leave. He will kill you on sight.' I cough then vomit. With the sound of a lion roaring and a jolt my body screams against, I am carried from the barn.

I draw in a deep lungful of clean air before seeing two black anorics head in our direction. Lazarus swerves, then gives a violent shudder before I black out.

'PLEASE, BEAUTIFUL. WAKE up.' I hear Lazarus' soft voice. 'I'm so sorry. Please wake up.'

I try to open my eyes but they stay closed. I can smell the stench of burnt skin and hair and wonder how badly I'm hurt.

His voice fades and I again black out.

The voices return and, even though I try, my eyes refuse to open. My voice rattles but only a murmur escapes. There's a fire crackling nearby and a cool compress is pressed against my body.

'How long before she wakes up, Jenny?' I hear Lazarus ask.

'She gonna be sleepin' a while. You need be patient.' I recognise the accent of an Aboriginal woman.

'Come hunt with me, brother. You no good to her hungry,' says a male Aboriginal.

'I can't leave her.' Lazarus' voice quivers.

'Bugger off! I take care of her,' the woman insists.

I hear several sets of feet move away. A cool compress is gently placed over my arms, chest, legs and face.

'What them things on her legs and face?' a young Aboriginal child asks.

'Look like tattoo to me. Not our business. That's white man's stuff,' the woman says. 'Go get more berries, son. Need to feed her. She's wakin' up.'

I try to open my eyes but nothing happens. I try to move my hand but the woman takes a gentle hold, restraining me.

'Keep still, girl,' she says in a gruff tone. She wipes my eyes with a wet liquid then pries them open, one at a time. I see her dark face staring at me, her small brown eyes calm and caring. 'You'll be good no time,' she adds, smiling her white teeth at me.

It takes a few minutes to react to the pain in my body. I cry out and try to sit up to see my injuries. She lifts me into a sitting position with her rough, strong hands.

My body is covered in large palm leaves. I lift one of them from my stomach to see my burnt skin covered in a brown-green coloured mud.

'It bush medicine,' the woman says, answering my silent question. 'My medicine make you sleep. You getting better but your spirit keep talking.'

'How long have I been asleep for?'

'Five days sleepin',' she says before a young boy walks out from behind a bush. His hands are full of berries. He comes towards me with hesitant steps, his torso slightly bent over as if he fears me.

I glance over the length of my body and notice I'm completely naked. I rearrange several leaves to cover my private areas. To my relief, the mud covers my breasts, giving me a little privacy.

The woman releases a boisterous laugh. The small boy moves closer, a tiny smile on his lips. I force a smile onto mine and try to shut out the shocking pain.

Their campsite is primitive. A campfire is the centrepiece, with a small shelter made from broken branches close by. Large river rocks, which have well-worn grooves in them, are filled with bush medicine and wild berries. There is animal flesh and skins hanging off large sticks over the fire which smells as burnt as I do.

The young boy squats and hands me a small ugly-looking berry. I open my hand and he drops it in my palm as if he is too scared to touch me. He picks one up and puts it into his mouth, then holds his tongue out, showing me the berry sitting on his tongue. Then he chews it and puts several more in his mouth.

I lift my hand to my mouth and place my berry on my tongue, chewing it as he has done. It tastes like a spicy apple.

He hands me a fistful and, with a polite smile, I take them.

'You eat good tucker.' The little fella smiles.

'It's delicious. Thank you.' I feel my cheeks crack with mud as I smile back.

I turn my head to see a large Aboriginal woman sitting cross-legged on the ground. She nods once at me as I take in her near-naked features. She has a skirt around her waist which resembles kangaroo hide and her large breasts have drooped and are sitting on her round belly. Her brown skin looks dry, as does her hair.

I wonder what I look like and where the hell I am. 'How did I get here?'

'Laz brought you here.'

'Lazarus?' I ask and she nods. 'What are your names?'

'Me Jenny. Boy is Jack.' Her face is a blank canvas showing no emotion. Her only reaction is her hand constantly shooing away several annoying flies.

'Thank you for taking care of me, Jenny.' I smile. 'How severe are my burns?'

'Don't know. Can only give you bush medicine. Your tattoos didn't burn.' She points to my legs and face.

I lift a leaf from my shin to see my markings darker than before but no visible burn marks.

'They heal good.' She shakes her head, looking away. Then she points to my face. 'Not my magic. That one came from the spirits. I put bush medicine on but it still came.'

'What do you mean? Do I have more tattoo markings?'

She waves her hand over one side of her face then mumbles something in her native tongue.

'I need to see it. Do you have a mirror?'

She laughs beneath her breath.

'I show you,' Jack says.

'Yes, please do.' Tears fill my eyes.

Jack stands and, with cautious moves, comes to sit beside me. He holds his hand up and as if in slow motion, points his index finger out. His small, thin finger touches the side of my face and trails a vine shape up my cheek to my forehead.

In an instant I picture the markings—they're the same as Raven's. The memory of her flashes before me and I see her radiant smile. She is a beautiful woman and her markings are attractive on her but I shudder to think how they look on me together with my burnt skin.

I gasp in horror at how I must look, making poor little Jack jump back.

'No, I'm sorry. I didn't mean to scare you. Thank you, Jack.' I try my hardest to smile but I burst into selfish tears. 'Jenny, where is the river or waterhole?'

'Just beyond these bushes.' She points to a large cluster of bushes behind me.

When I try to stand, my whole body yells at me and I crumble to the dusty ground. With a determined breath, I push to my feet, crying out in pain. Jenny is beside me and helps me walk to the river with young Jack several steps behind us.

I shuffle my feet into the cool river water. She walks me in deeper, where she washes the mud from my body. Her rough hands feel like sandpaper as she scrapes it away.

Now I can see my burns for what they are. My arms have skin missing, with vibrant pink sticky skin visible. I gag, trying to keep the handful of berries in my stomach.

I glance at my other arm as she scrubs it. She yells in her native tongue to little Jack. The next thing I see is my undies floating down the river, with little Jack in fits of laughter as the slow current brings them to us.

Jenny snatches them before they pass by and hand them to me. I reach under the water and slip them up my legs.

She helps me lay back and washes my hair and face. She gives my face a hard scrub where little Jack had said my new markings are. I smile and she shrugs her shoulders. The magical tattoos that keep appearing are a mystery and I fear my whole body will one day be full of ink.

She helps me stand up but I sink back under the cool water, relieving my pain.

'I had to cut your hair,' says Jenny, pulling her fingers through it. I lift my hand and feel chunks of it missing and the length is shorter than it has ever been. It's now above my shoulders and feels dry and knotty. I know now how the Elephant Man must have felt and wish I had a bag to put over my head.

Little Jack yells something and Jenny lifts her head. I panic and squat further under the water in case Ronan has found me.

'Laz is back. I will cook and you come up later.' She stops tugging at my hair and starts to head towards the river's edge.

'Please don't tell him I'm here.'

She stops and turns to look at me. 'Why? Because of this?' She waves her hand around her face, indicating my new facial ink.

'I know I'm vain but yes, and because of my scars.'

'Stupid white girl. He seen them already,' she snaps before walking up the riverbank with little Jack at her heels.

I look around and there's no recognisable landmark. I search for somewhere to hide then drop my head, remembering Lazarus will sniff me out where ever I hide, especially smelling like a burnt sausage. But if I keep under the water he may not hear my heartbeat.

'Jasmine.' Lazarus' voice is as soft as silk.

My heart flutters when I turn to see him standing on the river's edge.

He enters the water with his jeans on.

'No! Don't come any closer,' I say, through a flood of tears.

'Don't cry, babe. Everything will be all right.'

'I mean it. Stop or I will fire at you.' My threat stops him in his tracks.

'I would never hurt you on purpose. You know that. The fire was to get your attention away from the dark sorcerer.'

'You started the fire?'

'Yes. I never thought you'd endanger yourself and go in the barn.'

'Did you think I'd let innocent horses burn to death? Are you crazy?'

'I needed you out of the pub and into the clearing so I could grab you.'

'How did you know where to find me and that he was a black sorcerer?'

'I have been watching you for the last month. It has taken me all that time to find you. I've been miserable without you.' He drops his head as if ashamed.

I stand up so the water is lapping around my belly button. 'Look at what your misery has done. I'm a burnt freak!'

'Oh no, babe. You become more beautiful every day.' He walks deeper into the river.

I lift my hands out of the water and draw on the energy I've tried so hard to ignore. My white anorics ignite in my hands as I stare daggers at Lazarus.

'I said don't come near me and I meant it.' I force my words through gritted teeth.

He stops and withdraws, walking backwards out of the river. 'I am sorry for your injuries. But I can't live without you.'

'I'm not yours to love anymore.' Tears fall down my cheek. I close my hands and slam them into the water. It explodes around my fists, surging away from me as if I have just jumped into it.

'Don't say that. Please let's talk about this.'

'I forgave you once for puncturing me with your talons. I don't think I can forgive you again. Please do as I ask and leave. As you can no doubt see, I am naked and I need to find some form of clothing.'

My words are like a slap to his face. His eyes drop, as does his head, before he turns and heads back towards the campsite. I hear him mumble under his breath—he loves me.

My heart tightens like someone is squeezing it dry. I slowly swim to the edge of the river and sit, hugging myself tightly. I cry and rock my body, staring blank-minded at the river's pebble floor.

A small rock plops into the water near my legs. It doesn't scare me; my body and mind are too numb. I look up and see little Jack sitting in a gumtree with a leg either side of a thick branch.

'He gone.' He tilts his eyes to look at the sky.

I drop my head onto my folded knees and sob.

The air becomes cooler and my feet and hands are wrinkled from sitting in the water for so long. I hear the crunching of branches and leaves and pray that it's Falcon or Ronan coming to snuff me out, but instead, I see the stern face of Jenny carrying a black t-shirt.

'Stand up,' she orders. She breaks a thick stem of a plant, similar to an aloe vera branch. She wipes it over my wounds, then, with an abrupt movement, tosses me the black t-shirt. I'm shocked at how her attitude has changed and wonder why.

'He got shirt for you,' she snaps. I gather she is talking about Lazarus.

'I didn't ask him to follow me,' I murmur. 'Why did he have to follow me? I was dealing with not having him in my life and now I'm hideous for anyone to look at.' I fall back onto my bottom, curling my legs back up underneath me.

'Let me fix your hair.' She sits behind me, tugging at my knotted hair while trying to rake her fingers through it. When she comes to a knot, she rolls it in her fingers, breaking the hair to remove it. I doubt I will have any hair left on my head by the time she finishes.

'You can't blame him for this,' she says after a while. She waves her hands over my burnt arms and stomach. 'You ran into the fire. He didn't push you.'

'I didn't say he pushed me.' I receive a hard tug on my disappearing hair.

'Don't let your spirit darken.'

'I'm not,' I reply and she grunts at me.

'Blame you, not him. You did this. He watched over you for long time. He loves you and it breaks his spirit not being with you.'

'Trust me, my spirit broke the day I drove away from him. I have never loved someone that much and my mind refuses to let me forget him. But death follows me and there are people who will kill anyone I love to get to me.' Fresh tears start to roll down my cheek.

'Two of you together make one strong spirit. You can fight together.'

'He will die because he loves me. I won't allow it. I can't lose him too.'

'Isn't that my decision?' Lazarus says in a soft tone.

I whip my head around to see him standing behind us. Jenny struggles to her feet and hands Lazarus another branch of the shrub she'd previously rubbed all over me.

'Wash her in river. Then put on burns,' she orders before walking away.

'I can do it myself!'

'Stop it, Jasmine! And if you ever raise those hands at me again, I will bite them off.'

I stand up, holding up the t-shirt over my chest, shocked at his outburst. It takes several minutes before my shock turns to anger.

'Leave now!' I say, gathering up my courage. I hold one hand out to the side, threatening to ignite my white anoric.

Lazarus' eyes flicker and narrow. His heat radiates towards me before the red swirl kicks up around his feet. 'What the hell. You wouldn't dare!'

Unsure if his threat was more than just a scare tactic, I close my fist. He slows and stops the transformation and moves towards me. I step back, unsure of his actions.

He cocks his head to the side then points to the water. 'Now that we have an understanding, I will wash your wounds.'

'I can do it—'

'Enough!' With one stride he is beside me, tugging at the t-shirt I'm gripping to my chest. 'I've seen your naked body before.'

'That doesn't mean I want you to see it again.'

He inhales deeply through his nose and exhales a smoky breath. I cough and roll my eyes at him even though I'm a little intimidated. I have pushed his buttons before and I'm probably close to the edge of him losing it.

'I've inhaled enough smoke to last me a lifetime. So douse it, you cold-blooded lizard.' I wait for his eruption.

He moves around me, dragging me into the deep water. He pulls the t-shirt from me, throwing it onto the riverbank.

'Cold-blooded?' he questions in a whisper, moving behind me. The heat from his body is electric. He leans against me so his hot stomach is against my back while his hands run water up my arms and down again.

I close my eyes and try to keep my heartbeat sedated. I refuse to let him hear me.

'I'm very warm-blooded and you know it because you have felt it on more than one occasion, Jazz.'

His soft hands wash over me, my stomach and eventually my breasts. I try my hardest to sit on my heartbeat but it slips and releases a deafening thud. His lips are on my shoulder so I can feel his smile when I can't contain my heartbeat.

I listen to his and he is fighting to control it but it's calmer than mine, which irritates me more. He presses his body firmly against mine; his stomach to my back. The heat from his body is as welcoming as the evening breeze, which is cool on my skin.

'I'm not letting you out of my sight again,' he whispers, biting my earlobe and sending a surge of adrenaline through me.

I fight my heart with everything I have but the build-up is too much. I let go, allowing it to pump freely and loudly. His arms loosen around me and, within a second, he is facing me, his lime-green eyes locking with mine. He pulls our bodies together and the heat of it bites at my burns. I gasp in pain and he pulls away, dropping his eyes to my chest and stomach.

'I'm sorry; I forgot that my heat would do that.' His eyes are still looking at my chest.

'Excuse me, but my eyes are up here.'

'And what beautiful blue eyes you have.' His eyes widen with lustful delight. 'Let's get you dry. I want to drip this all over you.'

'How can you make something so basic sound so sexy?'

'I am known as a 'sex god' amongst the elite.' He chuckles, swoops me up and cradles me in his arms. In a blink, he as me on the banks of the river.

Lazarus stands dripping wet in his jeans as he rips open the plant and starts to gently rub it over my burns. He seems scared that he might hurt me as he glides it over my arms. He timidly trails it over my chest and stomach but this time I keep my breathing relaxed due to the stinging.

'Are you in pain?'

'Yes, but I have learnt how to push the pain away from my mind, whether it be physical or mental.'

'Did you push me out of your head?'

'Yes.' I drop my head before reaching for the black t-shirt. 'Every day I'd push you out because every morning when I woke you would be in it. I needed to stop loving you.' I slide the t-shirt over my head, wincing when it scrapes against my chest and stomach.

'Did it work?' He tilts my face up with his index finger so I am looking into his questioning eyes.

'Did what work?'

'Did you stop loving me?'

'No.'

'As each day passes I love you more and more.'

'I think I fell in love with you the day I met you.' I smile, then roll my eyes. 'Maybe not the first day I met you, or the second.'

'Hmm, the first day I met you I wanted to eat that delicious heart of yours. That is after I ripped it out of your lying chest.'

'I had to protect Drake from your evil claws.'

'I'm glad you did.' His smile drops as does mine. 'I would never have really hurt him. He was my friend.'

'Then you made me an unsuspecting villain in your crime to steal cows.' I playfully punch him in his arm, trying to move away from the subject of Drake.

'I did.' He chuckles. 'That was the night before I kissed you and after you kissed a gargoyle.'

'Oops!'

Lazarus growls deep in his chest but I know he's playing. He holds my face in his soft warm hands and I wait for the sting of my burns. Nothing.

I frown and he follows suit. 'What?'

'My face is burnt but I don't feel the pain like I do on my chest and stomach.'

'Your face has healed.' He takes a breath before continuing, 'You have fresh markings on your face, similar to Raven's.'

'I know. Little Jack traced them on my face.' I drop my head, feeling self-conscious about the way I now look.

'I think it makes you look more irresistible. You are the

most beautiful woman I have ever laid eyes on. Plus, your markings are as hot as hell. The way you're going, you will have more ink than I do.'

'If I looked like you, I wouldn't mind.'

'I'm kind of glad you don't look like me as that would be a big turn-off on my part. Babe, you are unbelievably beautiful, and it rips my heart out to hear you doubt my words. Anyhow, your markings aren't seen by the human eye, only the elite creatures.'

'Jenny and little Jack see them.'

'Aboriginals can see—'

I hold my hand up to stop Lazarus from telling me about their spiritual connection to nature, even though it would help me to understand what the men at the cattle station saw in me and why they kept clear of me. 'Don't tell me. I don't want to know.'

'Just know Aboriginals are healers and carers for all creatures and the land. Without them caring for the land, the elite would be drawing tainted energy from the earth. Elite creatures that are filled with tainted blood are dangerous, especially to the human race.'

He lifts my face and places his forehead against mine. Our eyes lock, green on blue, while his warm breath heats me. He slowly and tentatively leans his lips to mine and softly presses them together. I melt at his touch and am thankful his supporting arms are there to hold me without putting his body against mine.

His kiss becomes urgent, as if he needs it to breathe. I return the same passion, wishing he could hold me tightly in his arms. I need to be held by this loving man; the man I've tried so hard to eradicate from my memory. My mind constantly argued with my heart, which refused to give up the memories or the love I have for Lazarus.

His hot, heated tongue finds mine, starting the electric build-up between us. I pull back, panting from our marathon kiss.

'I can feel that electrical current start to build. If we keep going, I will singe the little remaining hair I have.'

He smiles, then it drops from his face. 'What?' I ask.

'The black sorcerer, Ronan. He has been stalking you for the last two weeks. He searched you out and has sat outside the pub the last few Friday nights but you walked out with several men and drove off in their truck. I heard him ask around, trying to find out which station you were working at, but either no one knew, or they didn't want to get involved.

'He waited for your return and I watched his every move. He may have killed a dragon and gained its senses but he doesn't know how to use them efficiently because not once did he sense me.'

'I killed Attor and I don't have any extra senses.'

'You haven't tapped into them yet. Raven was going to explain it to you, but you were so adamant on leaving, she thought best to let it lie dormant.'

'I don't think I want my hearing heightened. I don't want to hear what everyone is saying. I think it's rude.'

'It comes in handy sometimes.'

'I can already hear your heart.'

'Hmm, there's so much more to hear, babe,' he purrs, giving me a quick peck.

'Oh, that reminds me, have you eaten recently?' I wonder if my heart is sounding juicy to him.

'Yes, every day with Tom and sometimes with little Jack, much to his excitement.'

'You go in dragon form?'

'Sometimes. They believe all creatures have their own spirits and—'

I stop him talking with my lips by pressing them firmly onto his. 'Please don't tell me if they turn into dingoes or kangaroos. I don't think I could take it.'

He laughs. 'Come on. They're sitting around the campfire waiting for us to return. They were making bets on who would arrive back at the campsite alive.'

'And who did they bet on?'

'Little Jack said me, as did Tom. But Jenny told them they were "silly buggers" because you were one angry white woman.'

'It would be a good fight; me with my sorcery and you with… a little flame.'

Within a split second, Lazarus has me scooped up in his arms, making my head spin. 'You forget that I can move quicker than your eye can see and can have your sweet delicious heart in my razor-sharp talons before you knew it.' He nuzzles my chest with his warm nose.

As sneakily as I can, I draw a small current through my body and release it, shocking him.

He shudders but keeps his tight hold on me. 'Hilarious,' he growls with a smile.

'I don't know what you mean.' I play innocent before he latches onto my lips, kissing me hard and desperately.

Tom introduces himself with a nod and a swish of his hand to brush away the few flies that linger around his meal. Little Jack sits staring at both Lazarus and me as we eat the cooked flesh from their latest kill. Thankfully it's kangaroo, which I quite enjoy.

We sit around the fire, drawing in its warmth, as night-time in the Outback can become extremely cold. I shiver and Lazarus moves closer, wrapping his toned arm around me.

'I slept with you every night when you were sleeping,' he says.

'You seem to do that a lot.'

'I'll take advantage where I can.'

'Even when I'm incoherent?'

He laughs cheekily, showing his perfect white teeth. 'I can change form now and keep you warm. I don't want you to get sick.'

'Thanks, that would be great, as long as you've had enough to eat.' I grin and little Jack giggles.

'I'm fine. I haven't eaten little Jack yet. Have I, Jack?' This makes Jack laugh then roar as Lazarus does in dragon form.

'Were you roaring in front of them? Someone could have seen or heard you.'

'He screams 'coz you not wake up,' Jenny interrupts. 'And 'coz he got hurt.'

'What?' I swing my head and look directly into Lazarus' eyes.

'I was worried, that's all. It's not as if I was crying or anything.' His shoulders tense and he seems a little embarrassed.

'You got hurt?' I feel selfish and pathetic as I only ever seem to worry about myself.

'The sorcerer threw two black anorics and I could only avoid one as I didn't want to puncture your torso with my talons. I'm fine.'

I lean back and look over his toned chest, running my hands over it, trying to find his injury. He grabs my hand, stopping it from trailing further. 'Touching me like that could be dangerous when I'm about to change form. I can control myself to keep from eating you but...' He winks and gives a cheeky grin.

I smile, lifting my face to kiss his rosy lips. 'I love you too.'

He instantly relaxes his shoulders then pulls me in tightly. 'You need to sleep, babe.' He stands up and moves into an area clear of shrubs. 'Keep your voice low if you're talking to me as little Jack curls up on the outside of me. He enjoys my warmth as well.'

The ground swirls at his feet as he collects particles from the earth. It thickens and expands into an oval shape, filling the entire campsite. Rocks, branches, leaves and a small part of the fire are drawn into the swirl, breaking down and becoming lost in the hurricane. Within seconds, I'm staring at the magical creature I love.

He moves his large frame with great care, watching everyone with his eagle eye. I stand and move a distance away from the fire, letting the others get its heat, as I will have Lazarus.

As I lie down, he approaches and nuzzles me with his warm snout. I kiss it. 'I wish you had kissed me before you changed form. Now I will ache for it all night.' He growls and shakes his head then gently sits beside me. He lifts his wing over me, then pulls it in, folding me against him. I lie with my eyes open, spotting a large scar on his wing. I can tell by the paler colour that it has just recently healed.

I lift my face and kiss it. 'Thank you for saving me, Lazarus. I love you.' He purrs like a full-grown lion. I hear the shuffle of small feet and gather that little Jack is snuggling into him too. I smile and wrap my fingers around my pendant and drift off into the best sleep I've had in a long time.

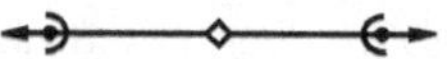

CHAPTER THREE

I WAKE TO the smell of something cooking. Lazarus feels me move and immediately lifts his wing.

The three Aborigines are sitting around the campfire.

'You gotta put more bush medicine on.' Jenny points to the river before handing me the plant.

I turn and Lazarus is standing in human form before me.

'I'll give you a hand.' He scoops me up and we arrive at the water in seconds. He slides me gently down and lifts my t-shirt over my head. He trails his hands down my sides stopping at my petite waist.

His eyes are heated and I wait for him to say something. Instead of speaking, he kisses me, taking my breath away. In a blink, he removes his jeans and lifts me up before carrying me into the cool water.

'You talked in your sleep all night, babe. I found it so hard not to change back and make love to you,' he whispers against my neck.

'What was I saying?'

'How much you love me and that you wanted me to touch you and…' He stops talking to kiss me.

The water cools my body enough for him to lean against me. His arms slip around my waist and my back, holding me to him. I clasp my fingers behind the nape of his neck to keep his lips moulded to mine. Oh, this is heaven! I wrap my legs around his waist and let the water hold my weight. I leave one hand on his solid neck and let my other hand race over his back; the back I have missed touching for the last four months. He pants next to my ear, his breath heating my entire body.

'I need you.' My whisper is full of lust.

'Oh, hell! Not as much as I need you, babe.'

His words ignite an adrenaline rush through my body. I shiver and he smiles into my neck.

He lifts me so we become one. I nibble the soft lobe of his ear. He growls and it vibrates through his body into mine. His lips return to mine and they mould together perfectly.

The familiar electric current builds in my body. I try to control it but it's too strong and runs wild. I stop kissing Lazarus and stare deep into his hooded eyes as the electric jolt shoots out of me. He holds me tight and sniggers before kissing me again.

My mind and senses are oblivious to what is going on around me. Everything that I am is locked on this very moment, on Lazarus.

After washing my burns, he lifts his head and nose up. I know he has sensed something. I panic for a split second then a grin creeps over his face.

'We have a visitor coming.' He winks. 'Little Jack and I would swim together if I couldn't take him flying.'

'You took him flying? How can you trust them?'

'I have been living with them for the last month so I could watch over you. They have been nothing but kind. Would you like me to put the plant extract on you before he arrives?'

'No, you go have fun.'

He dives under the water and pops up under a willow tree which overhangs the river. Little Jack jumps out of the tree and into the water, splashing him. He pretends to be surprised, amusing little Jack. Lazarus tosses him high into the air, making the boy squeal with excitement.

Sitting on the riverbank, I lather my skin with the healing

plant while watching the two boys play. I'm not alone for long, as Jenny comes down to check on my progress. She grabs my arms and rolls them back and forth, then lifts my t-shirt up without asking, revealing my chest, as she pokes my healing blisters.

I glance up at the boys in the water and spot Lazarus with the biggest smile on his face. I try to lower my t-shirt but Jenny smacks my hand away and continues to poke my skin. Lazarus falls into the water to smother his laughter.

After getting her approval that my skin is healing we sit by the river and talk about each other's amazing lives. She has a large family but for several months of the year, the three of them come further along the river as the fish breed in the deeper pockets and it's easier to catch them.

She's fascinated to hear about my life back in Melbourne. I divert the conversation away from anything that is not human. She mentions she knew I wasn't a creature that changed form but sensed a confused spirit within me. I keep my sorcery a secret and thank her for caring for me.

The day flies past with Tom returning with a dead goanna for our dinner. I eat a small amount and return to the river to sit alone and sort out my future.

Ronan is on the hunt for Raven, and now me since he knows I have a connection to the dragons. Lazarus will be in danger if he stays with me and there's no chance I can leave without him knowing. Plus, I don't know where I am.

The patter of Lazarus' heartbeat breaks my concentration. He sits behind me and wraps his legs around me. I'm grateful when his warm stomach presses against my back, as the evening air has brought a cool breeze with it.

'What are you up to, beautiful?' he says, kissing my cheek.

'Trying to work out where my life is heading.'

'Where *our* lives are heading.' He softly squeezes my torso.

'You will die with me, and you know it. I won't risk your life.'

'Do you love me?' He places a hand under each of my armpits and grips tightly. He lifts me up with ease and spins me around so I am facing him.

'Yes, I do,'

'If I was a human, would you hesitate at the thought of being with me?'

'I don't know. I think you'd be a bit boring and cold.'

'I'll take that as a yes.' He shakes his head.

'So confident.'

'In loving you, I am.' He kisses me quickly but with meaning. 'I want to take you back to the Elyograg Castle, or we can live at Nogard Hollow as it's now vacant. I can protect you there and more importantly, we can be together.'

'I refuse to put your life in danger.'

'Enough, Jasmine! Life as a dragon is dangerous. Maybe you should be afraid of living with me.'

'You don't scare me and I can look after myself!'

'Well, why are we arguing? You admit to being able to look after yourself and I can definitely look after myself. Plus, you should be nearer Jet, Raven's son,' he says, holding my eye contact.

'Raven had a son? Why didn't you tell me earlier?'

'I want you to return because of our love, not to be an aunty to Jet. Selfish on my part but I needed to know how you felt about me without Jet in the picture.'

'You're right. It would have changed my mind, but it does the opposite as now I really don't want to go there.'

I fold my arms across my chest, ready to argue further. He pulls my arms free and puts them around his solid neck. I smile at his actions and he rewards me with a heated kiss.

'When you're ready, we will travel home. Tom and I will fly

out tonight and pick up the truck and your precious fella, Blue Boy. He is still at the station under the close eye of an uncle of Tom's. My only concern is that you will get cold without me here and I'll be gone most of the night.'

'I don't want you to fly anywhere, especially with Ronan sniffing around. He can shoot you out of the sky and—'

'I love you so bloody much,' he says, kissing me hard. 'I'll be fine and will return first thing in the morning. I have several skins I've collected and, without arguing, I want you under them before I go.'

'Yes, sir!' I salute him with my right hand.

'About time you realised who is in charge.'

'Really? Do I need to bring out my anorics?'

'Depends if you need your hands to eat your breakfast in the morning,' he says, licking his lips.

'You are all bluff. I could put a hole in that chest with one small toss of my hand.'

'You already put a hole in my heart once.'

'I did it to protect you.'

'You ran away. I won't let you do it again.'

I am about to argue but something inside me agrees with him. I ran away from him and the love of a family who will protect me, as I will them. I've been so stupid!

I look up into his hypnotising eyes and see his love radiating from them. Hearing the pain in his voice twists a knot in my heart and I get a flash of nausea. If I wasn't so stubborn and could properly grieve for Drake, I might have avoided the pain I've caused us both.

'I'm sorry. In my mind, I was doing the right thing by everyone. I don't want to spend another day without you.' An elusive tear runs down my cheek.

'Hey, babe, I'm about to fly off. I don't want to remember you in tears. I'd prefer to remember you kissing me.' He pulls me in tightly and kisses me softly. I kiss him as if it's our last kiss.

I pull myself up onto his lap and mould our bodies together, deepening our kiss to a more passionate and heated one.

'Wow! Maybe I should stay tonight,' he purrs.

'Please fly safely. How does Tom travel with you?'

'He refuses to sit on top and prefers me to grasp him with my talons. Don't worry, his skin is as tough as an elephant's hide and hasn't punctured yet. Plus, if you remember, I carried you out of the fire and never left a mark.'

'Yes, I remember that night clearly.' My eyes drop to my burnt arms.

'I'm sorry. I started the fire in my natural form. If I was in human form it would have been a smaller fire.'

'It was my decision to run into the barn. I was wrong to blame you. I should be the one who is sorry.'

'I shouldn't have started the fire in the first place.' He takes a deep breath before continuing, 'When I saw him grab your arm… your heartbeat belted out a beat that stopped mine. I had to do something.'

'What's done is done. We need to move on. I don't want you to be with me because you feel guilty for what's happened. I want you to love me because of who I am and not what I look like.'

'I love your heart and soul and, trust me, I very much enjoy looking at and touching all of you.' He grins. 'Shit, I need to leave before I attack you again.'

He jumps up and leaves me standing on my feet. 'Come and let me cover you before I leave. I don't want to return to you sick.'

'Sure,' I say, even though I can cover myself without his help. I keep my fears of Ronan and returning home to myself. I don't want to take his mind away from the job ahead.

He gives my hand a few quick squeezes as we walk back.

He must have heard my fearful heart.

Jenny and little Jack are lying beside the fire with several skins covering them. Tom stands with a broken branch in his hand and taps the trunk of a gum tree. He seems impatient to get going.

I lay beside the fire and Lazarus covers me in the fur of our recently eaten dinners. He leans over and kisses my forehead. 'Sleep and I will be back before you know it.' He gives me a reassuring smile and I return it.

They leave and, within minutes, little Jack is snuggling in beside me. He lifts my arm so he can get closer; similar to how Lazarus warms me under his wing. I pull him in tightly and re-adjust the skins to cover us.

His heartbeat is singing within minutes. I lie staring up at the millions of stars; uninhibited by the bright city lights. They twinkle and shine so brightly. It makes me wonder if there's another life form sitting on one of those stars looking down at us. Elite creatures exist, so anything is possible.

My thoughts drift back to Lazarus as I tuck my head under the skins. I inhale several deep breaths, trying to relax my stiff body. If I lose him after re-opening my heart to him, it will devastate me.

It takes hours before I drift off to sleep.

I wake when little Jack drags off the warm skins. 'Get up, you sleepyhead,' he says, shooing several flies away from his face.

I stretch my stiff body and scan the campsite to see Jenny stoking the fire. I jump up and walk back and forth, trying to see over the shrubs, looking for Lazarus. 'Where are Lazarus and Tom?'

'Not back,' she answers, shrugging her shoulders.

'Oh, hell! I hope they are all right.' I continue to pace the small campground trying to occupy my time and mind.

'Go wash your skin and put this on it.' Jenny throws the healing plant at me.

'I can't, I—'

'Go! You put hole in ground if you keep walking in same spot.'

Her tone brings me back and I stop. I look at the healing plant on the ground near my feet and pick it up. I walk to the river and wash my flaking skin as quickly as I can then douse it with the soothing plant extract.

I try to tap into my deeper senses, the ones I received when I killed Attor. Closing my eyes, I lift my nose and inhale the air's scent, drawing it deep into my lungs. My olfactory ignites when I'm inundated with heady aromas. It makes my head hurt so I shut down my sense of smell and concentrate on my hearing.

I narrow in on the smallest of sounds and, once I have one, I push further.

A loud pop in my eardrum deafens me. I cringe in pain and hold my hands over my ears. The pain quickly eases, and as I draw my hands away I notice something.

I hear everything! The running of the river sounds like a gushing waterfall. I can hear the buzzing of a bee and the flapping of its wings. There's an earthworm slithering into his hole on the river's edge. I hear it, then I when I direct my eyes to it, see it. Wow! It's a total overload of my senses.

I lift my head and listen to the orchestra of birds and critters around me. I force past them and hear the large wings of a dragon. Lazarus is on his way back but I don't know how far he is; the distance a blur.

I whip my t-shirt on and race back to the campsite. Lazarus and Tom walk in, both looking exhausted.

'Hello, babe.' He smiles.

'Is everything all right?'

'The bush was too thick to get the truck here so we corralled Blue Boy with the truck. He is safe but we had to give Ronan the runaround.'

'Did he see you?'

'No, but he's camped nearby the station. Tom's uncle took your truck for a drive while we took Blue Boy. We met him several hundred acres away and loaded Blue into the float. The sorcerer was still camped out, none the wiser.'

'When you say took Blue Boy, what do you mean?' I'm curious to how they moved him.

Tom chuckles and pats Lazarus on the back before walking away. He speaks in his native tongue, with Jenny and little Jack laughing.

I throw my hands onto my hips and narrow my eyes at Lazarus. He shrugs his shoulders and smiles his sexy grin.

'What was I supposed to do—put him on my back and carry him?' Lazarus moves like lightning to hold me in his arms.

'Ride him!'

'He is fine, babe,' he says in a soft tone, leaning forward to kiss me. I turn my face and he nuzzles my cheek instead. 'I know you want me to kiss you because I could hear your heartbeat when you heard me flying. I told you how good it was to hear everything.'

He nuzzles his nose around my face until his lips are on mine. I clench them shut but he continues to leave soft little kisses on them. Darn, he knows how to push my buttons!

'If there are any puncture wounds on my horse, you better run, lizard,' I murmur through my tight lips.

'He is one whole fat heavy horse, my grumpy little witch!' He chuckles and I join him before he kisses me.

We say our goodbyes before Lazarus changes form and I climb onto his back. Little Jack's eyes are wide with wonder until I wave goodbye and his smile drops to his feet. I think he enjoyed having Lazarus as a big brother for a while.

Lazarus stretches his wings wide to check where I am on his back and, with a downward thrust, we are soon flying low over the red dusty earth. It isn't long before we land and are driving back towards Elyograg Castle with my puncture-free horse.

As Lazarus drives, I scavenge around the truck for clothing. I find clean shorts and a t-shirt that fits me instead of the black t-shirt that fitted like a short dress.

We drive until dark then pull over to sleep until dawn. I wake to the rocking of the truck. Lazarus has resumed driving as he's eager to get me home. I jump over the front seat and snuggle against him as he drives. My mind races ahead with excitement at seeing Raven again and meeting Jet.

My heart jerks at the thought of Drake. I wonder if Raven used Drake's soul and if he is a part of Jet.

'Why are you anxious, babe?'

'Is Drake a part of Jet?'

'Yes, he is. It was strange at first but I soon learnt to love Jet as I did Drake.'

'Oh, boy.'

'Oh boy, what?'

'Will I have feelings for him like I did Drake?'

Lazarus pulls the truck over and turns to face me.

'Before you left, you told me you were *in* love with me and the love you had for Drake was a bond. Or have I got it wrong?'

'I was *in* love with you and I still am. My love was different with Drake. There was an unexplainable connection between us, plus I felt the need to protect him. It's as though I have gargoyle blood in me.'

'I can't share you, not again. I will rip any creature's heart out and toast it on my claw before eating it if I taste him on your lips. Do you understand? You're inked on my soul; you are my mate for life.'

'You will never have to share me. My heart *is* yours. But you will have to share me when it comes to loving other people, as I'm sure you do.' I lift my hand to cup his cheek.

He leans forward and kisses me, hard and desperately. 'I can live with that… just.'

My heart skips when I see the elaborate castle I once called home. Lazarus reaches over and squeezes my hand. There is a gargoyle flying overhead, giving us a welcome escort.

'Is that Jet?'

'Yep.'

'He is magnificent!

'He has been waiting for you. It has taken all of Raven's convincing to keep him here. He desperately wanted to follow me to find you.'

'Is it Drake that I will be talking to or is Jet a completely different creature?'

'Since Jet is Raven and Lysander's son, he has a mixed natural form—gargoyle and human. He will appear to be in his late teens. He has the knowledge and strength of Drake, and with that, all his memories, including his love for you.

'Jet has inherited Raven's sorcery, but we are yet to find out how powerful he is.'

'Is Jet in love with me?'

'I bloody hope not!' he growls. I squeeze his hand and he smiles.

'I love you, lizard.'

'You'd better, witch!'

I see Raven running out of the castle with Corbin landing close by, transforming into his human form. The gargoyle above shrieks a wild growl before landing beside Raven. With a quick and skilful action, he shreds his hard rock exterior to form a handsome young man.

'I love watching you creatures change form. It starts a fire in my soul. And he is so handsome,' I say, staring out the front windscreen with my mouth gaping open.

'Hmm, you keep drooling over Jet and I *will* set you on fire.'

I giggle and roll my eyes at him, 'Don't get jealous.'

'I am a dragon, that's what we are—jealous! The big, scary, razor-sharp teeth, fire-breathing, scary beast that will rip your heart out with one of my claws type of jealousy.'

'You said "scary" twice. And you are *my* scary dragon and I love and admire every inch and red scale you have. Trust me, I do more than just drool over you when you change form.' I look over at him. He rolls his shoulders back and sits tall, knowing I adore him.

Lazarus pulls the truck to a stop and, in seconds, Raven is at my door, whipping it open and pulling me into her loving arms. 'You're back! I missed you so much.'

'I missed you, too.'

'Welcome home, Jazz,' says Corbin, sneaking in-between the embrace I have with my cousin.

'Corbin, how are you?'

'Better now you're back as I don't have to listen to Lazarus whine.' He laughs, then heads towards the float. 'I'll grab Blue Boy out of the float for you.'

'Have you…'

'Yes, I've eaten. Anyhow, Blue and I are mates and I never eat a mate.'

'How have you been?' I ask Raven, returning my attention to her.

'I'm a mother, and you, my sweet cousin, are an aunty to Jet.'

My heart thuds when she says his name and my eyes focus

on the young man standing in front of me. His arms are open wide, inviting me into his hold. I swallow hard and move into his embrace. He holds me tightly and breathes me in. Slowly he rocks me side to side with no sign of letting me go.

'All right, Jet, that's enough unless you want a broken arm,' murmurs Lazarus from behind me.

'I'll arm wrestle you anytime, uncle.'

'Uncle?' I tilt my head around Jet's broad body to frown at Lazarus.

'Well if you're his aunty, it would only be logical that I am his uncle.'

'So confident I'd return.'

'One look at me and I knew you'd come running.' Lazarus grins.

'Is that so?'

'Gee, you two haven't changed,' says Corbin, walking Blue Boy over to the paddocks.

Jet steps back and runs his eyes over me. I do the same and take in his human form.

His six-foot height matches most elite men. He has the gargoyle trademark—blue eyes and a solid build. But his hair is a light brown which breaks away from the traditional gargoyle look—dark brown. His chin, which is covered in stubble, is square but curves around to his broad cheekbones. He is a handsome and strong-looking boy.

A dark shadow looms over the top of us, giving me an unexpected fright. I drop to my knees in fear that Ronan has found me, or Falcon has returned to avenge his father. I had been preoccupied with Jet and didn't keep any of my senses on what was happening around me.

With a gentle touch, Jet grasps my shoulders and lifts me to my feet. The shadow covers me again. This time I glance up and spot Lolana gliding above me.

'No need to worry, Aunt Jazz. I will never let anyone hurt you. I will protect you. You can trust me.' He has a reassuring smile on his face. I gaze into his glowing blue eyes and see Drake staring back at me.

'Thank you. I do trust you, handsome.'

I hear Lazarus sigh and Jet gives him a cheeky wink before giving me another hug. Lazarus releases a low warning growl.

'Stop stirring him, Jet. He will rip your arm off for the fun of it,' I whisper, and he chuckles.

'Jasmine!' Lolana says. She runs over then stops and rolls her eyes over me, head to toe. 'You're hurt and you've got new markings.'

'I'm a lot better than I was.'

'What's wrong with markings?' Raven laughs, pointing to her face and we all join in. Lolana hugs me, expressing her happiness at my return.

The angels walk out with large smiles on their faces. Malachi greets me with a small peck on the cheek. He stands back and gazes over my burnt limbs.

'I can heal you better than that. I have a recipe of herbs and bush medicine that will heal and eradicate all your scars. After you finish saying hello to everyone I will bathe you and apply my lotion.'

Lazarus' heart thuds louder than a drum next to my ear. I lasso mine so he doesn't hear it beat out of control at the handsome angel's offer.

'Thank you for your kind offer but the burns I have cover ninety percent of my body so it'd be more appropriate for Gabby to apply the lotion,' I say, trying to contain my smile.

'As you wish,' he says, not realising the trouble his offer has just caused.

We move indoors. The smell of the castle hits me head-on. I have missed its warm aroma and the secure feeling of a home.

With dusk falling quickly, everyone gathers for an early dinner—an amazing spread the angels have supplied. Jet sits next to me, with Lazarus on the other side. I hear Drake in Jet's stories and he expresses how much Drake loved me and protected me as he will do now.

I see the connection between Jet and Drake, both being similar in personality, but Jet is more determined to fight for the gargoyles' survival.

Everyone is silent when I repeat what the black sorcerer, Ronan, told me about black sorcery and the likelihood of an invasion from the Europeans. Raven gasps in horror when I say his name.

'I was suspicious of Ronan the first day he approached me,' she says.

'When did you meet him?' I ask.

'Several years after Grandfather's death and leaving you. He approached me when I was training with a well-known sorcerer, who has since passed away. I wondered if Ronan had something to do with the sorcerer's death. The circumstances were unusual and could have only been committed by some-one with sorcery or elite powers.'

'You were lucky he didn't turn on you.'

'He was always trying to make me practice dark magic, saying I'd be a stronger sorceress if I did. It wasn't until I witnessed him killing a good and kind sorceress for her powers that I took off and hid from him. He was blasé in his kill and it worries me how many more he has killed and that he will one day unstoppable,' Raven says.

'Why haven't you mentioned Ronan to us sooner?' asks Lazarus.

'I contacted Falcon the next day and he has his scent from a t-shirt I grabbed. He has been watching out for him.'

'Great help Falcon is now!' I say.

'I have his scent. It's not one I will forget. And you're right, Raven, he has killed many elites—he reeks of death,' Lazarus says.

'I'm glad I pretended I had no advanced powers. But now I fear for your life, Raven.'

I yawn, tired from the long day and the excitement of being back with my family. Lazarus excuses himself to go feed while I, in slow steps, climb the stairs to my old bedroom. When I grasp the timber handrail of the staircase, I get a sense of belonging; a sense of home.

I arrive at the door and push it open. The room is filled with everything I remember. The four-poster bed is inviting, soft and warm. My body sighs with relief at the thought of dropping into it. The hard ground that has been my bed for the last week is embedded into my backside. I can't wait to have it replaced by the soft cushion mattress and a feather-warm doona, even though I enjoyed Lazarus' heat over me.

Malachi walks in with a brown bottle in his hands. 'Gabby is busy so I'm happy to rub this lotion on your wounds.'

Within a split second Lazarus walks in the door. 'I'll do it, thanks Malachi,' he says, trying not to snarl.

'I have the time and am more than happy to help,' he insists.

I walk over at a quick pace and place my hand on Malachi's. 'That is such a kind offer.' I smile, then hear Lazarus' heart thud hard and angrily. 'But I am more than capable of doing it myself. Thank you so much for caring.' I kiss him on the cheek then take the lotion from him.

'Shall I run you a bath?' Malachi asks, then bows out of the room when Lazarus roars at him.

'Really! Did you have to scare him?'

Lazarus grabs me and kisses my annoyed lips. 'I said if I ever tasted another man on your lips I would rip his heart out. You're lucky I only scared him.'

'Your jealousy will get you hurt. And now I don't have a handsome man to bathe me and cover me in lotion.' I flutter my eyes.

'Oh, yes you do.'

'I thought you were too busy and needed to feed.'

'I am hungry so you'd best do as I say, witch.' He flicks his eyebrows before scooping me up in his arms and carrying me into the bathroom. I squeal then shut my mouth, remembering that everyone has sensitive ears around here.

I wake early with Raven sneaking in beside me in my warm, soft bed. I sit up and there's no sign of Lazarus.

'He's gone to feed,' she says, cuddling into my side. 'How are your wounds?'

'Malachi's bush and herb medicine has worked a treat. I feel great!'

'You have more ink than any other elite—they'll be jealous.' She laughs.

'Your son is a credit to you and Lysander.'

'He is my world and placing Drake's soul in him was the best decision we could have made.'

'I find it difficult when I hear him say something Drake would say or when I look into his eyes I see Drake.'

'His love for you is unconditional, with the strong need to protect you. Drake died trying to protect you and it has been intergraded into Jet's soul. He will be your guardian angel whether you want it or not.'

'As soon as I saw him flying above me I knew I loved him like a son. I promise you here and now—I will risk everything I have to protect him from what is coming.'

'I know you will. And that is why I am glad you have returned. Jet was eager to leave Elyograg Castle in search of you, but now you're here, it will hopefully keep him home. His powers need to be kept secret, as creatures will hunt him to use him for their personal goals. I need you here and to be a family again.'

'I love you, Raven. I know how stupid I've been in leaving. It took my heart breaking every day and seeing Lazarus again to realise it. But I'm here for good.' I slip my arms around her and squeeze her tightly.

'I love you too, sweet girl. Now tell me about you and Lazarus.'

'I would be happy to, but he has just landed on the roof and will hear everything I say.'

'So you've tapped into your extra senses?'

I inhale through my nose and try to pinpoint what Lazarus has eaten. 'And I believe he has just consumed a deer.'

'Wow, I'm impressed, Jazzle,' she says, raising one eyebrow.

'I'm in love. My heart skips a beat every time he looks at me and my breath falters when he kisses me. I can't get enough of him. He is etched on my heart and soul, as I am on his,' I whisper as softly as I can.

'Sounds like poetry. I'm happy for you.'

'Good morning,' Lazarus purrs, standing in the doorway. 'It wasn't deer but you're very close.'

'I'll see you downstairs for breakfast.' She winks before wiggling out of the bed. She skips out of the bedroom, slapping Lazarus on the bottom as she passes. He laughs, closing the door behind her.

'Good morning, handsome. I missed you when I woke up.'

He is in a playful mood and moves towards me like he is stalking his prey. I draw my legs up and move on all fours, ready to scramble away from his prowling. I watch his slow, calculated moves and am ready to fly from the bed to avoid him catching me. I love playing games!

'It's not a good idea to run from a dragon when he has you in his sight. A fleeing creature is attractive to the palate and

I can't be held responsible if I bite.' His low tone is seductive. My heart kicks into gear.

'Oh, Jazz, will you ever learn?' he growls, licking his rosy lips before pouncing on me, pinning me on the bed. He gazes at me as I wiggle beneath him. My efforts are lost on his strong frame and I relent willingly. He leans close and whispers warm into my ear, 'Even when you whisper I can hear every word you say. I can hear every breath you take from ten miles away. We will never have secrets.'

'What is my heart saying now?'

'That you are hungry for breakfast.'

'You're wrong. It says kiss me!' He smiles then shakes his head before a serious look glazes over him.

'I am in love with you. And I can't get enough of you.' He releases my wrists from his playful hold and kisses me softly. I push him back and he playfully falls onto his back. I jump up and straddle him, lifting his large hands so they are beside his ears, pinning them, making him chuckle. When it comes to strength, I am a toothpick compared with him. 'Do your worst, witch.' He laughs, and it's music to my ears.

'Oh, I intend to.'

I kiss his forehead and leave a soft, wet trail of kisses all over his face. He tries to kiss me but I 'tut' him and continue along his neck. He growls when I reach his chest, which rises and falls at a massive speed.

I loosen my grasp on his wrists and slide my hands slowly down his contracting arms. His skin crawls when my nails glide over his chest and I smile into him.

He sits up and flips me onto my back, his eyes searching mine, back and forth.

'Damn, Jazz, you're killing me,' he pants. He kisses my lips hard, demanding me to return the passion he so desires. I grasp his toned back, pulling him harder into me. I realise we won't be eating breakfast and will most probably miss lunch.

AFTER ANOTHER RESTFUL night's sleep, Lazarus returns to our warm bed after feeding.

'I want to take you out today and teach you how to tap into your extra senses more effectively. So if you need me you can zone in on what I am doing. I will always be near or within our hearing limit.'

'I thought we could have another day in bed.'

'As tempting as your offer is, I need all your senses working to their fullest capacity in case Ronan or the European drag-ons come visiting.'

'We can exercise all my senses right here.'

'Jazz, you're killing me here.' He kisses me before dragging the warm feather doona from me. 'The quicker we go the quicker we can come back to more exciting activities.'

'Fine!' I snap, rolling out of my comfortable bed.

'I need you to take in someone's scent. You have mine and I want to teach you how to link it to your other senses. You can use it to locate an elite or smell where they have been.'

'You want me to start sniffing someone?' I giggle.

'Be discreet, babe.'

'I need to grab something for breakfast, so I will get Malachi's scent, as he will be in the kitchen,' I murmur, seeing if Lazarus' green jealousy dragon makes an appearance.

'I'd prefer if you connected to Jet or Corbin. Listening to your heartbeat every time you sense Malachi will drive me crazy,' he says in a calm tone, to my surprise.

'So how is this going to work?'

'We will fly out far enough away from any distractions but close enough for your senses to work. I will stay in dragon form and fly around you. I want you to sense when I am approaching and how far away I am. Use your eyes to narrow in on me and when we're flying, scan the ground for critters. Your vision will be altered as if you're looking through a magnifying glass.

'You will need to control your senses; there will be hundreds of animals around and you need to pinpoint what is a threat and what isn't.'

'I'm in the Outback; what threat is out here apart from Ronan and Falcon? I'm sure I'll spot them.'

'Every elite creature alive can be a threat. You've made enemies you haven't even met yet.'

'That's ridiculous.'

'Do you think Falcon is sitting sulking in a corner and that Ronan is doing the same? I need you prepared for anything that may come your way. And if what's predicted with the Europeans invading Australia comes to pass, we need to be at our best to stand by the gargoyles and fight.

'Plus, if anyone finds out about Jet and his powers… we need to protect what's ours.'

I nod in agreement. He is right—Falcon will seek revenge on me for killing his father and Ronan saw me fly off in the claws of a dragon. And I refuse to stand by and let any group of foreigners take over this country and use it as their training ground. I will stand with my family and use every inch of my power to protect them.

'Will I get x-ray vision?'

'I've never seen or heard of that power transferring to a human but, knowing my luck, you will inherit it.'

'It's not fair that you and Corbin have all the fun.' I smile, before moving to stand in front of him.

'It's how you'll use the power that worries me.'

'Would it worry you or make you jealous? I'm not like you, who strips people of their clothes.'

'Just let me know if your sight loses its colour. And the answer is jealous, with a very big, razor-sharp teeth "J"!' He pulls me into his strong arms and plants a heated kiss on my lips before smacking me on the bottom and leaving. 'Razor-sharp!'

I head downstairs and walk up to Jet, wrapping my arms tightly around him.

'Good morning, Aunt Jazz.' Jet seems surprised at my warm embrace and gives a nervous laugh. 'I'm running late, the sun is rising and everyone else is in stone sleep, even though I don't need to recharge like a full-blooded gargoyle.'

I inhale him deeply, collecting his scent—a mix of Raven, Lysander and Drake. It is a unique bouquet and one I will always remember.

'Have you got me?'

'Yes, you cheeky bugger.' I playfully slap him on the arm.

'You're supposed to be discreet when gaining someone's scent, Aunt Jazz.' He glances down as if using one of his senses. 'You were never one to hold back with what you had to say or your actions,' he adds as if someone had spoken telepathically to him.

'And how would you know?'

'When I received Drake's soul, apart from the physical transformation, I was blessed with a huge overload of information. As our souls adjusted to become one, I was constantly inundated with his knowledge. It was a history lesson I could never turn off.'

'Do you know everything he knew or is he still relaying it to you?'

'The information has slowed, and I have learnt to control it, so I receive it when I want to. I re-open the connection when in stone sleep. I can draw on his knowledge and ask questions anytime but he gives me the answers before I have time to think. He is an amazing creature and I am blessed we are now one.'

'Is he at peace? Will his soul eventually die?' I force back the lump forming in my throat. I still get teary when I speak about Drake.

'He is a part of me—our souls are one. And I am at peace, especially now you are home safe and under my protection. But the odd information slips through about your mannerisms.'

'I loved Drake… no, I *love* Drake. I couldn't accept him dying because of me so I ran away and left behind everyone I have ever cared for. I tied my feelings up into a big painless knot so I didn't have to deal with it.

'It took someone to threaten Raven's life to give me the wake-up call I needed. Plus, an overzealous dragon who swooped down and dragged me back to reality.'

'Well, this overzealous dragon is becoming impatient,' interrupts Lazarus, who is standing behind us. I didn't hear him enter the room. I need to be in tune with what is happening around me, even when I'm in conversation. 'We should have left by now, Jasmine.'

'When he calls me "Jasmine" I don't need to use any of my sorcery senses to know he's in a mood,' I mutter into Jet's chest as he draws me in for another hug.

'We'll finish this conversation later.' He kisses me on the cheek before glancing at Lazarus. 'She has my handsome scent now, dragon. Yours will make her gag.'

'Keep thinking that, pebbles.' Lazarus laughs.

I ignore them both. 'We will chat later, handsome. Come on, Laz.' I wave my hand as if I was waiting for him. He shakes his head and we leave through the front door.

Corbin is returning from the paddock with a horse brush in his hand when we exit the castle. I walk over to him as I want to take in his scent before leaving. The more I have to play with, the better I will become at distinguishing the different scents.

'Hi, Corbin! Did you go for a ride?' I move beside him and try to inhale him without his knowledge.

'No, I just gave them all a good brush.' He smiles. 'Looks like you're going riding.'

I turn to see Lazarus in his glorious dragon form. 'He is teaching me a thing or two about senses. Can you give me a boost? I don't like the way Lazarus lifts me up onto his back.'

'It's my pleasure.' Corbin moves towards the vibrant red creature. 'As I'm a bit overhearing his heartbeat every time he is around you. I've permanently blocked him out.'

'I'm sorry.' I blush.

'I'm stirring, Jasmine. Get him to show you how to block out a sound you're connected to. It comes in handy sometimes.'

'I enjoy listening to his heart.'

'Trust me, you will get over his irregular beat.' He chuckles before elbowing Lazarus in his shoulder. Lazarus bumps Corbin, making him stagger sideways.

'Watch it, you oversized gecko.' Corbin laughs before bunking me up. 'Enjoy your flight, Jasmine.'

'I will and thanks for the boost.' I wiggle into my safe spot in front of his wings.

Within minutes, we are flying over the magical landscape I call home. We fly low beside the running creek. I use my eyes to scan in and it doesn't take long to lock onto small unsuspecting critters. They all go about their business until Lazarus' shadow covers them and they sink to the ground before scattering off under a shrub or rock.

I close my eyes and sit tall. I open my arms wide and let the warm country breeze rush against me. My hair flies behind me and my clothes flap against my skin.

I inhale the surrounding aromas. Wham! An overkill of

strong heady smells hits me head-on. I gasp and cough, trying to eradicate everything I have inhaled.

I hear Lazarus rumble as he lowers and hovers before landing. I slide down his scaly leg, with the usual groan from him, and then step aside as he takes off.

I stand, mesmerised, adoring this magical elite creature. He soars over the tops of the trees and I know he is nearby.

I close my eyes so I can use my sensitive hearing. I hear his heartbeat loud and clear and work out that he is sitting just over on the other side of the creek.

'You need to move further away, babe. I can hear you chewing on…' I swap senses and inhale deeply, forcing aside anything that isn't attached to Lazarus' scent. I smell fresh blood and zone in on the creature. 'A rabbit.'

I hear a low growl and the gush of his strong webbed wings. I keep the connection and notice his wings have stopped pumping. He is gliding. I can hear the air running along his wings.

I search the sky, presuming he will try a sneak attack. I spin around on the spot, taking in every bird and insect flying around. I force their existence aside and keep my sole focus on him.

I see him as he pops over the top of the trees. He roars, and a flame shoots from his wide mouth. He's careful to aim it high in the air so as not to start a bushfire.

Lazarus heads straight for me, like an arrow shooting for its target. I stand with my arms open wide and yell at the top of my lungs, 'I heard you. You're losing your touch, dragon.'

He roars—he's amused—and takes off towards the river's mouth. I wait and wait, wondering if he has found something a little more entertaining or attractive to eat. I listen and inhale his scent, but nothing returns.

I focus on Jet and Corbin, receiving them both strongly. I gather Corbin is still at the castle, as their scent seems the same distance away and they are both in a calm state.

I try to contact Raven by telepathy.

'Hello, Raven,' I echo.

'Hey, Jazzle.'

'G'day, Aunt Jazz. How is the training going?' echoes Jet.

'Wow, this is trippy, guys. I can hear you both and I'm miles away.'

'You are a strong sorceress with the added powers of a dragon,' Raven echoes. *'You need to keep this quiet. Ronan will hunt you out and kill you for your powers.'*

'If he kills me, I'm no good to anyone,' I echo.

'He will inherit your powers. All sorcerers inherit their victims' powers,' echoes Jet.

I sense something close by.

'I've gotta go, guys. There is a dragon who thinks he can sneak up on me.'

I listen for Lazarus' heartbeat but it's faint, as is his scent. Inhaling long and slow, I draw in on the creature I fear may be stalking me.

There are several heartbeats, two large and three small. I've pinpointed where the scent is coming from, under the tree-lined area beside the creek. The two larger heartbeats increase in flow and I panic; I might be their prey.

In a blink, I open my hands and draw my power from the earth, feeling it creep up my legs. I stop when it hits the pit of my stomach and I let it fume inside me.

Drawing in the scent again, I recognise the smell as something from my past. It has been blocked and I try to force down the brick wall surrounding it.

Adding to my confusion is the sound of Lazarus' wings frantically flapping. His heart is pounding and his roar is deafening. I estimate him to be at least five kilometres away. I swap my senses back and forth from the creatures that prey on me and the dragon racing towards me.

Out of the corner of my eye, I spot Lazarus, but I keep my eyes glued on the beating pulse of my stalkers, hidden behind the scrub. Lazarus is metres away when I see two dingoes pounce at me, flattening me like a pancake. My body shoots out its electrical current without me saying so, shocking the two enormous dogs. It knocks them down, leaving them lying motionless beside me.

I scramble to my feet and stare at the two panting creatures. I look into the eye of the largest dingo and get a feeling of déjà vu. I know these eyes, I know these souls. They are not here to hurt me.

Lazarus flies towards us with his eyes locked dangerously on the dingoes.

'No, Lazarus! Stop!' I jump in front to protect them from his charring flame. He releases an angry roar before landing with a thud. He moves to my side and uses his snout to nudge me away from the subdued creatures.

'They're not here to hurt me.'

A low growl rumbles through his large dragon body before he nudges me hard.

'Enough, I've got this!' I stop myself from flicking his nose as I remember how quick he is and decided my hand is more attractive attached to my arm.

I kneel between the two oversized creatures and place my hands on them. One flinches at my touch, so I coo at them. They roll their eyes so they are both looking at me.

'I'm sorry, I didn't mean to hurt you,' I say in a calm tone.

One dingo sits up and shakes its body like a wet dog, while the other lies still under my hand. In a blink, the dingo under my hand changes form into a female human. I recognise her features, but I can't pull down the wall to see how I know her. The other dingo changes form into a male human.

I sit mesmerised at the transformation before me. Lazarus

has changed form and has moved in behind me. I sense the three other creatures creeping up under the cover of the long grass. Their heartbeats are small and full of fear.

'It's all right to show yourselves,' I say.

Three small children scamper out of the long grass and over to the female that sits before me.

'Hi, Jasmine,' says a small girl.

'Hello, Nelly,' I reply, shocked that my mind has released this child's name. I look at the two small boys behind Nelly and their names float before my eyes. 'Kip and Tag.'

'You know these creatures?' Lazarus asks his mood gruff.

'No. I mean… I believe I might.'

'We have met before. Over six months ago when you first started your journey,' the female says. Her name flashes before me.

'Ellie?' I question and she nods. 'And you are her husband, Rhys. Am I correct?'

'Yes, that is correct.' Rhys slowly stands. Lazarus growls and moves towards him. 'We are no threat to either of you.'

'Lazarus, please stop.' I shake my head.

'If you're not a threat why did you pounce on Jasmine?' Lazarus snaps.

'We thought you were attacking her. We saw you swoop at her once and wanted to move her away from the clearing and closer to the creek where she could shelter from your next attack,' Ellie answers.

'Yeah! You big old mean dragon,' spits Nelly. 'I'm not scared of you.' She pokes her tongue out, making Lazarus question her with a raised eyebrow. 'And nor are my tough brothers. They will eat you 'cause we enjoy eating red things.'

I laugh out loud, much to Lazarus' disgust. 'He was training me, Nelly. He'd never hurt me.' Nelly stalks him on her two little legs. Lazarus growls and Nelly cowers away behind her brothers and they all hide behind their mother. 'How do I know you and what are you?'

'I see it didn't take long for your ink markings to show. It's obvious you have met other elite creatures apart from us and the dragons,' Rhys says, pointing to my face and scarred arms.

'I've had a run-in with one or two. How did you know about my markings?'

'Our eyes can see all your markings. They stay invisible until you earn them or show when you've had an injury,' Rhys explains. 'We first met you on the banks of a river and we spent several educational days together. You accepted us and our transformation but you, we believed, weren't ready to accept your sorcery. You were full of guilt and lacked trust. You focused on the negativity of your past instead of your positive future.

'We didn't want to be the ones to open you to dark sorcery, so we wiped your mind of our meeting and our existence. When you woke, you saw three pups playing on the opposite side of the river. Ellie and I stayed hidden, as our size would've made any sane mind question what steroids we'd taken. The children look to like full-grown dingoes and you acknowledged them as that.'

'You said I was the cutest!' Nelly sings.

'No, she didn't. She said I was the cutest,' Tag says, bumping his sister.

'You both can be the cutest because she said I was the handsome one,' adds Kit.

'I remember thinking how stunning the three of you were, equally!' I say.

'So what do you want?' Lazarus snaps.

'As I mentioned before, we are not your enemy,' Rhys says.

'Since our meeting we have kept tabs on Jasmine, watching over her. When we believed it safe, we would show ourselves to her again. We monitor the dragon and gargoyle feeding routines and we try to avoid those areas,' Ellie explains. 'It's safer for us to stay near the river so we can swim under the water when the dragons fly overhead as they can't hear our heartbeat. The water absorbs the sound.'

'I would have smelt you,' Lazarus sniffs, sounding insulted.

'We have ways of covering our tracks and, if you don't mind, I need to keep some of these a secret,' she adds, standing up and brushing off grass and dirt.

I jump up and help her to her feet. 'I'm so sorry I shocked you.'

'No harm done, but you've got a full body punch going on there. It knocked me out for quite a while.' Ellie laughs.

'You still haven't answered my question. What do you want?' Lazarus sounds unconvinced they are genuine and not a threat.

'Like you, the gargoyles, the fairies and several other elite creatures that are yet to disclose themselves to Jasmine, we are here to protect our identity and to protect her,' says Ellie.

'What can a dog do to protect her?' Lazarus scoffs.

'We're not dogs. We are dingoes,' Rhys spits.

'Any dingo could take your big fat red belly down before you know it. We can hide from you and stop you from finding our scent. I wish we could stop smelling you, fat scaly beasts,' snarls Nelly.

'How about we both change form and meet in the middle of the clearing and see who wins, wolf?' Lazarus jests.

'Gee, you aren't very educated. I am a dingo, which is neither a dog nor a wolf. And I will gladly kick your scaly butt.' Nelly gets a tap on her head from her father.

'Nelly, remember your manners and Lazarus, please don't disrespect us,' Rhys says.

'Well, put that child on a leash,' Lazarus murmurs.

'Lazarus, be the adult!' I spin my head to glare at him. He

holds his hands up as if I am about to shoot him. Nelly pokes her tongue out and I catch her, narrowing my eyes, making her cower away. 'We are not enemies, guys.'

'No, we are not, but you are getting a long list of them, Jasmine,' Ellie says. 'The dark sorcerer from the north has followed you here, and the whisper is that the dragon, Falcon, is still here, waiting for the European clan to arrive. We are waiting for information as to where their new training ground will be. There was talk of them taking over Elyograg Castle and Nogard Hollow, which will give them more than enough room and cover from humans.'

'I found my way here so who's to say another human won't?' I say.

'You didn't stumble across this life, Jasmine. It's a part of you. You followed your soul, and that's what brought you to all of us. Our kind has watched over you since the day your grandfather died,' Ellie says. 'It is our way of thanking Grandfather for keeping the peace amongst the Australian elite.'

'I've never seen you or your kind anywhere near home,' I say. 'I've seen dingoes but not as large as you guys.'

'We are timid by nature and show ourselves only when needed. And we believe now is the right time to enter your life,' Rhys says. 'We did the same when we thought Raven was ready.'

'She never told me dingoes change form or that they're apart of the elite creatures.' I'm disappointed she has kept this secret from me.

'It's not for you, Raven or anyone to disclose other elite creatures' secrets. They must evolve as naturally as possible. If a creature reveals themselves to us there must be a purpose,' says Ellie.

'And what is your purpose?' Lazarus asks.

'We are your link to what goes on beyond your senses. Our

kind, and others we connect to, send messages through a long and extensive chain, relaying any information.'

'Like the telephone game but Aussie style,' Nelly pipes up.

'An Outback telephone line. That's cool.' I smile at Nelly. 'I am glad you revealed yourselves to Lazarus and me. You are welcome at the castle at any time. Everyone will accept you there.'

'Oooh, can we go to the castle, Mummy? Please!' Nelly jogs on the spot.

'Thank you, your offer is warming, but we need to stay near the river so we will know when danger is coming.' Ellie smiles. 'Most creatures are connected to the earth, whereas we are connected to the rivers and the Aboriginal people.'

'How will I hear from you?'

'If an emergency arises, we will approach the castle. We can call out to you, as I know your hearing is sensitive.'

'Call out to me?'

The three children start to howl while changing into their healthy dingo coats. I laugh as they rub up against me while continuing to howl. I inhale their scent, capturing it for future reference.

'All right, we get the picture.' Lazarus laughs, dropping his tough persona.

Nelly runs at him and stops and squats in front of him as if she is ready to pounce.

'Come on, Nelly, do your best.' His attitude towards the pup has done a three-sixty. He seems keen to play.

She pounces, growling and snapping her teeth, but Lazarus is too quick. He catches her in mid-air and forces her gently to the side.

The other two pups join in and Lazarus playfully falls to the ground. He throws them in the air, only to have them come pelting back at him. He laughs and I hear the pups giggling.

With Ellie and Rhys fully recovered from my shockwave, we walk down to the creek bank. Ellie and Rhys drink the water so I follow suit. It's cool and refreshing. We sit and chat about what I witnessed when meeting Ronan and Falcon.

'I believe we could persuade Falcon to change his ways and give him a second chance. It's his father who was evil and a poor role model. Even though he has burnt, choked and abducted me, I still get a feeling he has good in him,' I say.

'I'm glad you're seeing the good in people. You've grown so much since we met six months ago. It's a good trait to have, but don't be naïve,' says Rhys.

'I didn't say I forgive him. The pain I went through is still fresh in my mind.'

'What gives you the impression he would change his ways?'

'Falcon and Raven were an item. I know Raven, and she's not a silly woman who would date someone with evil intentions. Attor was a powerful dragon and from what I can remember, highly regarded amongst the elite creatures. Falcon may not have been strong enough to go against his father. I've always believed everything my father has told me. Plus, I'd stand beside him and his judgements for one reason—because he is my father.'

'What if his judgement was wrong?' Ellie asks.

'I trust my father, so I believe his decisions are right. Falcon is probably the same.'

'We know of Falcon and found it out of character for him to attack the castle,' says Ellie.

'Lazarus and Corbin walked away from Attor and Falcon, even though they were the leaders of the clan.'

'Lazarus had an ulterior motive.' Ellie winks. 'A dragon becomes "inked" to another creature, or in your case, you. Once inked, they are devoted, protective and committed to staying with this partner for life. Only on the death of one's partner will they no longer be inked.'

'Do you mean inked as in getting a tattoo together?'

'This is something Lazarus should explain to you.' Ellie reaches over and squeezes my hand. I take it that she'd prefer not to say anymore.

Before long, Lazarus joins us, exhausted from the pups' playtime. He has several scratches and teeth marks on his arms but brushes them off to child's play.

I sit staring up into a large gumtree where a well-fed koala sits perched between two tree branches. I stare for hours, wondering what his story is.

'You've been staring at the little fella for a while. Is everything all right?' asks Lazarus.

'I'm waiting to see if he will talk or change form.'

'I think he is what he is.' He laughs. 'What do you think he is going to say?'

'I imagine him to be a "stoner" because he sucks on those leaves all day then sleeps the rest of the time.' I giggle. 'I reckon he'd be deaf because of his fluffy ears and blind because of his small eyes. And if I ask him a question, he'd give me the finger for interrupting him.'

'You have put a lot of thought into it. Sorry to burst your bubble, but he is as you see him—a koala minding his own business,' says Ellie.

'I'm going to question every creature now.'

Nelly jumps onto my back in human form. 'Can I ride the dragon?'

'No, it's too dangerous,' snaps Rhys.

'I don't mind. We need to be heading back home so I'm changing form anyhow,' Lazarus says, smiling at Nelly. It's obvious he's changed his mind about liking the dingoes, especially the pups.

'Oooh, pretty please, Dad,' Nelly says.

'What if she rides with me?' I ask, then turn to Lazarus, 'That's if you can carry two of us?'

'Of course, I can.' He sits up tall and rolls back his strong shoulders.

'Yippee!' Nelly yells.

'Remember to move slowly around a dragon,' I warn.

'I know the rules.' Nelly's smile is so big it reaches her ears.

Lazarus moves over to a clearing so as not to knock anyone. With an amazing display of red swirling particles, he transforms into a handsome dragon. He snorts loudly and drops his tail to lie flat on the ground.

Unafraid, Nelly runs over and clambers up his scales. Lazarus rolls his eye and snorts a puff of smoke. I ask for a bunk up from Rhys, despite Lazarus' growling; he wants to lift me up with his snout.

We wiggle into place and, after Lazarus feels comfortable with our position, he takes off, flying low over the vast Outback.

'Shoot a flame, Lazarus!' Nelly yells with excitement. And he does, several times.

The other two children jump up for a ride before I bid them goodbye and again tell them that they can visit the castle anytime.

We arrive back and Lazarus heads up to the top of the castle while still in dragon form. He slithers around the gargoyles' stone frames and I presume he is relaying what the dingoes have mentioned.

I see Jet break from his stone sleep and spread his wings to glide down. He is magnificent to watch and I shake my head, wondering what other elite creature will reveal itself to me.

I glance over at Blue Boy, who is oblivious to anything except grass. There's no elite blood in him. He's definitely a horse.

'You must stay in the castle, Jasmine,' demands Jet, drawing my eyes away from my fat horse.

'I'm fine when I'm with Lazarus.'

'He said Falcon is here and Ronan is close by. I can't protect you if you're off flying with a dragon!'

'My powers are stronger than all of you put together. Ronan doesn't know of my powers, only Raven's, so we need to protect her. I can handle Falcon. I killed his father.'

'So killing one dragon makes you an expert?'

'Why are you so angry? I never left the land and if I hear a threat is near, I will stay in the castle. But until then, I refuse to be told what to do.' I walk towards the castle's entry. 'I understand you're anxious but I can protect myself.'

'Like when Drake died,' he mutters. 'If he hadn't stepped in front of you, to protect you, you'd have been the one stabbed with Attor's razor-sharp tail.'

It hits me in the chest like a sledgehammer. I stagger and force my legs to hold me. 'Is that what Drake told you?'

'No, it's my opinion on how I saw it when his soul was transferred. I will do the same to protect you, but your inexperience will cost lives. You need to leave the fighting to the elite creatures.'

'Please, don't say another word,' I whisper, my voice lost amongst my emotions. I hold my hand up to stop his approach.

I walk into the castle slowly and hunched over as if I've received a violent punch to the stomach. Climbing the staircase to my bedroom, I pass everyone in a daze and lock my door behind me. I fall onto the bed and burst into a hysterical sob for the man I regrettably killed—Drake.

Chapter Four

The night is interrupted with several attempts to comfort me. Lazarus, on the fourth time, asks me to open the door, threatening to burn it down. But after my calm voice tells him to leave me in peace, he does, leaving my cousin to continue to persuade me.

Soon everyone leaves me alone with my thoughts. Covering myself in a dome of silence, I cry myself to sleep.

'You sleep too much, human,' says Xandria to wake me.

'What do you want, fairy?' I squint my eyes from the morning sun which is pouring in through my open window.

'Xandria is checking on your progress.' She moves so she is beside my face.

'So you can report back to Falcon, no doubt,' I snap, sitting upright. 'I don't believe in fairies. I don't believe in fairies.'

'You silly human. We don't die if you don't believe. That is a horrible bedtime story human parents tell their children, trying to keep their thoughts pure.'

'Then please tell me, what does kill you?' I flop backwards onto the bed making her little body bounce.

'Be careful human, or you will tap into your dark sorcery. Or have you already done that?'

'If I had, your wings would have been plucked from your tiny shoulders by now.'

'You may need Xandria's help in the future so plucking her wings would not be a good idea. You have obviously woken up on the wrong side of the bed so maybe Xandria should come back later when you're in a politer mood.'

'My mood won't change so what do you want?'

'Xandria heard the dingoes have revealed themselves to you.'

'Maybe and maybe not.' Annoyed, I roll my eyes at her. She laughs and drops onto the bed, rolling her petite frame around. 'What is so darn funny, fairy?'

'You thought koalas could talk and change form. It gave all us creatures a good belly laugh at how silly you are.'

I flick the bedsheet and she tumbles to the end of the bed, which renders her silent. Ignoring her, I head for the bathroom.

'Where are you going? We haven't finished talking.'

'Follow me in here and I will flush you and your precious wings down the toilet!'

'That temper that will get you into trouble and that's what Ronan is planning on getting from you.'

Hearing the dark sorcerer's name stops me in my tracks. I spin around and she is standing on the end of the bed with her hands on her hips. 'Xandria thought that might get your attention, human.'

'What do you know of Ronan?'

'He knows all about you. He doesn't want Raven anymore but will kill her so he can gain her powers.'

'What does he know of me?'

'He knows you are stronger than Raven and Grandfather. His plan was to kill Raven and gain her powers, then if you didn't join him, he was going to kill you too. But he senses your dark side and believes he can draw you across to join him.'

I hear a loud roar and banging on the roof as if a thunderstorm is rattling the castle. Lazarus must have heard the fairy's story. I hear his feet scamper down the stairs.

In a blink, he is before me and holding Xandria tightly in

his grasp. The bedroom door swings on its hinges and is now in disrepair due to Lazarus' entrance.

'What does he know of Jasmine?' Lazarus barks, staring daggers at the little fairy.

'Xandria told him everything.' She blinks several times, looking back and forth between us. 'He asked me a question and I had no reason to lie or hide the truth.'

'You're supposed to keep creatures' identities a secret,' I say, moving over to calm Lazarus and loosen his grip on the fairy. She annoys me but I don't want her dead.

'You are not a creature. You're a human and mean nothing to Xandria.'

'Pluck her wings,' I snarl, changing my mind.

'With pleasure,' Lazarus growls, a small puff of smoke escaping his mouth, covering the fairy.

'Wait, Xandria has a message for the human,' she pleads.

'The last message you gave me put me in danger and killed someone I loved.'

'I deliver the message. Your actions are your doing, not Xandria's,' she huffs, pulling her wings tightly into her body.

'You told me I'd be safe. You lied and have now lost my trust.'

'Tell me what the message is,' slurs Lazarus through sharp gritted teeth.

'Dragon, put Xandria down and she will tell you the message,' she says, crossing her little arms.

He places her down on the side table, 'Speak!'

She jumps back in fright and dusts herself off. 'Dragon spit, yuck!'

Lazarus growls again, making her stand to attention. 'Patience, dragon! Ronan wants to meet Jasmine alone or he will go to her Melbourne home and meet her parents.'

I gasp and stagger backwards. My parents! I need to return home and protect them.

I glance up at Lazarus and he is shaking his head. 'You will not meet him or return home.' He quickly moves to hold my shoulders square to him. 'Fairy, where is Ronan now?'

'Xandria is to meet him at Nogard Hollow by midday.'

'That gives us enough time to surprise him,' he says.

'I'd prefer to go alone. I would never forgive myself if something happened to anyone else,' I say.

'Xandria will leave you now and return to Ronan to let him know you will both be coming,' Xandria says.

'No, tell him I will be the only one coming, but I can't get there until early afternoon.' I wink at Lazarus, who has his mouth open, ready to disagree with me then realises I'm up to something.

'Well, if you want to face him alone, I won't stop you.' He winks at me. 'And if he wants Raven, tell him she will be here waiting for him.'

'Very well, Xandria will tell him to expect Jasmine in the early afternoon.' She flutters her wings over to the window, which is open. I give myself a mental note to shut it tightly before I go to bed tonight.

'Terrific. You'd best get going or I will beat you there.'

'Huh! Humans don't beat fairies at anything,' she scoffs, before flying away.

We stand in silence until neither of us can hear her little wings flapping.

'Get any deluded idea out of your head, Jasmine. We will deal with Ronan. Not you or your cousin.' Lazarus' tone is stern.

'Who is "we"?'

'Corbin and I can eradicate one backward wizard and if the gargoyles want to join in that's up to them.'

'It's my battle to fight, not yours.' I throw my hands onto my hips, trying to show authority.

'As sexy as that pout is, I will do everything in my power to stop you leaving the castle.' He steps closer and pulls my hands down.

'My powers are stronger than yours. Don't make me prove it to you.'

'Enough!' interrupts Lysander, in his larger-than-life gargoyle form. I realise now why the doors and rooms in the castle are so large—to allow them to move around in their natural form. 'You're echoing through the whole castle.'

'Ronan is here and—'

Lysander holds his hand up to stop me and, if he was in his human form, I may have continued, but his gargoyle form renders me silent.

'As I said, your loud voices have told everyone living here what is happening. Your silencing spell wore off a while ago. And I agree with Lazarus—you and Raven are to stay here under the protection of Jet and Lolana while Jarius, Demona and I follow the dragons.'

Jet bursts through the already damaged door with Jarius two steps behind. I pray that none of the others come in as my bedroom is already full of these oversized stone creatures.

'But gargoyles don't attack. You only fight to protect yourselves. That won't help the dragons,' I say.

'Gargoyles protect and if that means protecting you and Raven, we will fight.'

'I will fight!' Jets shouts and moves into the centre of the room, making his presence felt.

'No, you won't,' Lysander says.

'We don't have time to argue. Are you with me or not?' Lazarus asks Lysander.

'We're with you. We won't stand by and let our friends and family be hurt by this rogue. Jet, you are to stay here with

Lolana and protect Raven and Jasmine. They are your only priority. Do you understand?'

'I understand,' Jet says, but his head echoes loud and he forgets I can hear him. *I understand that as soon as you leave, I will follow and destroy the enemy.*

'No!' I yell, and everyone looks my way. 'No Jet, do as you're told.'

'Do not disobey me, Jet!' Lysander's voice makes the walls of the bedroom rattle.

Raven comes to the doorway, a look of fear etched on her face.

'Jet, do not disobey,' he scolds. 'Please, son. Protect your mother.'

'Plus, if he happens to escape us and sees we have the only living hybrid, we'll have every rogue attempting to abduct you,' says Lazarus.

'Jet's a hybrid?' I murmur.

'I'm going before it's too late.' Lazarus moves towards me. He smiles and leans forward for a quick kiss. 'I won't be long. Don't do anything stupid. Your senses will let you know what is happening. I love you.'

With a stride, he is out and down the stairs. Lysander leaves, stopping to hold eye contact with Raven. 'I love you. Stay safe.'

'I love you. Hurry back,' she replies, giving him a warm kiss.

They leave with a thunderous noise of roaring and growling. I race past Raven and head up to the rooftop. In the distance, I spot the two dragons flying with the three gargoyles gliding beside them.

I whisper so Lazarus can hear me, 'Watch out in case Falcon is waiting for you. Fly safe and remember I love you.'

I hear a loud roar. He's letting me know he has heard me.

I listen to them fly over the forest but struggle to hear

much more. Closing my eyes, I inhale and focus on Lazarus' scent, but the overpowering scent of the dingoes is present instead.

I run around the top of the castle roof, searching for them. Jet and Lolana have joined me there and have stayed in gargoyle form.

'What is it, Jasmine?' Jet lifts his nose into the air trying to grab hold of the same scent. 'Why are the dingoes here? It must be an important message for them to come personally.'

I ignore his question and concentrate on the land below. 'Something is wrong for them to be so close to the castle.'

My eyes scan the area and I see nothing but Raven in the paddock with Blue Boy. I inhale again and the dingoes' strong scent still pierces my nostrils.

I hear the pups howling. Then, seconds later, two deeper and stronger howls join in— Ellie and Rhys.

I block out every sound but heighten and tune in to the dingoes.

'He is here! Raven, shelter in the castle before it's too late,' Ellie cries.

Raven spins and her eyes lock with mine. She has heard the dingoes cry. We have been tricked! Ronan knew the dragons would protect us and leave us alone in the castle.

'Run, Raven, run!' I scream before taking off down the staircase, heading for her.

'What is it?' growls Jet.

'Ronan is here!'

Jet follows me down the stairs. His heavy impatient feet break the timber steps. It sounds like a stockwhip being cracked beside my ear. He growls, frustrated by my slower pace, before leaping into the air and gliding down to the base of the staircase just as Raven runs through the doors.

He shelters her with his large wings as the front door is

blasted off its hinges. I take a deep breath and feel a disgusting taste in my mouth. Ronan!

He stands square-shouldered with his hands open wide, black anorics increasing in size in his palms.

'It's me you want!' I yell as I continue to run down the stairs, stopping bedside Jet and Raven. 'Leave them and take me.'

'I'm a greedy man, Jasmine. I want everyone's power.'

Lolana glides from the top of the staircase with her claws exposed and targeted on Ronan. She picks him up by the shoulders and flies out the castle doors.

We race out after them. She is trying her best to take him higher, but his weight is drawing them both down. A gargoyle can glide from a high point, but they have great difficulty taking flight from the ground. She will never be able to keep him up from the ground from which he draws his powers.

Jet growls and takes off behind me, climbing the steep walls of the castle.

Lolana has Ronan dangling less than a metre from the ground and I fear he will hurt her before coming for us.

'Split him in two,' I yell out, surprising myself. 'Kill him! Kill him now!' As the words pass my lips, I wonder if I would be able to kill him if I were in her shoes. I pray I have the strength to kill a human enemy.

'Jazz, we can bring him down together,' Raven yells, running towards where Lolana is heading.

I run after her and am soon shadowed by Jet flying above us. Lolana drags Ronan along the ground giving him the power he needs.

'Drop him and go,' Raven yells while continuing to run towards them.

My heart has a frantic and deafening beat, making it hard to hear anything else. But I can sense Lazarus coming towards me. I look up but there's no sign of him or the others.

'Where are you?' I yell and listen for his reply. I hear his roar. He is still several minutes away.

Lolana lets out an ear-splitting screech when Ronan fires a deadly black anoric into her. She drops him and hits the ground hard, rolling uncontrollably before stopping in a bloodied pile.

Ronan rises quickly to his feet and has two anorics already thrown in Raven's direction. In a split second, I draw up two white anorics and throw them, hitting and stopping the advance of his.

Before I can shoot one at him, he has another two heading for Jet. Again, I muster up an anoric as quickly as I can and fire at his advancing black swirls. I hit one and it explodes, but the other strikes Jet in the wing, throwing him back before he crashes to the ground. Ronan throws another two small ones at Jet, tearing his other wing in half and blowing a chunk out of one of his arms.

'Jet!' yells Raven. I hear her run backwards and presume she's seeing to Jet.

The noise from the two injured gargoyles is deafening but before I can blink, I hear two howling sounds from behind my heels. Too scared to turn my head away from Ronan, I inhale the scent of the dingoes behind me. Ellie and Rhys have joined the fight.

'You must choose,' says Ronan, with large anorics swirling in his hands which have increased to a size I have never seen before. 'Who will you save, dear Jasmine? Will it be your precious cousin Sky or the gargoyle?'

'What kind of sick person kills another human or creature?'

'It's easy after your first accidental kill.'

'Killing isn't accidental, you deluded twit!'

'Your best friend, Kelly, was my accidental kill.'

'What the hell do you mean?'

'I located you in Melbourne and waited until you left the protection of your home. I saw a young woman run from the house and I presumed it was you. She jumped into a car and sped off. I stood in the middle of the road, but she never slowed so I launched a small anoric at her windscreen. She swerved off the road and hit a tree head-on. Once I realised it wasn't you, I walked away, leaving her to die.'

My heart thuds before skipping a beat. 'You bastard! It makes sense. The police never found the cause of her swerving off the road. They blamed it on her being distraught after our fight. You could have saved her! Her family and friends blame me for her death. I blamed myself for her death!'

'When I returned to your house there were elite creatures roaming the area and your scent was gone. But with you being away from the elite's protection and letting your guard down, it was easy to hunt you down.'

I twist my feet into the ground, covering them with the red dusty earth. I need all the earth's help to bring this sorcerer down. I dig deep and draw the earth's powers into my soul.

I hold my hands out to elevate Ronan from the ground, but he's anchored, a sarcastic smirk plastered over his face.

'He's grounded, like a tree and its roots,' Raven yells, returning to my side.

Raven throws her white anorics, but they are deflected when only a metre away from him.

He laughs and tilts his head sideways. 'You should have stayed with me, Sky. If you'd killed as many dragons and sorcerers as I have and sucked all the power from their corpses, you'd learn how to place a barrier around yourself for protection against mere beginners like you. So make your choice, Jasmine. Shall I kill Raven or the gargoyle?'

I look over the top of Ronan's head and see Lazarus and the others returning. They are less than a minute away. I need to keep Ronan occupied until then.

'Neither, Ronan. I will leave with you quiet and calmly. I am the stronger sorceress and will join you in your quest to eradicate the dragons. No one here needs to be hurt.' I draw up my energy but keep my fists clenched so he can't see my light.

'Save my son, Jasmine. I beg you,' Raven whispers.

'Oh, this is precious! Is this gargoyle your son, Raven? If I'm not mistaken, he will be a hybrid and have extraordinary powers. Now that's a power I can use. What's your decision, Jasmine?'

'Me! Take me!' I run towards him with the dingoes moving with me.

'Wrong answer!' With Satan's grin, he throws two anorics the size of basketballs. One heads for Raven and one for Jet. In a millisecond I hear Raven's sweet voice begging me to save her son and raise him as if he was mine.

I open my fists and throw two at his torpedoing black ones. I draw again and throw two towards Ronan. He avoids one but the other strikes him in the arm. My anorics have passed through his shield!

He staggers, his face a mask of shock. I take the opportunity to put distance between us. If I can render him helpless, I will let the dragons deal with him as they see fit.

I keep my eyes glued to his as he holds what's left of his arm; his fingers and forearm lie motionless on the ground. I pray my legs hold me as the distance between us is only several short metres.

I keep my hands open wide and hear the gargoyles land behind me. I hear Jarius order the dingoes to drop back. The dragons are still hovering above me, but I don't take my eyes or senses away from Ronan to see which one is shadowing me.

'No! Raven!' screams Lysander. I spin and see him in human form bending over Raven's lifeless body. I search for Jet and see him on his knees with his head bowed. I scream like a madwoman as the dark fluid from beneath the earth fills my veins. I turn back to Ronan, who is smirking at me.

'Join me, Jasmine. Take your cousin's power and we will be unstoppable,' he pants, with blood flowing free from his severed arm.

I take several steps forward, eliminating the distance between us, my lips curving upwards. I hold my right hand out as if I was holding the handle of a sword and crook my finger at him as though I want to whisper in his ear.

As we lean toward each other, a lightning sword shoots from my hand and stabs into his torso.

'I will never be like you. You disgust me.' I step away, withdrawing the sword from his body.

He falls to his knees and smirks up at me, his eyes glazing over. 'You've found the darkness,' he gargles.

I look down at the lightning sword and it's glowing black. I clench my fist and it disappears as quickly as it appeared.

A deafening roar vibrates my body before a heated flame hits the ground, setting Ronan on fire. I stand motionless, staring at the devilish grin on his face before it melts away.

Seconds later, I am being dragged away from the human inferno and from the face that mocks me by a set of strong gargoyle hands.

'You don't want to draw in his powers, Jasmine,' Jarius says, his claws loosening their hold. 'Let them burn.'

I stare coldly at the burning body, too scared to turn to face the reality behind me. A heated pair of arms encase me from behind.

'Please don't touch me,' I say, and Lazarus' hands drop away. I am frozen in fear and hate.

I can hear Lysander and Jet both crying and Lolana scream-ing in pain. Again, death follows me wherever I go and now I fear I have tapped into my dark side. I am a threat to everyone I love.

The chargrilled remains bubble on the dusty ground and, once I am convinced that there's no return for Ronan, I turn to face my ultimate fear.

I move towards my cousin. Her stomach has taken the brunt of Ronan's aim. My legs walk as if on autopilot and I stop and drop beside her.

She is just conscious and gasping for breath. Tears fill my eyes and my throat tightens, stopping any words from flowing. I force a smile to my lips and inhale long deep breaths, trying to regain control of my voice.

'Raven, I'm sorry I didn't protect you.' I can't stop the flood of tears.

'Take my power,' she whispers through faulting breaths.

'You will be just fine. The angels are here to help you. They've fixed me up several times.'

'Take my… power,' she insists through gasping breaths.

'No, Jet is the better one to take it. I've drawn on my dark side. I need to leave.'

'You promised me… to be Jet's guardian. I trust in you.'

'I will never break your trust, Raven, I love you.'

'Grandfather is here to take me away. He sends his love, Jazzle.'

'No! Don't leave me. You're all I've got!'

'Sweet cousin, look around you. This is… your family.' She rolls her eyes to Lysander who is kneeling beside her, covered in her blood. 'Tell Jet I love him.'

'I'm here, Mum,' Jet gasps through pain and tears. 'I will always love you. You will always be a part of me.'

'Yes, son, I will. There is so much I haven't taught you but together with Jazz… you will work it out.' She forces a smile on her lips, but her glazed eyes stay focused on Lysander. 'Ly, you had my heart and soul… the day I met you. I love you.'

She closes her eyes and inhales a deep breath. Her chest falls as she exhales from her open mouth. I wait for her to inhale again but there's nothing.

Lysander's head drops to her chest and he bellows a painful cry.

Without warning, a warm surge floods through my legs, up through my stomach, stopping in the middle of my chest. It's the warmest and most unusual feeling I've ever felt. Raven has merged her powers with mine and my soul feels light for a split second.

I stare at her lying on the ground. Her blood has stopped flowing and her face has become peaceful. I listen for her heartbeat, but it is silent. I see her body lighten as if her soul is being released.

A white light shoots from her torso, and up into the sky, similar to the one I saw shoot from Grandfather when he passed away.

'*Grandfather,*' I echo.

'*Sweet child, don't be sad. Raven is with me and is at peace. Together we will watch over you and Jet. We will be here to guide you when needed. Live the life that is before you and embrace your gift. Stay true to your heart and soul as together, they are an explosion of positive energy. We love you. And keep your promise to guide Jet on the right path.*'

'*I love you both,*' I echo before collapsing onto the ground, sobbing.

Lysander is slow to stand but lifts Raven into his arms with little effort. He walks back to the castle. I wipe my tears so I can see him carry her lifeless body away. He cradles her head in his arm, letting her long brown hair cascade down, catching the slight breeze.

I inhale her scent for the last time and, when it hits my senses, I wish I'd never done it. With an uncontrollable cough, I try to dislodge it from my sense of smell, but it sticks like mud to a boot.

The smell of death and blood is not how I want to remember her. I fight it, in-between crying, until the warm hands I know so well slide over my shoulders. Lazarus lifts me as softly as he can so I am sitting up, then he scoops me up into his strong welcoming arms.

I burrow my head into his bare chest and inhale his scent. As I breathe out, I quickly inhale again, not wanting to have any other scent but his in my nose.

'Store that new scent under something else and keep your cousins as it was. I will teach you how to remove a scent. Just keep it separate for now.'

'Don't put me down. I want no scent except yours.'

'I'm happy with that, babe.' He pulls me in tightly, giving me the comfort I so desperately need.

CHAPTER FIVE

WHEN I WAKE, I'm in my bedroom, securely wrapped in Lazarus' warm arms with my hand clutching my pendant. I must have cried myself to sleep. It is still daylight and I lift my head to see him staring out the window.

'Hi, babe,' he whispers. 'We were planning to bury Raven as soon as you woke. Lysander didn't want to disturb you.'

'What? That is ridiculous! He doesn't need to wait for me! It must be killing him to not be able to put her to rest.'

I jump up but my head spins, making me stagger.

'Take it easy. You have just lost someone you love. You've also been given new powers.'

'Don't tell me what to do! I can handle the powers so don't doubt me.'

'I do not doubt you. Take it easy.'

'Don't tell me to take it easy. I killed my cousin!'

'No, you didn't. Ronan killed her. You saved Jet.'

'Where were you when I needed you? You said you'd protect me and you weren't here!'

'I flew back as quickly as I could.' He moves towards me and tries to pull me into his embrace.

'You need to get far away from me. Everyone I love dies.' I push him away with both hands.

'You can yell at me, hate me and blame me, but I will never leave you.'

I fall to the floor and sob. I can't get the picture of Raven's breathless face from my mind. I recall the scent of her death and it hits me like a punch to the face. I taste blood in my mouth and gag before I throw up on the floor.

I hear the door open and feel the presence of the angels. A glass filled with red wine is placed in front of me.

'Are you deluded? I don't want to drink bloody wine!' I say to Malachi, whose face is inches away from mine.

'Don't cuss at the angels, Jasmine. Take it out on me, not them,' whispers Lazarus.

'It's not wine, Jasmine. It will help calm your senses,' says Malachi.

'I don't want them calm. I want to remember what the death of my loved one tastes like.'

A hand rests on my shoulder and a warm wash flows over me, like a hot shower. My shoulders drop and I glance up into Gabby's soft eyes. She smiles and I return the gesture.

She helps me to my feet but keeps her hand on me. Malachi gives me the glass and I take a small sip. It's not wine. It tastes like a fruity cordial. I drink until the glass is empty.

My mood and mind are calmer now and I can see everything as it is. I am no longer being selfish and grieving for my own loss. Instead, I smile, happy that I loved and knew Raven and can still draw on her when I need to. Jet needs care as he matures, and Lazarus needs me to love him. I have a family to protect and they will protect me just as much.

I smile at Lazarus and he nods at me. I think I am forgiven for my outburst.

'We need to bury Raven,' I say, softly and calmly.

'Lysander has everything prepared, so when you are ready, everyone else will be,' Malachi says. 'Would you like me to help you clean up? Maybe with a quick refreshing shower?'

I hear Lazarus' heart thud hard before I politely decline Malachi's kind offer. 'Thank you for being so kind and I apologise for my snappy tone.'

'You are welcome. We will see you downstairs when you're

ready.' He and Gabby leave the bedroom.

'I owe you an apology.' I move towards Lazarus, who unravels his folded arms. He opens them and I fall into his warm embrace. 'I know you would have been frantic trying to get back to me. I'm sorry for accusing you of anything different.'

'As soon as we got to Nogard Hollow, I could smell he had been there and had left along the creek's edge. We found Xandria hanging in a tree, locked inside an old honey jar. She said Ronan had predicted that the dragons and gargoyles would head over to confront him, leaving you and Raven alone.

'I flew back as fast as I could, babe. If I had lost you, I'd…' He takes a sharp breath.

I squeeze him tightly and kiss his bare chest. 'I know because I feel the same way about you.'

After throwing some cool water over my face, we head down the staircase. When I avoid several steps that are broken, tears flood my eyes at the memory of Jet racing down to protect his mother. Lazarus is by my side, squeezing my hand to show his support.

I arrive at the base of the stairs and everyone stares at me. I open my mouth to speak but my words fail me when I spot Raven's body lying on the couch.

'It's time to lay Raven to rest,' whispers Lysander.

I nod and he picks up her covered lifeless body. He has wrapped her in a white bed sheet and cradles her in his strong arms. Jet walks beside his father with his hand on his shoulder and his head lowered in respect. With a soft tug of my hand, Lazarus encourages me to follow.

Everyone walks in silence to the rear of the castle. We head towards a stunning willow tree on the creekbank where someone has dug a large hole. Jet jumps in and Lysander passes him Raven's body. With tears filling his eyes, he lays her down, making sure she is covered by the sheet before he jumps out.

Corbin and Jarius shovel soil over her. The sound of it as it hits the sheet is sickening.

I fall to the ground, bawling. Lazarus is beside me, drawing me into his comforting arms. I have no will to fight or argue, my mind is numb and my heart is truly shattered.

It doesn't take long before the two boys have her grave finished. We take it in turns telling stories about Raven and what she meant to us. I want and need to keep her memory alive through these stories.

I call her Sky and explain the impact she had on my life from such a tiny age. I can't choose one story to tell as I have so many fond memories. I promise everyone that I will continue to remember her by telling these stories to them.

I listen to everyone else as they talk about her and watch Lolana as she struggles to compose herself, fighting with her own emotions. She is the only one still in gargoyle form and is still badly injured.

Everyone leaves in turn, with the gargoyles returning to the rooftop to rejuvenate and heal. I watch Jet move gingerly towards the castle, his face frowning in pain. He refuses to disclose his true injury to us.

Lolana stays back and struggles to sit beside me. 'I should have ripped him apart, but I didn't have the strength to hold him off the ground. If he'd attacked at night, I would have been strong enough to kill him.'

'You did a very brave thing by dragging him away from us. No one is to blame for Raven's death.' I try to smile but it's hard. I lean over to rub her rough rock hand. 'You need to rest and repair.'

'Like you, I want the pain to remind me to fight harder next time.'

'We need to remember but we must also allow ourselves

time to grieve; I have learnt that much. I tried to shut out Drake's death and run away from it all, but it did me more harm than good. Maybe together we can talk about what we are feeling and help heal each other?'

'Maybe.' She drops her eyes to the ground where she flicks small rocks with her large fingers.

'Is something else bothering you?'

'I've lost my orgle and can't change to human form. I can't be with Corbin looking like this.'

'If you were a fat ugly cane toad, he would still love you. Leave the orgle to me. If I can't find it, I have a great connection to a sorceress who can help me create one.' I lean over to kiss her cold cheek. 'Now stop worrying and go heal.'

She tries to stand, but her injuries are too severe. I jump up to help her. She is in a bad way and I see Corbin leaning up against the castle, waiting for her. He moves at lightning speed towards us and helps her to walk.

She stops and turns to look at me before leaving. 'Thank you.' Then she smiles. 'A cane toad?' She shakes her head and so does Corbin, as he would have listened in on our conversation.

I sit for hours staring at the fresh grave, letting my mind race around with memories, spells and eventually fear. Fear of what is coming if Falcon joins forces with the European dragons.

I sense the presence of the dingoes. I glance up to see Ellie and Rhys wading across the river in human form.

'Hello, guys.' My smile is weak.

'We are so sorry for your loss. Raven was one of our closest friends.' Ellie's tone is genuine.

'She touched our kind in a positive way. It will take time for everyone to come to terms with what has happened,' says Rhys.

'I missed her terribly when she first left. Having her back in my life seemed like a miracle. It's unfair that I have to grieve for her again.'

They sit beside me. 'She would speak of you often and said that leaving you was her only regret.' Ellie smiles.

'My regret is that I didn't kill Ronan earlier.' I sniff.

'He would have killed both Raven and Jet. He was always one step ahead of you,' Rhys says.

'Raven has passed on her powers and knowledge to you. Learn them quickly, as it will make you unstoppable.'

'I worry about drawing on my dark side.'

'You drew on it, but you controlled it. I have never known a sorcerer who can control their dark side. You can switch back and forth without it controlling you. With practice, you will learn which power you are drawing on and when to shut it down,' Ellie explains.

'I pray I have time to practice before the Europeans come.'

'The word on the grapevine, even though it's conflicting, is that Falcon stayed in Australia and is waiting for the Europeans to arrive. He offered to go over there to help in the fight against the gargoyles, but they declined. They want him to collate where and how many gargoyles are in Australia.

'The English gargoyles had an informant telling them of the oncoming attacks and were ready to fight back. Only two castles have been taken over by dragons,' Rhys says. 'The gargoyles are standing strong.'

'You said conflicting. What else have you heard?'

'That Falcon has turned over a new leaf and is going against his father's wishes,' Ellie answers.

'Huh!'

'You once said he could change, that you saw something in him.'

'I believe your grapevine has been compromised.' I shake my head.

'As I said, there are conflicting reports from the creatures loyal to Falcon,' explains Rhys. 'The Europeans also have a new leader since Attor died. He is the most powerful sorcerer. They call him King.'

'King? Isn't it a bit vain to call yourself that?'

'Promise me you'll never confront King alone.' Ellie frowns and her body tenses.

I hear footsteps behind me and turn to see Lysander walking over to us. He stops and nods to the two beside me.

'Our condolences.' Ellie smiles sympathetically.

'Thank you. She will be sadly missed by many. I don't mean to intrude, but I overheard your conversation and need to get word to our Australian relatives. We need to band together and soon.'

'If the dragons aren't winning the fight over in Europe, they have no need to come here,' I say.

'I disagree. I think it will have the opposite effect. They will come over here to train up an army and, after taking over Australia, they will return home to fight.'

'We have so much open space. How would we know if they are here or not?' I ask.

'That is where we come in,' Rhys says, full of pride. 'We will know as soon as they set a foot on Australian soil.'

'Our gargoyle families are so spread out we need to come together or they will pick us off one by one. Falcon knows each and every one and their exact location. We need to notify them of the dangers as soon as we can,' says Lysander.

'Leave that to us. They will be notified within the next twenty-four hours.' Rhys nods with confidence. 'Where do you want them to gather?'

'We can cater for most of them here and I'm sure Lazarus will let us use Nogard Hollow.'

A soft rumbling roar vibrates the air. We turn to see Lazarus in dragon form, wrapped around the tall conical spire of the castle. His lime green eyes stare at us, his mouth open, revealing his razor-sharp teeth. He approves of Lysander's suggestion. I smile and whisper, 'Thank you.' I hear his heart surge out a few quick beats, making me smile wider.

'What can I do to help?' I ask.

'There will be plenty to do when everyone arrives. For now, you need to grieve and to understand your powers.'

'We will always be close by, but we will need to keep our identity hidden from your relatives. We don't have powers to protect ourselves as you do. So we will reveal ourselves only when necessary,' Rhys says.

'I understand and am grateful for all you have done and will do in the future,' says Lysander.

'And we don't want to be dinner for your rooftop dragons,' Ellie adds with a snigger.

Lazarus growls and puffs out a small flame of laughter. Corbin joins him on the roof, wrapping himself around Lolana, who is in stone sleep.

'I don't think dingo is on his menu.' I chuckle, but I stop when I recall their bravery earlier today. 'I don't want you two putting yourselves in danger. I appreciate you standing by me but please don't risk your lives for me. You have three beautiful pups to raise and I don't want to be the reason for them not having their parents.'

'We don't normally get involved physically, only verbally,' Rhys states.

'I heard you loud and clear when you warned Raven.'

'I wish I had heard about Ronan's movements earlier, but he used a spell disabling our senses' ability to locate him.' Ellie's face drops.

'Death is a part of life.' Lysander places his large hand on Ellie's shoulder.

'Yeah, well it sucks!' I blurt.

'Yes, it does but Raven... sorry, Sky, would want us to

remember her happy and loving. Not her last dying moments.'

'We better get a move on and send the message to your clan. I will be in touch, Lysander, as soon as I hear anything. Again, our condolences.' Rhys stands up and shakes Lysander's hand. He and Ellie kiss my cheek. 'Goodbye, Jasmine. We are only a whisper away if you need us.'

'Thank you both. But let's not say goodbye. It sounds so final. I will see you guys later.' I stand up and hug Ellie before they leave.

I watch the two cross the creek and change form into ginger-coloured dingoes. They acknowledge us with a howl before running off.

'How are you holding up?' I ask.

'My heart is breaking with every thought of her. I know I will wake up tomorrow and the next day alone. But I also know she loves me as much as I love her and we have a son to show for it. Jet is my main focus. His training will be my top priority.' Lysander takes a deep breath before looking up to his son who's sitting on the castle rooftop in stone sleep.

'Both he and Lolana have serious injuries.'

'They will both heal physically if they stay in stone sleep for the next twenty-four hours. But mentally will take a little longer. Lolana's mother was killed by a sorcerer so this must bring back horrible memories for her.'

'I'll keep an eye on her.'

I stand motionless, staring at Sky's grave. Lysander moves to encase me in one arm as if he is supporting me. I slip my arm around his waist and we stare at the disturbed ground, not saying a word.

We must have been standing arm in arm for over thirty minutes when Lazarus snorts behind us, still a dragon. I didn't sense his movement, my mind lost in the memories of Sky.

'I need to rest. Will you be all right?' Lysander asks.

'I will be. I'm always here for you when you're ready to talk about Sky. And please let me know how I can help.'

'Gabby is gardening but Malachi is inside if you need anything,' he adds, before leaving.

Lazarus rumbles deep in his dragon chest. Lysander shakes his head and walks towards the castle.

I move to Lazarus and he drops his head to my height. I rub my hands over his large, scaled head. He inhales deeply, taking in my scent.

'You are a jealous, dragon. Malachi has nothing on you. You should be a green dragon, not red.'

His warm nose nuzzles me.

'I might go for a ride.'

He pushes me back towards his front leg and sits.

'I don't mean ride you. I mean Blue Boy.'

He blows out a puff of smoke and shakes his head.

'Don't get jealous of a horse. I won't be long. I need to clear my head.'

He rumbles a disapproving growl.

'I'll be half an hour and will stick to the creek. If I'm not back in time for dinner, you can yell at me and no doubt I will hear you.'

He blinks and walks back to the castle like a moping dog. His body language tells me he is sulking, but I don't back down.

I whip on Blue Boy's bridle and throw myself up onto his broad back. We head to the creek, passing Sky's resting place. I force a smile on my lips, remembering her sweet face when she was sitting in bed with me giggling under the sheets.

'I'll see you later, cousin,' I whisper and spur Blue Boy forward.

I relax my body and flop my legs against his wide stomach. He has his ears pricked and a spring in his step. He loves being ridden, which gives me the guilts for leaving him alone for so long.

I block out my thoughts and listen to the Australian Outback as it sings its magical tune. Birds call out to each other, creating a harmonic sound. Critters scamper on the dusty red ground, together with the water cascading over the rocky creek floor. It is nature's orchestra. I inhale its unforgettable aroma of gumtree, cattle and rusty earth—I love it!

I remember my late cousin, Sky, and the promise I made to raise and educate Jet. I feel honoured she thought so much of me to ask me to care for her only son. I already love him as though he's my own.

I turn my mind to the last year—the good, the bad, what I have learnt and the people I have met. I've found happiness living amongst the elite but there's an unnerving feeling in the pit of my stomach. I miss my parents and, with Ronan threatening to visit them, it makes me uneasy. I want to return home to see them, plus I need to be the one who tells them about Sky's death.

This is the life I am meant to lead; what Grandfather nurtured me for when I was young.

I shiver, feeling the air cool, and realise that night is falling. Blue Boy has wandered for hours without my guidance, placing us close to Nogard Hollow. I kick him on and canter the rest of the way to the dragons' den.

As we approach Nogard Hollow, the sky lights up with a dragon's flame. Pulling on my reins, Blue stops and jogs on the spot. I force my ears to listen to the beat of the dragon's heart as night is approaching and I can't clearly see which dragon it is.

'Is that you, Lazarus?'

He answers me in the way I recognise, with a deafening roar. He takes off and lands in the pasture in front of me. Blue Boy jumps around, unsure if he is this large creature's prey. I grip my legs tightly, careful to not fall off, rubbing his neck to soothe him.

'I'm sorry I lost track of the time.' I smile. 'Please don't be mad and blow smoke because you will spook Blue.' He snorts and shakes his head. Then, to my delight and amazement, he changes form.

'Can I yell at you now?' He stands before me with his hands on his hips. I say nothing. He moves as if I am a mouse and he is the cat ready to pounce. He stops beside me and places his hot hand on my leg. 'Scoot back.'

I do and, in a blink, he's in front of me on the horse's back. I wiggle forward and wrap my arms around his waist.

'Hmm, I missed you,' he purrs.

'Does that mean I'm forgiven?'

'Squeeze me tighter and I'll think about it.' He kicks Blue Boy into a canter. I hold him tightly, drawing my body to his, so we are one.

Approaching and entering Nogard Hollow makes my skin crawl. The memory of Attor imprisoning me here is raw and has left a bad taste in my mouth.

Lazarus reassures me that he scanned the property for any creatures before I entered. 'You're safe with me.'

'This place gives me the creeps.'

'This place has fond memories for me. We had our first kiss here.'

'Yes, we did.' I grin, remembering him losing his head because he tasted Drake on my lips.

'Your increased heartbeat better be because you're remembering our kiss.' He opens the curtains, which allows the evening light to brighten the dreary room.

'It is.' I chuckle, and he growls deep in his chest, moving quicker than lightning to stand in front of me.

He draws me into his arms, creating a comforting and

secure embrace. He lowers his face and presses a soft kiss on my lips. The gentleness of his touch spurs my heart to flicker.

He smiles a knowing grin. 'Are you hungry?'

'I'm sure the food here has gone mouldy.'

'We have a cool store in the cave. Why don't you soak in the bath for a while and leave dinner to me?'

'Do I smell?'

'Not at all, but if I don't occupy my mind and hands, I will do more than give you one small kiss.'

'Will you be in the cave long?' I feel a little nervous about being alone in this house.

'No creature will enter with me inside. Relax, babe. You're safe.' He rubs his hands up and down the length of my arms to comfort me.

'You're not scary enough to keep creatures from entering.'

'I may not be to you, but I am at the top of the food chain and everyone knows it. Trust me, they will keep their distance. Plus, we would have had word if the Europeans had arrived. And I flew the area to see if I could catch Falcon's scent; he's not here. I can take you to the cave with me if you wish.'

'No, thanks. I've seen enough caves to last me quite a while. A bath sounds good.' I shudder at the memory of the cold caves I have been in.

'I won't be long.' With a swift kiss, he disappears through the large doors.

I stand still, letting my eyes take in the mansion's surrounds. The evening light shines through the large windows, giving slight warmth to the oversized living area. I blow out the lungful of air I have been nervously holding and listen for any alarming noises.

There are birds chirping and the usual scatter of small critters. Lazarus' loud heartbeat indicates he is in dragon form and, due to it fading, is heading down into the cave. I drop my tense shoulders and head for the bedroom, which was once deemed for me.

The room is still in a shamble from the last time I was here. Shutting the door, I head along the timbered corridor until I smell Lazarus. Pushing open the door, I find a masculine bedroom.

I take a pillow from the four-poster bed and inhale his scent. Heaven! This is his room. I open two large timber doors, thinking it's the bathroom, but it's filled with clothes. Some are dusty and some still have the price tags on them.

I wonder when he has had time to go shopping and where he would go. I imagine him flying onto the rooftop car park and changing form, only to walk into the shopping centre to purchase another pair of jeans as the last pair were torn in a dragon fight. Then he would fly home with the shopping bags hanging from his killer-sharp talons. The thought makes me smile and I relax.

I open the remaining door to find a waiting bath. I turn the large tap and hear the water rattle and whine as it surges up the old copper pipes.

As I remove my clothes, I sense the nearby presence of a creature. I turn to look at the bath and Xandria is standing on the edge with a small bottle of essential oils.

'Why do you have to interrupt all my baths, Xandria?'

'Xandria was visiting relatives close by and heard you were here. She wanted to give my sincere condolences for the sad loss of my friend, Raven.' Her tone is authentic. She pours the entire contents of the bottle into my bath.

'Thank you, but I'd prefer you stopped coming into my bathroom. I enjoy my privacy and I'm not sure I want to speak to you. You must have known Ronan was going to double-cross us.'

'When Xandria returned and relayed your message to Ronan, he said he was going to the castle to kill any remaining elites. You told me you were coming here. You lied to Xandria. Then Ronan captured Xandria, placing her in an old honey jar. I can't see how I'm to blame.'

'Well, I do, so leave and give my privacy.'

'Huh! You humans and privacy.' She screws the lid back onto the empty bottle.

The aroma is delightful and the bubbles fill the tub. 'That smells nice, but I don't think I needed the whole bottle,'

'Yes, you do. You smell like horse. Trust me, Lazarus was being polite saying you smelt fine.' She screws up her nose. 'His last girlfriend left her oils here, so why not use them?'

'His last girlfriend?'

'You're not the first human he has brought here. Did you think you're that special?'

'Yes, I did, but I can see I was wrong.' My heart thuds with jealousy. 'But I've also learnt not to trust you.'

'Dragons aren't known for being faithful. They enjoy having at least two women each.' She tries to turn off the tap with her two small hands. I lean over and help her. 'I've heard Lazarus likes one human and one dragon, just to spice it up.'

'Great, so I will smell like his last girlfriend.'

'But you don't believe Xandria.'

I hesitate, stepping into the bath, but then have the devilish thought of soaking myself in these essential oils and watching his reaction when he smells his ex. He lectures me about controlling my heartbeat so I will see if he can restrain his when the aroma hits his olfactory.

I drop into the scented water, closing my eyes so as not to see the annoying little fairy. I push away the jealous thoughts and force my mind to go blank.

After a long while several droplets of water drip onto my face. 'Xandria is still here, human. Why don't you talk to her?'

'Because Xandria is annoying!'

'She only wants to be of help and be a friend, as she was to Raven.' She splashes several drops of water on my face.

'Her name is Sky!' I splash a fistful of water over the little creature.

'You are not the only one who is sad and missing her.' Her tone is mournful as she jumps up and flicks her wings dry.

Her tone makes me sit up straight. She is right; I'm not the only one who loved her. 'I'm sorry, but I get the feeling you enjoy stirring the pot and only tell me information that will agitate me or get me into trouble.'

'Xandria is a friend to many and can be to you if you allow it. You must stop seeing the negative in creatures.'

'Negative? Me?' I jump up and out of the bath, sloshing the water over the edge, knocking her into the tub. She spits and spatters, waving her arms and legs in a panic. Her wings have stuck together, and she is having trouble keeping her head above the water.

I reach in and grab her, placing her onto the small vanity.

'I can't swim, Jasmine! If my wings get wet, I can't fly. Just like a bird can't fly when their wings are wet. You never see a bird flying in the rain, do you?'

'I didn't mean to drop you in. I only wanted to splash you. At least you called me Jasmine and not human.' I shrug my guilt-ridden shoulders.

'Hmm, one day you will be surprised when we see eye to eye.'

'What do you mean, eye to eye?'

'There's no time for an explanation as your dinner is ready. Xandria will see you again soon and you will understand.' She turns her back on me and tests out her wings.

'Fine!' I leave with a towel wrapped around me. I open Lazarus' wardrobe and pull on one of his t-shirts, which fits me like a short dress.

I walk into the large living room and follow my nose to the kitchen. Lazarus is madly cooking when I enter, and it smells mouth-wateringly good. He turns then stops cooking.

I walk over to him, his eyes never leaving me. I want him to breathe me in, to smell the scent of his ex.

I listen hard to his heartbeat and it quickens as I approach. I stop several inches away from him, his emerald green eyes heating as they stare down and into me. He breathes me in and I smile at him. His eyebrow questions me but he says nothing.

'Do I remind you of someone?'

'No one in particular, but you must have been searching through Attor's room.' He moves closer so there's nothing between us. The heat from his body is intense but he doesn't touch me.

'Are you sure it doesn't remind you of one of your ex-girlfriends?'

'My ex-girlfriends?' Like switching on a light bulb, he realises something. 'Xandria was telling stories again. I sensed she was in the bathroom with you but your heartbeat stayed calm, so I thought all was well.'

'She told me your girlfriends bathed in your tub using these oils.'

'That was Attor's favourite thing, not mine. It sounds as though you're a tiny bit jealous, babe.' He blinks his large eyes and I roll mine. I am about to move away when he encases me in his warm arms. 'Don't go getting grumpy, I've cooked us a lovely dinner.'

'Which smells like it could be burning.'

'Oh, bugger!' He turns off the stove. Within seconds, he is back holding me. 'Now, where was I? Hmm, I was disciplining you then I was going to kiss you, even though you smell like one of Attor's women.'

'I will kill that little fairy!'

'Why would you want to smell like my ex-girlfriends?' He gives me a curious look.

'I didn't! But Xandria said your ex used it when she was with you, so I wanted to hear your reaction.'

'The only reaction you heard was when I laid my eyes on you wearing my t-shirt and nothing else. You are one beautiful woman and you always smell delicious.' He kisses me softly, then with more passion. 'Maybe there's a little bit of dragon in you after all.'

'I'm not jealous of your exes!'

'Hmm,' he rumbles, smiling at me.

'But I do have one question.'

'Ask away.'

'Do dragons need more than one girlfriend? Do you need a human girl and a dragon girl to be happy?'

'Huh! Why do you listen to that little pest? Of course not. Trust me; you are more than enough woman for me.'

'I don't know if your answer offends or pleases me.' I frown, but then smile as I know Xandria is playing her little annoying games again.

'Come and sit. Dinner is ready.'

He points at the table set for two. There are two glasses of wine and a vase that has wildflowers shoved roughly into it. Judging by his attempt at arranging them, I can guarantee he will never be a florist. I smile—it's his way of being romantic. None of my ex-boyfriends ever spoilt me this way. With a melting heart, I take my seat.

His movements are quicker than my eye can see and, in less than a minute, he has my food plated and placed before me. He sits with a proud grin. He has cooked steak with wild mushrooms and a side of salad. The vegetable garden must be thriving even though it's been unattended for a while, as my salad looks divine.

'It looks delicious and smells even better,' I say, and his smile reaches his ears. He holds up his wine glass to toast mine. Our glasses clink and our eyes lock.

'I love you, Jazz.' His face becomes serious. 'To us and to our future together.'

'To our future together.'

I polish off the whole plate of food and it is scrumptious. We talk like two people who haven't seen each other in a long time. Then we sit on the small balcony watching the evening stars until I fall asleep under his warm arm.

I stir from a happy dream to find that I am tucked into Lazarus' bed. I reach out for him, but I am alone, so I listen hard to find him. Nothing.

Heading into the corridor, I stop, stand still and listen. The only sound is the singing of night-time creatures. I close my eyes and dig deeper, smiling when I hear his beat—soft and calm.

I move to the cave and the sound increases. He is in dragon form. I leave, wondering why he'd prefer to sleep in the cave than with me. I climb back into bed clasping my pendant before falling into a deep sleep.

'Good morning, beautiful,' he whispers, spooning in behind me.

'Morning.' I roll over to face him. 'Why didn't you sleep with me last night?'

'To be honest, I miss the cave. I was in dragon form the majority of the time whilst living here. I'm sorry if I scared you.' He nuzzles into me.

'I wasn't scared. I was wondering where you were.' I roll back over so he can cuddle in. 'I'm going home for a week to see my parents. I need to tell them, face to face, what happened to Sky.'

'Fine. I will come with you.'

'How can you be public with your eyes looking like a pair of cat's eyes?'

'Contact lenses, babe. We're not that prehistoric, you know, and we have been mixing with humans for centuries.'

I spin around, amused at his eyewear.

'There are elite creatures that prefer to live as humans amongst the humans.'

'So I leave home running away from a dishonest boyfriend and come back with a new one? I'm sure that will go down well with my parents since I left home to get away from my last boyfriend.'

'Don't bring up your exes. Remember, I *am* the jealous one and might accidentally burn down his house or sit on his precious car in dragon form. All male humans love their cars.' He flicks his eyebrows at me.

'I'll keep that in mind, dragon. Anyhow, I will have to keep hidden with these markings I have.'

'Only creatures of the elite nature will see them, and of course, sorcerers, so you will be fine.'

We spend the day rearranging Nogard Hollow's interior, allowing more light in and trying to give it a homier feel. I get the impression Lazarus wants to live here, even though it gives me the creeps.

We return to Elyograg Castle to find the gargoyles in stone sleep and the angels in the kitchen with Corbin. I advise them of my plans to return home to my parents for a short time so I can explain in person what has occurred. No one seems surprised or alarmed by my plans.

Before nightfall, I search for Lolana's orgle. I eventually find it, broken into two pieces. Crossing my legs, I sit on the ground and draw on my grandfather's presence. I hear and feel his energy.

I sense Sky is here, but I can't yet hear her. I ask for guidance in repairing the orgle and to learn the secret of creating one from scratch. I need to have them ready for when the other gargoyle relatives arrive.

Placing the broken pieces in one palm, I squeeze my hand shut. I pull deep from the earth's energy, concentrating on the mineral in my palm and where it originated from, deep below me.

A cool wet force floods my legs and up my torso before flowing along my arms, stopping in the palm of my hand. A vision of the two pieces joining fronts my mind, before I feel the stones move in my clenched hand.

I open my hand and witness the magic. Wow! I really am a powerful sorceress.

'Lolana, glide down to me,' I yell.

She stands on the edge of the castle roof in gargoyle form, then steps off, gliding on a soft breeze. She is a beautiful creature, but if I didn't know she was kind, I'd die of fright seeing her glide toward me. She smiles, which from a human's point of view, isn't an attractive site. A mouthful of razor-sharp teeth speeding toward you would stop anyone's heart.

I smile and hold out the orgle in the palm of my hand. She growls with appreciation, landing with an earth-shaking thud. She is graceful while flying but is an elephant on landing.

'You are amazing, Jasmine. You fixed it! How can I ever thank you?' She wraps her large webbed wings around me, squeezing me too tightly.

'Can't breathe,' I squeak.

'Oh, sorry.' She giggles, which sounds more like a hiccupping growl.

'You are very welcome. Go test it out before you thank me. It's my first one and it might turn you into toad instead of a human.'

She looks afraid to place it against her skin. Surprising her,

I move fast and press it against her.

Her eyes lock with mine as she crumbles before me. I see her human face appearing from under the rubble. I take a relieved breath when she grabs me with her human arms for a warm embrace.

I pull back and frown.

'What's wrong?' Her voice is full of fear. 'Am I not the same as before? Have you changed my features? Will Corbin recognise me?'

My lips curve into a large smile. 'Just joking. You're the same.'

'Phew! You had me worried. You should know it's not a good idea to trick a gargoyle. Especially a love-struck female,' she nervously laughs. 'Thank you.' She kisses me on my cheek several quick times.

'Don't waste your kisses on me. Go find Corbin.'

'I love you,' she yells, running off towards the castle.

The evening is filled with laughter and talk of Sky. I leave them chatting and slip off to my bed. I want to get up early to have a full day's driving under my belt. I can't remember how I got here and which way to go, but no doubt Lazarus will know. I smile as I try to picture him with contacts in his eyes and drift off to sleep dreaming of home.

CHAPTER SIX

LAZARUS WAKES ME before dawn. I grab my bags and, on exiting my bedroom, I find Jet pacing the hallway, impatiently waiting for me.

'I want you to reconsider going back to Melbourne. You don't know who or what is waiting for you,' he blurts in one quick breath.

'Lazarus is with me, Jet. I will be fine. My powers are much stronger now.'

'Let me come with you.'

'No, you have to be here to welcome your relatives. I will return in two weeks. You must promise me you will stay here and obey your father.'

'It's my job to protect you. I can't do it when your miles away!'

'I'm not arguing with you. Let me leave remembering you happy, please.'

'Well I'm not, and the dragon can't look after you like I can.'

'Yes, he can, and he will,' interrupts Lazarus in a stern tone.

'She should stay here where we can protect her.' Jet puffs his chest out.

I step in-between them, knowing Lazarus has a short temper and may burn the castle to the ground.

'As I said, I am stronger than you know.' I reach up, cupping his cheek in the palm of my hand. 'I love you and will see you soon.' I reach up to kiss his cheek. 'See you later, Jet, and behave.'

Jet lets out a wall-shattering growl and storms up the stairs towards the roof. I'm about to follow him, but Lazarus grabs my arm. 'He will calm down. We need to get moving.'

I hesitate before picking up my bags and moving to the truck, eager to get away from the young gargoyle's tantrums. I throw Lazarus the keys then put my bags in the back.

I scan the rooftop and see my gargoyle family in stone sleep, staring in my direction. All except Jet, who, in gargoyle form, is storming around the roof growling his disapproval.

WE DRIVE FOR most of the day, stopping only once to eat the picnic lunch the angels had packed for us. I don't recognise any of the landscape and shake my head at how stupid I was to drive off the beaten road without leaving any breadcrumbs to follow out. We roll out the swag and sleep under the millions of stars, both of us exhausted from the long drive.

I wake to the gentle rocking of the truck. Lazarus is driving. He says he couldn't sleep and wanted to get as many kilometres done as possible. He's anxious; I can sense it. He's becoming edgier the closer we are to civilisation.

We hit the outskirts of Melbourne after dusk and pull up to my parents' home late in the evening. My father stands in the doorway, lifting his hand to his brow, sheltering his eyes from the glaring security lights my truck activated on our approach.

I fling open the door and run towards him. 'Dad! It's me!'

'Jazzy?'

'Dad!' I hiccup, running flat out until I am locked in his loving arms.

'Jazzy, your home! I don't believe it! Let me look at you,' he says with a quivering voice.

'I missed you guys so much.' I suddenly realise how true that is and tears flood my eyes.

'Gloria, come and see who is here!'

I hear movement and a heartbeat so warm it would melt an Eskimo's heart.

'What's going on, Geoff?' she says from behind the door. She steps out, her face lighting up when she spots me.

I release Dad, opening my arms wide to her.

'Oh, my goodness! Jasmine, my baby girl,' she shrieks, wrapping me tightly in her arms.

'Mum, I missed you so much.'

'Are you home for good?' she asks, holding me at arm's length, racing her eyes up and down. She stops at my face and studies me for a long few seconds.

'No, Mum, I'm not. I have something to tell you.'

The look on her face tears at my heart. She tried to keep this side of her life at bay and here I am bringing it to her doorstep. I drop my head, feeling as though I have let her down.

She uses her index finger to tilt my head up so I am looking directly into her eyes. She runs her fingers gently over one side of my face and I wonder if she can see my facial markings.

'Whatever it is we will deal with it.' She smiles but it doesn't reach her heart.

'You can see my markings, can't you?'

'What are you two talking about? And did you forget your manners while you were out travelling? Introduce us to your friend,' my father says, walking over to Lazarus with his hand stretched out. 'G'day, I am Jasmine's father, Geoff.'

'I'm Lazarus. I believe we've met before,' he murmurs, shaking my father's hand.

'I'm sorry. Mum and Dad, this is Lazarus… my boyfriend.'

I watch my mother's face, which instantly scans his. I look at Lazarus' eyes. He has slipped in his contact lenses. I try not to laugh.

'Lazarus?' she questions, holding out her hand to him. 'I'm

Gloria.' He shakes her hand and in an instant, her face drops and she turns to me. 'A dragon! For Pete's sake, Jasmine. A dragon!'

'Mum! Can we take this inside, please?' I quickly scan the front yard for anyone or any creature.

My father's hands shoot to his head, pulling back what little hair he has from his shocked face. 'Please, Lazarus, come inside.'

Lazarus nods and moves confidently towards me, escorting me into the house with his warm hand on my lower back. I walk inside with my mouth still wide open at my mother's outburst. How did she know he was a dragon? She must have recognised his heat.

'Would you like a coffee or a beer?' Dad offers, less phased by the situation.

'Beer, thanks,' he answers.

'Me too, thanks Dad,' I murmur.

His eyebrows shoot up in surprise. 'You don't drink beer.'

'I think I will need one with what I have to tell you both.'

My mother turns to Lazarus. 'Please excuse my outburst but I'm not happy that my daughter is dating a dragon.'

Lazarus nods as if to accept her half-hearted apology.

Then she turns back to me. 'When did you get your markings?'

'The ones on my legs arrived after I was burnt by...' I hesitate to finish my sentence. Am I supposed to tell her that Lazarus lured me to Nogard Hollow to force me to join the dragons in killing the gargoyles?

'A darn dragon!' she finished my sentence.

'It's not what you think. It's a long story and one I don't want to go into this late in the night. I came home because I had to tell you and Dad something important.'

'That you're a sorceress?' she snaps.

'What? But we protected her from all of that. Her orgle should have erased it all,' my father says.

'No, that's not it. I have been living with Sky,' I say, softening my tone. I hear my mother gasp when she hears the name of my lost cousin. 'She died in my arms last week, killed by a dark sorcerer.' I try to control my tears.

Lazarus reaches for my hand and squeezes it gently in support. I explain how I met up with her and how she died but kept the details of the elite creatures I have met a secret. I tell them Sky had a son with Lysander but nothing further. The less they know the safer they will be. I tell them of the connection I now have with Grandfather and how he guides me when needed.

I talk until my throat is hoarse, but my yawns become contagious and send all of us off to our beds. I slide into my old bed, feeling secure and at home. I drift off to sleep seconds later.

I wake to Lazarus sitting on the side of my bed with his contact lenses in his eyes. He blinks non-stop, making me smile.

Entering the kitchen, I find both my parents eager to continue the conversation from last night. They both fire questions at Lazarus and, to his credit, he keeps his heartbeat steady and answers as honestly as he can without putting them in danger.

'It's predicted there's going to be an invasion from the European dragons. Drake's father, Hudson, is over there trying to bring calm but no one has heard from him. Word is that many gargoyles have fallen. We're expecting the worst.'

'Then Jasmine should stay here under our protection,' says my mother.

'She is safer under the protection of our clan.'

'No one found her whilst she was under our protection,' says my mother. 'Can you say the same?'

'I am now known to be the strongest and most powerful

sorceress in Australia. My whereabouts are to be kept hidden and Nogard Hollow is the best place.'

'Ronan found you and killed Sky.'

'Maybe he followed me from the Outback,' I say.

'For the most powerful sorceress in Australia, you should have known to have all your senses switched on. You should have sensed him following you.' She sighs and shakes her head. 'I'm not convinced living with the elite is the best place for you.'

'I'm not leaving them. I made a promise to Sky and I love Lazarus.'

'You've known him for less than a year.'

My father grunts, clearing his throat. 'Maybe I can show Lazarus around the property and leave you two ladies to talk.'

'Good idea. Mum and I need to talk this through further,' I say, nodding to Lazarus.

He stands then kisses my cheek before following my father out of the house.

My mother and I spend the remainder of the day talking about our feelings. In the end, she understands why I want to live with the elites but isn't overly happy about it.

Dad and Lazarus walk the property and, thanks to my heightened hearing, talk about fishing, farming and an old sorcerer named Aldore. From their conversation, I gather Aldore was the sorcerer who placed the unbreakable cloaking spell over me when Sky and Grandfather left.

Waking fresh and with a weight lifted from my shoulders, I show Lazarus the small suburban town I grew up in. With me by his side, he says he can control himself against devouring the two-legged creatures known as humans.

We walk down the main street hand in hand, and I notice so much more than I once did. The smells and sounds of this bustling town are a sensory overload.

I would hate to walk down the main streets of Melbourne.

My head would explode with the sounds and smells of traffic, horse and carriages, people, machines, restaurants and everything else that great city offers. I laugh out loud at the thought, gaining me a firm squeeze of my hand from Lazarus.

After splashing out on a tub of ice cream and Lazarus getting his first 'brain freeze', we head back to my parents' place. As we drive up the driveway, I can smell Mum has cooked her famous roast dinner. Our mouths water before we have time to get out of the truck.

'There's a school reunion on tonight. You should go. I know Paul would love to see you again,' she says.

'Paul who?' Lazarus asks with a lifted brow.

'Jasmine's English teacher, Mr Tanner.'

'He was my favourite teacher. He spoilt me and all the other kids would tease me, saying I was the teacher's pet. I knew I was, and I didn't care.

'It was funny how every year he would be my teacher. He would often give me a lift home, refusing to let me walk alone because he worried about strangers. He was a bit like Jet with his protective mannerisms,' I say, smiling at the memory. 'It was so sad when his wife died in a hang gliding accident.'

'It was a very sad day. I think it would be beneficial for you to attend tonight and make sure you talk to Paul.' My mother pats my hand while pouring more gravy over my roast. 'Rick has also been visiting regularly, trying to catch up with you.'

'Rick?' Lazarus stops eating and glares at me.

'He's an old friend from high school.' I keep my tone flat because if he knows it's my ex-boyfriend he may go hunting tonight.

'I'm happy to accompany you,' Lazarus says as Mum adds the remainder of the meat to his plate. She must know how much dragons can consume. 'Thank you, Gloria.'

'I suppose I could go for an hour. I'd be lying if I said I

wasn't a little intrigued by how much my classmates have changed and what they are doing now. But only if you feel comfortable and in control, Laz.' He nods firmly.

I finish my dinner and leave Lazarus to continue devouring anything that was left on the table. That man can eat!

I fossick around my wardrobe, pulling out a short summery dress. I slip it on and add a small amount of makeup. It's the first bit of makeup I've worn in over a year.

After throwing on a pair of high heels, I head out into the lounge room to find Dad and Lazarus rolling around in fits of laughter. They seem to have hit it off and I daren't ask what they find so funny.

Butterflies circle my stomach as we walk into the timber school hall I once used for lectures. It is filled with familiar faces. Some have changed and some are still the same as I remember.

The walls of the room are lined with old photos, bringing back fond memories. There are colourful helium balloons floating above the dance floor and a five-piece band. The lighting is dim, which makes me glad. I am paranoid about my markings, even though no human can see them.

After introducing Lazarus to several old friends, I drag him onto the dance floor to escape the questions. In an instant, I'm drawn into his warm arms and his nose nuzzles into my hair. His heated body aligns with mine as if we're moulded just for each other like yin and yang.

He breathes me in and I muffle a groan to let him know I can hear him. His lips are on my neck, curving up into a smile. He's eliminating the human's scent and filling it with mine. He kisses my neck then moves to my ear. He nips my lobe. 'You need to learn to turn off your senses, babe.'

'Not when I have a hot boyfriend like you around. I saw how those girls were looking at you.' I run my hands over his toned shoulders and back. We dance slowly and out of rhythm, oblivious to what is going on around us.

The music stops as the band takes a break. We head for the bar and grab a drink each. We clink our cans together. 'Cheers, big ears!' Lazarus chuckles, wiggling his ears.

I stop smiling when I hear a racing heartbeat beside me. Turning, I see my ex-boyfriend, Rick, smiling at me.

I glance at Lazarus. His eyes have narrowed and a puff of smoke escapes his nostrils. I reach for his hand and give it a firm squeeze.

'Jazzy,' Rick kisses me too quickly for me to escape.

'It's Jasmine,' I correct.

'Oh, sorry. How have you been and where have you been?'

'I'm great, thanks. This is my boyfriend, Lazarus.'

'Oh. Um… That's an unusual name. Where are you from?'

'What do you want, Rick?' I jump in before Lazarus can answer.

'Could I have a moment of your time… alone?'

'Nope!' I shake my head uncaringly.

'Please, baby. I need to explain my side of things.'

'Baby?' Lazarus growls.

'I'm not your baby and there is nothing you can say that I want to hear.'

'I am so sorry for what I did to you. What I did to us. I have been nagging your folks for months, trying to find you, but they said they didn't know where you were. I need to tell you something.'

'They didn't know where I was. No one did. What did you need to tell me?'

'Can I speak to you in private, please Jazz?' he begs.

'No, you can say it in front of Lazarus or don't say it at all.

I'm leaving tomorrow so this will be your only chance.' My hand is sweating in Lazarus' which means he is becoming agitated.

'Fine. If this is the way you want it. I want to apologise…' his eyes shoot nervously around the room before he continues, 'for sleeping with Kelly. I made a huge mistake and I want to make it up to you.

'I miss you in my life; we were so good together and I was hoping you will give me another chance. There's no one in this shithole of a town who comes close to you.'

He moves closer. Lazarus growls and steps in front of me, becoming the meat between an old sandwich.

'Did you just growl at me?' he questions Lazarus.

I squish in-between the two men, 'I accept your apology because the last apology I received I didn't accept and now I have to live with that decision.'

'Kelly's death had nothing to do with you. You need to stop feeling guilty.'

'That's a bit hard when everyone in town blames me for it.'

'They blame me too. If she was upset, she shouldn't have driven her car, then she wouldn't have had an accident.'

'No one blames you, as you were still sleeping with her. They blame me as I was the jilted lover who never forgave her.'

'Can you honestly say you have no feelings for me? After everything we shared? The love we shared?' Rick frowns as if he is in pain, his body slightly slumping.

'No feelings at all. I am in love with this man right here.' I smile at Lazarus who is glaring daggers. I need to defuse him before he burns a hole in Rick's forehead. 'You broke my trust, which takes more than an apology to fix it.'

I hear Lazarus start to inhale his scent. Hell's bells, if he gains his scent, I know he will return to hurt him when I am not around. I blow in his face. He jolts as if I had flicked his nose with my finger.

He stares down at me with a devilish grin. He knows he's been caught. 'Come on, babe. The band is about to start up again.' I roll my shoulders back and stand tall before tugging him towards the dance floor. 'Goodbye, Rick.'

'Jasmine, please,' he pleads behind my back. I ignore it.

Lazarus pulls me in hard, holding me too tightly. He places his forehead on mine, locking our eyes. It makes me smile to see his pupils round instead of the black slits I've come to love.

He narrows his eyes and I know his brain is running wild. 'Let me burn him to a crisp,' he whispers.

'Behave, dragon.'

'What if I grill or toast him?'

'I said behave.' I try my best to quash my smile.

'At least let me singe him a little bit.' He flicks his eyebrows up and down.

'Behave or I will give you an electric shock.'

'Hmm, now that sounds like fun.' He spins me around in a circle.

'I'm proud of you for not making a scene and controlling your jealousy.'

'The night is young, babe. And there are a lot of juicy hearts beating in here.'

'The only heart you should listen to is mine, dragon. Or else we will see who has the stronger power—the little red dragon or the mighty sorceress.'

'Oh, I love a challenge, babe—' He stops mid-sentence. We both stop dancing, freezing like statues. I hear and sense another dragon and, in a blink, recognise it to be Falcon.

Lazarus' head spins to face a door at the back of the hall, lit with a green exit sign.

'Stay here amongst the crowd,' he orders before speeding out the back exit.

I follow with fisted hands, filling them, ready to throw an anoric at Falcon. I fling open the door and find him standing still with his hands open, palms up. Lazarus is pacing back and forth in front of him.

'Lazarus?' I murmur.

He whips his head around, 'For once will you do as you're told and go back inside?'

'I'm not leaving you,' I reply, a little timidly, due to his eyes throwing daggers at me.

'I'd appreciate it if you would relax your hands, Jasmine. I'm not here to threaten either of you.' Falcon's tone is calm.

'What do you want?' Lazarus asks, angling his body so I'm not in Falcon's firing line.

'I promise I am not here to hurt her, Laz, quite the opposite. I'm here to apologise and ask for you the clan's forgiveness.'

'Huh! There's a lot of that going around tonight.' I scoff.

Lazarus spins around to glare at me again. 'Jasmine, go inside, now!'

'No!' I feel my foot automatically stamp the ground. I look past Lazarus so I can see Falcon's face. 'Why the change of heart?'

'I've just returned from Europe and it's a bloody mess. There are men like my father, who have distorted views and are killing the gargoyles for no apparent reason.'

'They are greedy for the golden souls,' I snap.

'I have seen innocent gargoyles being killed and souls stolen. Some of them I've known for years and we were good friends.

'I warned families and tried to hide and protect as many as I could but they soon lost faith in me as they watched the dragons slaughter their families. They knew my father had instigated the attack and brainwashed the European dragons. That was before he was killed.' Falcon stares at me.

'I didn't want to kill Attor, but I will do it again if my family is under threat,' I say, returning his stare.

'Jasmine, will you please go inside and let me talk to Falcon.' Lazarus sighs.

'Fine, but a leopard doesn't change its spots or in your case, a dragon can never be trusted,' I mutter under my breath, knowing they both can hear me loud and clear.

'Thank you for that insight, Jasmine. Now leave,' he growls.

'Falcon returns and I get called Jasmine! Bloody lizard,' I whisper and hear a low growl for my efforts.

I walk inside the crowded hall and spot Rick leaning up against the wall talking to a pretty young girl. His body language is telling me he is flirting his butt off with her. So much for asking for my forgiveness.

Mr Tanner steps into view. 'Hello, stranger!' He smiles then hesitates as if he's scanning my face.

'Hey, how are you?'

'All the better now I have seen you.'

'I'm glad to see you too, Mr Tanner.'

'Please call me Paul. We're not in school anymore.' He continues to smile. 'I'm glad you're here. There was something I am desperate to talk to you about. Can we step out front for a quiet word?' He doesn't wait for my answer and guides me by my elbow towards the front entrance.

'Um, sure.' I shrug my shoulders, curious as to what is so secretive.

He escorts me to the side of the hall where the national park starts. He backs me up against a tree and smiles. Why is he smiling and running his eyes all over my face? Is he going to kiss me? Oh hell, was the special treatment he was giving me in class because he had an immoral crush on me?

Suddenly he is staggering sideways. Lazarus has shoved

him several metres away from me. Oh no! This can't get any more embarrassing.

Falcon is standing to the side with a huge grin on his face.

'Wipe that smile off your face, snake,' I snarl under my breath. He ignores me and keeps his eyes on the other two. 'Lazarus stop, it's okay. This is my schoolteacher.'

'No, it's not, he is a sorcerer,' he snaps, keeping his hands on Paul's chest.

'What?'

'Take your hands off me, dragon, before I break them,' Paul hisses.

'Wait, wait, wait! You're a sorcerer, Paul?'

'Yes, I have been watching over you since before Grandfather died,' he says, taking his eyes away from Lazarus for a split second. 'I'll ask you one more time to remove your hands, dragon.'

'Oh, thank goodness. I thought you were about to kiss me. Creepy, hey?' I sigh with relief.

'What? No! I was about to tell you what I was since I can clearly see the markings on your face. Mine are on my torso, hidden from view.'

'Lazarus, let him go!' I snap.

He backs away but keeps his eyes locked on him. 'I wish you would do what your bloody well told and stay inside the darn hall,' he growls, stopping beside me.

I take a deep breath and am about to tell Lazarus that I can look after myself, but he beats me to it with an angry glare. 'Don't!'

I huff and roll my eyes at him.

'Falcon, how you going, mate?' Paul says, nodding at him.

'Better than you.' Falcon laughs.

'You know this sorcerer?' Lazarus asks.

'I told you there was a sorcerer talking to Jasmine. I never said he was dark.' Falcon sniggers. 'He's quite the opposite.'

'I told you not to trust Falcon,' I snarl. 'You're here to cause trouble!'

'Thanks, brother,' Lazarus says, shaking his head in embarrassment. 'I'm Lazarus.' He holds his hand out for Paul to shake.

'I'm glad to see someone is protecting her,' Paul says, taking his hand. 'I've been trying to track you but the only information I could get was that you were with Sky living with a clan of elite creatures. My source is very secretive even though they know I am on your side.'

He turns to face me. 'I know what is coming and I want to help settle it before it gets out of control.'

'I only came back here to tell my parents some sad news,' I say, then remember that Falcon still has feelings for Sky and decide to tread carefully. 'A dark sorcerer called Ronan tracked me down and killed Sky.'

I watch the smile on the dragon's face fade. 'I'm sorry to tell you like this, Falcon.'

He shakes his head as if he doesn't want to hear this new information. As much as I don't trust him, I see her death has shattered him. My heart takes control, making me reach over to touch his arm in comfort. He stiffens so I pull back.

'Where's the dark sorcerer now?' Flacon grunts.

'I killed him.'

'Good!' Falcon takes in a deep calming breath. 'Did you receive his powers?'

'I was pulled away, so I didn't receive his black powers.'

'I heard Drake died and have been mourning his loss. He was a good friend and I miss him,' says Paul.

'How did you know him?'

'When Grandfather died, Drake took it upon himself to watch over you. Our paths crossed one night and, since our goal was the same, we became good friends.'

Interrupting our conversation, a long-legged blonde woman walks over. She's dressed in a sheer short dress similar to negligee. She walks elegantly over to Falcon and kisses him on the cheek before proceeding to Lazarus. She kisses him too and, luckily for him, his heartbeat doesn't alter. I raise my eyebrow at him, but he keeps his face expressionless.

She walks over to Paul and places a soft kiss on his lips, wrapping her arm around the back of him. 'Hello, handsome. I'm sorry I'm late,' she purrs into his ear. She turns and smiles at me and I have a distinct feeling I have seen her somewhere. She instantly irritates me, but I put it down to being jealous of her stunning looks.

'I'm re-introducing myself to Jasmine,' Paul explains to the blonde bimbo.

'And I presume she is being her moody little self.' She smirks. My hair stands on end and the draw in my hands heats so I clench my fists tight. I try my hardest to not hurl an anoric at her 'never-ending' long legs. Lazarus takes my hand and gives a gentle squeeze.

'And you are?' I snarl, raising one questionable eyebrow.

'You don't recognise me?' She sniggers, wrapping her other arm around Paul.

'Stop teasing her or I'll let her open her fist and you'll see what's brewing,' Lazarus snaps.

'She's not allowed to kill a fairy,' she huffs.

Then it hits me. 'Xandria?'

'It is me.' She smiles, opening her arms for me to see her in full. 'I told you that one day we would see eye to eye.'

'Only in height, fairy.' At least in human form, she doesn't speak in third person. 'How do you know her, Paul?'

'We have been together for two years, in secret, of course. Xandria, with the help of a few other creatures, was letting me know you are well but sadly, I never heard of Sky's passing.'

'I'm amazed the fairy could keep her mouth shut,' I say sarcastically.

'She told me you weren't the easiest to get along with,' says Paul, 'which I found very unlike you. It concerned me you may be tapping into negative energy.'

Lazarus steps forward, 'We can discuss this at a later time. Falcon and I want to get Jasmine back to Nogard Hollow.'

'You're trusting Falcon?' I stare up at him in disbelief. 'How can you trust him after he threatened my life?'

'I do and so should you.' Lazarus tilts his head sideways as if telling me not to disagree with him.

'You can trust him, Jasmine,' Paul says.

'Wow, hang on. You, Paul, have lied to me for as long as I've known you. Falcon has tried to kill me on more than one occasion, burning me to a crisp, choking and kidnapping me, and Xandria leads me into danger. I can't trust any of you. You're just as bad as my ex-boyfriend, who lied to me and hurt me.'

Lazarus reaches for my arm and I lift it up and out of his reach. 'No, don't touch me. I'm leaving alone. I can't trust any of you to tell me the truth.' I drop my head and leave them standing in the dark.

I walk home, shutting off all my senses, not wanting to hear, smell or think of anyone but myself. I am drained, alone and confused when I reach the front porch of my parents' house.

The front light is on and my mother is sitting on the front step. 'Hello, baby girl. How was the night?' The look in her eyes tells me she already knows.

'It could have gone better.' I drop beside her and lean into her.

She wraps her arm around me, pulling me under her arm. 'I tried so hard to protect you from this life, but I believe you are destined for it.'

'I don't know who to trust, Mum.'

'Do you trust me, even though I kept this life a secret from you?'

'I'll always trust you and Dad. And I trust Lazarus. I'm just annoyed he believes in and trusts Falcon.'

'Lazarus, Drake and Paul kept secrets from you to protect you. You lost faith in Rick and Kelly for other reasons. Don't let everyone else pay the price for their wrongdoings.'

'Are you saying I should trust these creatures?'

'I can't answer that, but you are a sensible and wise girl. Combine your heart and soul, and together, they will help you to answer your questions.' She kisses the top of my head, which instantly relaxes my tense body.

'Did you ever want to tap into your sorcery?'

'I did, a very long time ago.' She closes her eyes and tilts her head as if listening for someone. 'When I was a teenager, I would visit the castles with Grandfather. I met most of the dragons, as well as Hudson, who is Drake's father. We are still close friends so I pray he is well.' Her eyes drop to the ground. 'He and I were dating for several years before the orgle was created by Sky, which meant he was mostly in gargoyle form.'

'That must have been difficult. What stopped the relationship?'

'There were many things and creatures that interfered, making me lose trust in the ones closest to me. I returned to Melbourne, where I met and fell in love with your father. I pushed away my powers, never to use them again.'

'As I said, I trust Lazarus, but I'm annoyed he's accepting an outcast back into our home and one who threatened my life not that long ago. I'm scared he may be influenced by his return.'

I sense Lazarus is near and sniff the air to find him closer than I first thought. He must be listening to our conversation.

'Your body just went stiff as a board, so I presume we have guests. Your senses are strong, Jazzy.' She rubs my arms with her warm hands.

'I don't know what I want to do anymore.'

'Don't make any rash decisions now. Sleep on it and see how you feel in the morning. If you don't want to return with the elites, your father and I will pack up and start a new life with you somewhere safe.'

'After the effort you went to keep this out of your life, you'd pack up and live it?'

'No, baby girl, I'd hide you from it and them. That I can do.' She beams a confident smile.

'I wish it were that easy, but someone will find me and, unfortunately, it might be someone with dark intentions.'

'You can't return because you're scared of the future. You should only return if that is what your heart and soul wants. Come and sleep. Everything will be clearer after a solid night's sleep.' She stands and tugs at my arm to get me to follow.

I look towards Lazarus' heartbeat and so does my mother. 'Lazarus, I know you can hear me. You are welcome inside my home but the creature that threatened my daughter is not. One sniff of him and I will kill him.' I look up at my mother, shocked by her stern words and she smiles down at me. 'Threaten my daughter and you will see another side of me.'

I WAKE WITH Lazarus sitting beside me. I blink several times before focusing on his expressionless face. He has removed his contacts and I can smell that he has been out hunting.

'What have you eaten?' I ask.

'If you can't smell it, I won't tell you. That's what your senses are for.' His tone is flat.

'Why the attitude?' I sit up so I am face to face with him.

'I am hurt by the things you said last night.'

'You shouldn't have been listening to our conversation.'

'It wasn't what I overheard that hurt, it was what you said to my face—that you don't trust me. You put me in the same category as the other dragons, as Falcon.'

'I'm sorry you're hurt.' I place my hand over his.

'I thought you cared for me. But trust is love, and if you don't trust me… well.'

'I do love you, but you took Falcon's side before thinking about how I'd feel.'

'Your mother is right. You need to come home with me for the right reasons. If you don't want to be with me, I won't chase after you.'

I look into his eyes and listen to his heart. It's beating out of control in fear he may lose me.

I lean forward and kiss his salty lips, instantly tasting deer.

'You will chase after me,' I whisper, smiling, but his face stays motionless. 'I'm sorry. My emotions were whiplashed around all night. I shouldn't have taken it out on you. I do trust you and if my soul was golden, I would entrust you with it.'

'I'm not Rick. I won't hurt you.'

'I want to be with you but…'

'But what?'

'Do you ever wonder how a dragon and a human will work?'

'No one knows how any relationship will end up but not having one isn't the answer either. I will always love you as you are inked to me just as Sky is to Falcon. He is mourning her death, as he still loves her.'

'Huh,' I scoff.

His face hardens. 'Don't be so quick to judge, Jasmine.'

'That legged snake wanted to kill me, remember?'

He sighs, shaking his head. 'What will I do with you?'

'Love me, hold me and kiss me, then repeat.'

In a flash, his warm lips are on mine, kissing me fervently. He encases me in his hot arms, deepening our kiss. I feel so safe in his strong arms and oh boy, do I love to kiss him.

'I've known Falcon all of my life. We are not blood brothers, as you have previously pointed out, but we have a bond. He followed his father, as I did.

'It wasn't until he was overseas that he saw the destruction amongst the elites. Creatures Attor trained had killed many of his friends. Seeing unnecessary bloodshed woke Falcon up. He's returned to help protect us, not wanting Australia to fall to them.'

'He burnt and strangled me.'

'He knows it's a long journey in healing your fractured relationship. I wouldn't put you in danger. You said you trust me so trust my judgement.' He cocks his head waiting for my reaction. I say nothing. 'Paul wouldn't let Falcon near you if he felt there was any danger.'

'When it comes to Falcon, I'll take each day as it comes. But if I feel threatened, I won't hesitate to blast him, and there might be some descaling involved.'

'I'm sure you will, my little witch,' he purrs, nuzzling my cheek with his nose.

THERE'S HAPPINESS INSIDE me when I wave goodbye to my parents. They know who and what I have become, with no more secrets between us.

The car is crowded, with Paul and Falcon sitting in the back. Xandria has business to attend to, which I am grateful for, and will meet us back home. With her constant lies and misguidance, I would have de-winged her before we got to Nogard Hollow.

After driving all day, we stop beside the river for the night. Lazarus and Falcon disappear to feed while Paul and I share the picnic dinner my mother prepared. Sitting beside the river, we lift pebbles from the ground with the point of a finger then skip them across the river.

'It sounds as though I've been babysitting Australia's most powerful sorceress.' Paul smiles, flicking a small pebble at me.

'I thought I was lucky to always have the same teacher each year. I never twigged!'

'It took a lot of effort and convincing to make the school board allow me to teach a grade higher every year. In the end, Xandria gave me a potion to help persuade them.'

'How convenient it is to have a girlfriend who's a fairy with connections to elite creatures and their powers.' I smile.

'Together, with your parents, it was a hard task keeping you hidden and keeping this world hidden from you. I'd see you move objects around the classroom while students had their heads down studying. I'd quickly put them back and use Xandria's magic to make you forget you could do it. Most of your powers were suppressed using Aldore's powers.'

'Who is Aldore?'

'Have you never met him?' I shake my head. 'Oh, I've been misguided. I thought you had.' He frowns and shakes his head as if to shake a thought away. 'He was the strongest sorcerer in Australia but has gone into hiding. His last act was to cast a spell to protect you.'

'So you have spent all these years watching over me?' He nods. 'Why would you waste your time?'

'You have magical bloodlines which need to be protected. As a sorcerer, it is an honour to help raise you.'

'Well, your job is done.'

'It will never be done! After my wife died at the hands of a dark sorceress, I swore I'd never let you turn to it. I panicked when I couldn't find you and heard you'd killed Attor.'

'I'm sorry about your wife. I never knew she died that way.'

'It's kept me motivated to stay positive.' He's eyes glaze over with tears.

'Ronan killed Kelly. He thought it was me in the car and threw an anoric at her windscreen, making her crash. All these years I've blamed myself. People in town still blame me.'

'That explains a lot. We went into panic mode when we heard she crashed. Aldore sensed a sorcerer close by so he cast the heaviest spell he could over you and your property. It worked, as we never sensed him again. That's why it's extremely important you stay positive. Dark sorcerers thrive on anything negative. Keep your soul pure.'

'I'm in control of my powers. My sorcery is as white as snow.'

'You must be careful living with the elite creatures. They are creatures first, hence they think like creatures. Their actions are unpredictable.'

'If you're asking me to reconsider being with a dragon, you're wasting your time.'

'I've heard of Lazarus and of him being the alpha of the clan. But seeing him with you, he is very gentle.'

'Huh! Don't let that fool you. His calm attitude can change in a blink. He can quickly turn into a ten-tonne killing machine. I know how far I can push him and when to back down and let him win the argument. He has never hurt me on purpose.'

'What do you mean "on purpose"?'

'Falcon burnt me then pushed me off the roof of the castle. Laz caught me before I hit the ground. In doing so, his talons punctured me. It wasn't done on purpose, unlike Falcon's act.'

I hear the wings of two very full dragons in the distance. 'The boys are nearly back. Maybe you should ask your best friend, Falcon, why I'm covered in ink.'

'I can see why you don't have any faith in him. But I'm impressed how you can sense the dragons are close by. Your powers are so much more advanced than mine.'

'Have you ever killed an elite creature?'

'I killed the sorceress who killed my wife, but I didn't want her powers as they were dark.'

The dragons return with a ground-shaking thud, stopping my conversation with Paul and it isn't long before we all drift off to sleep.

CHAPTER SEVEN

WE ARRIVE BACK at Nogard Hollow just after dusk. Falcon changes form and heads into the cave for the rest of the night. Lazarus shows Paul around and offers him Attor's room, which he gladly accepts.

I crawl into a hot bath to soak away the stiffness of sleeping on the hard ground. I hear two gentle knocks on the door before Lazarus speaks, 'I might spend the night in the cave if that is all right with you.'

'I'd prefer you weren't with Falcon, but I know you need the cave. Can you wait until I fall asleep before you go? I drift off quicker when you're with me.'

'Put you to sleep, do I?'

I quickly jump out of the bath and wrap a towel around me. I spring to open the door. His lime green eyes scan my towel-covered body. 'Are you ready for bed now, babe?' he purrs.

'Yes,' I say with a cheeky grin.

He whips me up in his strong arms and carries me over to the bed. I gather by the look in his eye I won't be falling asleep for a while.

I JOLT UPRIGHT in fear, waking to the sound of screaming dragons. I race out of my bedroom and along the hall, meeting Paul on the way to the front door.

'What's happening?' he yells.

'I don't know but be ready to attack when we exit the

front doors. There's no cover out front.' I try to keep up with his fast pace.

He flings open the doors and plants his feet firmly on the ground. His head spins in every direction. I glance up with my hands open wide and armed with earth-drawn anorics ready for throwing. I see Lazarus and Falcon flying above the house bellowing large flames into the air while roaring like caged lions.

'It's okay, Paul. They are laughing and playing up there.'

I look at my hands and am happy to see that my anorics are white in colour. I flick one up in the air in-between the two singing dragons, then shoot the other one so they hit. They explode in the air, releasing a loud boom.

It startles the dragons and Falcon takes off towards the cave entrance. Lazarus flies down and lands quite a distance away. He walks towards us like a dog cowering after a scolding.

I close my hands, relaxing the energy pull. 'Did you wonder how we'd feel waking up to the loud noise of screaming dragons?' My heart is still pumping fiercely.

'I'll leave you to it now I know there's no threat,' Paul says, heading back towards the house. 'Thanks for the wake-up call, Lazarus.'

'Sorry, Paul. I will make us breakfast soon,' I yell to his back. He lifts his hand, gesturing a wave.

I turn to glare at the dragon sneaking up. 'I could have put a hole in you or Falcon! Trust me, I'd enjoy puncturing him. That was a silly thing to do and if you do it again without telling me I won't aim for the air, I will aim for one of your butts!'

He lifts his head high, angling his neck like a swan. He bellows loud, shooting a flame from his mouth. The heat is intense, but I stand my ground. I remember to keep my movements slow so as not to startle him. Even though he'd never mean to hurt me, he is in dragon form and a wild creature.

'Are you finished yelling at me?' I open the palm of my right hand, letting a small anoric brew.

He moves closer and puffs smoke in my face. I lift my hand, showing him my baby threat. He puffs smoke again as if to mock me.

'Do you want to play this game, dragon?' I close my fist and defuse my anoric. He turns his narrow head away from me and I'm unsure of its meaning.

I touch him on his scaly cheek and he rumbles deep in his chest. 'Go fly with Falcon and I will talk to you when you're ready.'

I turn to leave but Lazarus nuzzles me hard on my bottom, making me spin around. He drops his head in front of me so I open my arms and lie against his head. His nostrils blow warm air on my legs.

He breathes me in while my fingers caress his leathery red skin. 'You would make a lovely pair of shoes.'

He whips his deadly tail around so the spike is pointing at me but it's a safe distance away. I giggle at his threat. 'And looking at this size of your belly I could make a matching handbag, pants and jacket. Or better still, a new lounge suite for the house.'

He drops his tail to the ground and snorts a laugh.

'I love you.' I kiss his warm head. 'Go and play dragons and I'll feed our new guest.'

He nuzzles me and winks his lime green eye. He drifts passed me, so I keep my hand running along his side.

He is an amazing gigantic and dangerous creature who can also be loving and kind. I admire his elegance and beauty as he takes off with a warm gust of air. My heart skips with excitement whenever I see him in his true form. He turns his head to see if I am watching or maybe he heard my heart skip, but for whatever reason, he is happy and growling his acknowledgement.

Heading back into the house, I notice Blue Boy is in the paddock with Corbin's horses. Corbin must have brought him over here to keep the others company. I'm excited to see him and race inside to show Paul the kitchen so I can go for a ride.

I throw on Blue Boy's bridle and ride along the creek. It doesn't take long before I sense the dingoes. I smell Ellie before Rhys and the kids. They approach me in human form, which worries me. They may have information regarding the expected invasion.

'Jasmine! Hey, can I ride your horse?' Nelly yells, running through the long grass.

'Sure thing. How have you been?' I ask as she reaches me, leaving her family behind.

'Great!'

'Here, put your foot on top of mine and climb up behind me.' I hold my foot flat.

She steps up and jumps on. 'Can we go fast?'

'Sure, but you must sit still and wrap your arms tightly around my waist. And no squealing!'

'Okay, go!'

I squeeze Blue past the trot and straight into a canter as it's easier to keep a non-rider on board. She squeals as I predicted she would, but Blue Boy has his ears pricked at the others in front of us. I pull him to a stop when we are several metres away from Ellie.

'Hello!' Ellie yells.

'Hi, guys. How are you? Is everything all right?'

'We heard you coming and thought it easier to communicate in human form.'

'Oh, thank goodness, I was worried you had bad news for me.'

'No news is good news,' Tag says, moving to pat Blue Boy. 'Can I have a turn on the horse please, Jasmine?'

'Sure, but you mustn't scream or muck around as he is an animal and doesn't understand what you're saying.'

'I understand because I'm an animal. And I won't muck around, I promise.'

I slide off and boost him up onto Blue Boy's back with Nelly still sitting on top. 'These are the reins and, together with your legs, it tells him what you want. If you want to turn right, you gently pull the right rein.' I pull on one rein and Blue Boy turns his head.

'And if I want to turn left, I pull the left one,' Tag says, gently pulling the rein.

'Yes, and if you want to stop you pull both reins together. For your first ride I want you to walk and next time I come I will bring his saddle and teach you how to trot then canter. You squeeze your lower legs on his side and he will walk on and remember to pull both reins to stop.'

'I got it!' Tag smiles.

'Okay, off you go. Just walk or you will fall off.'

His little legs squeeze Blue Boy into a walk. Nelly quickly wraps her arms around her brother and they walk around in circles before us.

As his confidence grows, he makes the circle bigger and changes direction. Blue Boy is happy as he can snatch a mouthful of grass due to the loose reins.

Happy they are doing as they were told, I turn my attention to Ellie and Rhys.

'How was your trip back home?' Rhys asks.

'Could have gone better.'

'I heard Lazarus played up.' Ellie sniggers.

'Huh?'

'He burnt some poor guy's shed down which had his car in it.'

'I didn't know that.'

'Oops! Have we just got him into trouble?' She laughs.

'I'm presuming it was my ex-boyfriend's. Dragons are a jealous bunch!'

'We know Falcon is back. How do you feel about it?' Rhys asks.

'I don't know if I trust him. I'm wary of anything he has to say. I'm keeping an anoric on charge just in case.' I smile at the thought of biffing him again.

'We know he tried to save several families overseas and everyone is saying he is on board with the gargoyles, but we too are wary.'

'Can I have a turn now?' Kip asks, standing patiently, waiting to ride Blue Boy.

'Were you listening to the rules?'

'Yes, Jasmine.'

The other two slip off Blue Boy and I boost Kip up and onto his back. He gathers the reins and copies what his brother has done, walking in big circles. The other two dance around Blue Boy's legs but thankfully, he doesn't mind.

I turn my attention back to Rhys. 'Is there any word from overseas?'

'A dragon arrived here the other day. It's said she's no threat but we have been tricked before so we are all on edge.'

'I wonder if Falcon has anything to do with it.'

'They are connected but to what extent is yet to be determined. Keep your ears and eyes open, Jasmine,' Rhys advises.

'When it comes to Falcon they are. Anyhow, I better be heading home or there will be one frantic dragon screaming his head off.' I roll my eyes.

'I'm glad he has you to straighten him out.' Ellie laughs. 'Come on, kids. Jasmine needs her horse back.'

'Aw, we don't want her to go yet.' Nelly pulls a sad face and tugs on my t-shirt.

'I promise I will come back in a few days if it's safe.' I help Kip slide down from Blue's back.

'Have you met the relatives at Elyograg Castle?' Nelly asks.

'Of course she hasn't, Nelly. She only got home yesterday, you know that,' Kip says, shaking his head at her. 'You have too much fur between your ears, little sis.'

'Oh yeah, that's right. We know your every move. We knew you were riding along the creek, coming to see us,' she says proudly.

'I'm glad you've got my back, Nelly.'

'Kip and I do too,' Tag says, poking out his small chest.

'Thanks, guys. I don't know what I'd do without you.' I smile and Nelly runs up and hugs me.

'You're good with kids. Any plans?' Ellie asks with a grin on her face.

'I love kids, but Lazarus is kid enough for me.'

After several hugs and kisses, including kisses for Blue Boy, I wave goodbye and head home. I let Blue Boy have a loose rein as I'm presuming his mouth was tugged at over the last hour.

His head shoots up with his ears pricked. I shorten my reins and hear the flap of dragon wings but they're not Lazarus'. I glance around the skyline and see Falcon coming towards me. He lands a long distance away and is quick to change form.

I settle Blue Boy and hesitantly walk over to him. He has his hands on his hips and looks impatient for my arrival.

'Falcon, I won't hesitate to kill you,' I say.

'No doubt you will try.'

'Try, my butt! I will succeed, snake!'

I hear another set of wings and turn to see another dragon flying up behind me. I don't recognise it and fear I am being ambushed. I slip off Blue Boy and whip off his bridle. If there's a fight I don't want him anywhere near it. I slap him on the butt just as the dragon lands. I open my hands and instantly have two anorics spinning in my palms.

'Settle, Jasmine. I just want to introduce you. I didn't know you were out here otherwise I would have gone hunting elsewhere.'

'Stay where you are, dragon, or I will fire at you.'

The small dragon snorts and lowers its head in a submissive way.

I hear and sense the dingoes creeping from behind. Ellie and Rhys are by my side snarling and growling, rolling back their lips to show their pointed teeth and gums. Wow, I didn't know dingoes had such angry-looking teeth.

'She won't hurt you, I promise,' Falcon says.

'Your promise means toad shit!'

'I know you don't believe me, but I have changed. I've seen the monster of destruction my father has created and I want nothing to do with it. I lost many friends and it makes me sick.'

Rhys takes several stalking steps towards Falcon.

'I'm not here to hurt you. I asked Lazarus if my friend could stay here. Her family sent her to Australia to be safe while they stay in Europe to help the gargoyles. You could say she is my girlfriend.'

'Why doesn't she change form?'

'She has travelled here in human form for the last forty-eight hours and needs to hunt. Changing form takes all her energy, which she is not used to. After she feeds, she will gladly change form and speak with you.'

'I don't trust you and I hate you being near Lazarus. He cares for you so I won't interfere but if I smell one teeny-tiny thing out of place, I won't hesitate to blast you.' I close my hands, distinguishing my anoric.

'I understand I need to earn your trust and I promise I will.

I loved Sky and I never wanted her hurt.' His tone is soft and sincere. 'Once a dragon connects to another creature, whether human or not, it becomes a part of their soul. Sky and I had that connection. She is inked over my heart.'

I turn to the dingoes and place my hand on Ellie's furry shoulder. 'Thanks, guys, but I've got this.'

She licks her snarling lips then backs away, with Rhys doing the same.

'I'll see you next week,' I whisper so only they could hear, and then roll my eyes, knowing the dragons can hear me anyhow.

I turn to admire the small dragon. She is candy apple red and has kept her head low like a dog cowering after being disciplined. I smile and nod at her, but she keeps deathly still. 'What's her name?'

'Kite.'

'Are you kidding me?' I find it funny she's named after something that floats and flies in the air. It seems ironic.

'No, Jasmine, I'm not.' His tone changes to a more serious note.

'Oh, don't get me wrong, it's a fantastic name. Is she comfortable around humans?'

'She's never had one approach her, but she knows the scent. She was heavily sedated while flying here. I wouldn't approach her now while she is hungry. I couldn't promise she would refrain from eating you.'

'Rubbish. You're dying to push me right up in front of her and then tell Lazarus she ate me by accident.' I snigger.

'You got me!' He laughs but it doesn't reach his eyes. 'I better get her fed and we will meet you back home. Did you want me to give you a lift?'

'There's no hope in hell I will get on your back. Our friendship has got a long way to go before I trust you. I'm happy to walk until I find Blue again. Anyhow, I presume Lazarus will come looking for me and, by the sound of it, I can hear him already looking.'

'Your senses are strong, Jasmine. He is at least thirty kilometres away.'

'My powers have grown stronger since we last met.'

'Is that a warning?'

'Take it any way you want. No, wait—take it as a threat, because if you cross my family, Lazarus or me, I will kill you without blinking.'

'You're a charmer, Jasmine. I can see why he's in love with you.' He steps away and, with a warm red dusty swirl, transforms into the amazing creature I once believed existed only in dreams. As much as I don't trust Falcon, he is a stunning dragon.

He nods his head and the small dragon takes flight. He snorts at me, shaking his head, and then takes off, catching up to his girlfriend.

The dingoes howl and I can sense that they are back at the creek's edge.

'I'm fine, guys. Thanks for your support, but don't put yourself in danger like that again,' I yell, wondering if they have good hearing. They soon answer my question with loud howls vibrating through the Outback's serenity. Birds fly out of the trees that line the creek, telling me exactly where my dingo friends are.

I smile, remembering how the three young dingoes enjoyed riding Blue Boy and how affectionate they are toward me, and when Lazarus rolled around on the ground, tossing them into the air until they squealed with excitement.

I scan the flat land for Blue Boy and see him quite a distance away, heading towards home. I pick up his bridle and listen for my ride home. I hear Lazarus' anxious heartbeat together with his frantically flapping wings coming my way.

'I'm fine, Lazarus. Extinguish your fire and take your time,' I say, knowing he will hear me. I hear his roar before I see him. He glides over Blue Boy, making him take off at a gallop away from me.

'Thanks for spooking my horse, lizard!'

He roars and shoots out a flame of laughter. I stand mesmerised at the mystery and magic above me. I am in love with his dragon form as much as I am with his human form.

With a graceful landing and a determined walk, he heads towards me, pacing and circling around me, shaking his head. He is annoyed I left without him.

'Get over it, Lazarus! I went for a ride and caught up with some friends. Stop acting like a spoilt oversized blue-tongue lizard!'

He stops and growls, opening his mouth and showing me that his forked tongue is pink. He rolls it over his razor-sharp teeth and I believe it's a warning that he isn't impressed.

'Well, you're still acting like a spoilt… just spoilt!'

His growl rumbles through his core as he continues to circle me. I turn, following his eyes, waiting for him to make any move. He laps me several times before I snap again. 'You don't own me! I will ride my horse everywhere and anywhere I want, without your consent.'

He licks his lips and I'm presuming he is telling me he will eat Blue Boy. 'Don't you dare threaten my horse. I think you should leave as I'd prefer to walk home.' I don't really mean it as it's a very long hike back.

He stops and turns to face me, both green eyes staring hard at me.

Out of the corner of my eye, I see something move and sense it's a snake heading for my feet. Earthly energy pulses through my hand. I take several quick steps towards Lazarus and away from the snake.

I don't see or command my hand to move but it is already out in front of me, lifting the slithering creature into the air, preventing it from coming closer.

Lazarus' razor-sharp jaw is at the side of my throat. I freeze, statue-still, as a trickle of saliva rolls from his gaping mouth onto my shoulder. I keep my eyes forward, too scared to blink. My hand is still elevated, pointing at the snake that is still being held in mid-air.

In my peripheral vision, I see his lime green eyes blink several times before he lowers his head. I release the breath I was desperately holding.

I listen to his heartbeat and it's as erratic as mine. Holy hell! Was he about to attack me? He backs away, keeping his eyes on me. My breath is becoming panicked and I'm panting.

'I'm going to toss the snake away,' I warn before moving my hand. I watch as the snake is hurled at least one hundred metres away.

I look back at Lazarus and his posture has changed from the strong alpha male to a timid slumped creature. He's upset that he went to attack me. I must have moved like a flash as I didn't even see my hand go up.

'Don't worry about. It's not as if you're picking me out of your teeth.' I try to make light of his actions, but my blood is still pumping out of control through my veins.

He rumbles and looks away.

'Lazarus?' I take a slow step forward, holding my hand out to touch him, but he backs away. 'What are you doing?' He rumbles and opens his wings and, with a downward thrust, he takes off, leaving me.

I watch him fly away from me with his head lower than his shoulders. An elusive tear rolls down my cheek in fear I may lose the man I love. I know he will be angry with himself and presume that is why he left but why didn't he change form and talk to me?

I look around at my surroundings and fear nothing or no one, only the gut-wrenching pain I have in my heart from watching him leave. I keep my eyes focused on the skyline until his large eagle shape disappears over the top of the mountain. I hiccup and cry at the thought of losing him.

I pick up Blue Boy's bridle and head for a large tree, as the sun is intense and beating down on me. I drop to the ground and lean up against its large trunk.

How had everything gone to hell in a split second? My tears keep rolling down my cheeks and I don't want to stop them. I curl up in a small ball on the red dirt and cry myself to sleep.

I'm startled when I'm woken with a warm hand on my shoulder.

'Jasmine,' Corbin's soft voice says. 'I brought Blue for you to ride home.'

I blink several times before slowly moving to sit. Even though he is in human form, I don't want to startle another dragon.

I see Blue Boy tied behind Corbin's horse. My heart thuds hard when I see there's no one else here. 'Did Lazarus send you?'

'He is torturing himself that he nearly hurt you. He said his instincts took over when you moved quickly towards him. He is devastated.'

'I was agitating him before it happened. Then I saw the snake out the corner of my eye and, before I realised it, I'd moved to have the creature immobilised. His teeth were at my neck.

'It happened in the blink of an eye. I didn't know I could move that quickly and I'm always cautious to move slow around dragons. I was told to do so the first time I saw you. I never move quickly. I can't lose him, Corbin.'

'He's not blaming you but his is questioning himself. I thought we could go to Elyograg Castle for the night and give him time to settle down.'

'He doesn't want me at Nogard Hollow, does he?'

'He never said, but I'm presuming he must have scared the hell out of you. You need to speak to him when you've collected yourself. If you're nervous, he will sense it and if you're over-confident, he'll presume you are hiding your feelings.'

'If I don't return home, he will think I've left him. Even though he just flew off and left me.' I use my t-shirt to wipe away my tears.

'He knows I am with you.' He gently tugs my arm, encouraging me to stand.

'I can't leave him alone with Falcon, I don't trust that legged snake. No offence.'

'None taken. Lazarus isn't easily influenced but I understand your concern. I still believe you're best to rest a night or two with the gargoyles. Lolana would love to catch up with you.'

'I am desperate to see him, but you are right, it scared me. I actually scared myself when I reacted so quickly. I suppose one night won't hurt and I'd love to meet the relatives.' I follow Corbin to the horses.

We ride back, with Corbin telling me stories of dragons who lost control with humans and the devastating outcomes. He also tells me the success stories of different creatures fighting the odds to be with each other.

I understand the risks of being with these elite creatures and take it all on board, as this is the life I have chosen. I refuse to let one small incident change the relationship I have with Lazarus. I love him and what happened won't change that. I won't let it.

'That's a lovely sound,' Corbin says.

'Huh?'

'For the first time today, your heartbeat is pattering a lovely tune.'

'Because I've just promised myself that everything will be as it was. I love him and he loves me.'

'I hope you're right.' He gives me a sympathetic smile before kicking his horse into a canter. I squeeze Blue Boy and he eagerly follows close behind.

As we approach the castle, I get the giggles, as it looks like a concrete statue factory. There are gargoyles hanging off the side of the house, on the rooftop and even on the ground. There is one leaning up against the door entry with a huge grin plastered on its face.

We unsaddle the horses and wash away their sweat. Dusk has fallen and Lolana is the first to appear. 'Welcome home, Jazz.'

'Hey, honey, how are you?' I give her a warm hug. I hold on to her longer than normal as I need someone to embrace me and my heart.

'I'm fine. Um… how are you and where's Lazarus?'

Corbin sneaks out a cough and I hear his hand wave a gush of air behind me. I roll my eyes, knowing he is trying to warn Lolana about my miserable mood.

'He is back at Nogard Hollow.'

'Oh! Well, come and meet the family.'

As we walk towards the front doors I hear and see several of the gargoyles breaking out of stone sleep but staying in gargoyle form. As I approach the door the large gargoyle leaning up against it moves, making me jump back several steps. Corbin's warm hands stop me from going any further.

'Sorry, gorgeous. I didn't mean to frighten you,' the creature says.

'Nice one, Ash,' Corbin scoffs.

'Please tell me you live here with us,' Ash purrs.

'Back off. This is Jasmine, my brother's girlfriend,' Corbin huffs.

Ash moves toward me and, with his gargoyle finger, brushes several strands of hair back from my face. 'I don't see any boyfriend here.' He gestures with his other hand. 'So you are the one who is making orgles for those who don't have one. Is that correct, gorgeous?'

'Apparently, but if you excuse me, I need to meet everyone and get myself a glass of wine.' I smile up at him and walk past his large presence.

A growl rumbles in his chest when I pass him. 'Hmm, you smell as good as you look.'

'I said back off, Ash!' snaps Corbin.

'What's your problem, dragon? You've got your girl and I know you guys can't handle more than one,' Ash stirs, making me grin.

'Do you want to find out what I can handle?' he snarls.

'Corbin, I'd love a glass of wine,' I interject, stopping the testosterone overload.

'Sure thing.' He keeps his eyes locked on Ash's. 'You, I will deal with later.' He disappears in a blink, leaving Ash towering over me.

'I will work on getting an orgle later but for now please let me catch up with my family,' I say.

'I can't *wait* until later.' He smiles.

I catch up with everyone and am introduced to thirty relatives of the gargoyles. I can't remember half their names, but they are all eager for me to work on the orgle stones. Luckily, some don't want to have one and others already have ways of changing form, gifted from their sorcerer.

After Jet stops hugging and kissing me and the angels fill

me with a delicious dinner, I head to the river, taking with me the remainder of the wine. I have the need to drink. I sit cross-legged on the bank with the dozen precious pebbles Lysander has collected from the base of the creek.

I pour myself a glass of wine, placing it beside me. I clasp the first pebble in my hand and ask Sky for guidance to create an orgle.

'Hello, cuz,' she echoes.

'Hello, Sky. I miss you.'

'We can't waste time talking as it will drain you too quickly. You need to draw the colour red from the earth, like the colour of the Outback's dusty roads. Don't picture an animal or creature, just the earth's energy. You will see flashes of gold, which is the warmth the gargoyles need to heat to human temperature.

'Draw deep below the dusty soil to the Earth's crust. It is a cool, wet feeling, and you should never leave it to roam around your body. Send it straight to your hands and force it into the pebble. Once it changes to a marble colour, it is ready to use.

'Only you personally can give it to the creature. One orgle is dedicated to each creature. You will learn if you draw a certain colour through your body, it will offer you different powers.'

'I understand and I remember the feeling when I repaired Lolana's orgle.'

'I love you and please tell Lysander and Jet I love them and to stay happy.'

'I love you and I will tell him,' I echo, and then she's gone; my mind is empty.

I sit for hours in the cool evening air, sipping on my wine, in-between making my small but special creations. I sense someone coming and it's not one of my near family members. It's heavy-footed and I presume it's a gargoyle.

'I thought I'd keep you company,' says Ash, squatting beside me. His huge frame looks awkward with his large wings getting in the way as he tries to get comfortable.

I giggle at his expense. 'I'm halfway done. Would you like to have your orgle?'

His face lightens with a smile. 'I'm a little nervous, to be honest.'

I look at this huge strong creature before I laugh out loud.

'What is so funny?'

'Look at the size of you. How could you be scared of a small pebble?'

'I'm glad to amuse you.' He sounds hurt. 'Which one is mine?'

I glance down and they all look similar. 'I don't know.' I reach over and touch his hand then run my other hand over the top of the marble pebbles. When I pull my hand away one is glowing bright red.

'This one.' I pick it up, holding it in the palm of my hand. His glowing blue eyes stare at it. 'Take it. I promise it won't bite.' I laugh and realise I'm giggly because I've finished the bottle of wine.

He takes it from my hand and stands up, looking like a giant.

'Step away from me or I will be covered in your concrete ash,' I say and then fall backwards, laughing until my stomach hurts. 'No pun intended, Ash.' I roll around on the ground, holding my belly until the moonlight is hidden by a man standing over me.

'Are you finished?' His tone is half-serious, which stops my laughing fit.

I spring up to see a handsome man standing before me. Wow, he is one hot man.

His face is more chiselled than the other gargoyles and his chest is thicker. He's solid and stands around six-foot-three. His eyes are traditional blue, as is his brown hair, but the short crew cut style is different. 'Ash, is that you?'

'Yes, it's me. Do I look all right as a human?' He runs his eyes over his body. He looks to be a young adult in his twenties but it's always hard to guess an elite's age.

'You look better than all right,' I blurt, then cover my gaping mouth with my hand.

'Why thank you, gorgeous. I bet you'd be a stunner as a gargoyle as well.' He runs his hands over his arms, bludging biceps and chest.

'Nah, the stone would dry out my skin,' I joke, and he laughs.

'Thank you, Jasmine.' He bends his tall frame to kiss my cheek.

'You're welcome but remember you must recharge your batteries and only change form at night.'

'I know the rules and thank you.'

I shiver due to the cool evening air. I still have quite a few orgles to make.

'You're cold. Let me sit behind you to keep you warm.'

'I have a boyfriend, Ash.'

'I'm well aware of that but I am a gargoyle and it's my job to protect you. So hush up and let me sit behind you. Jet will have me crushed if you get sick. And I promise I will keep my hands to myself.' He smiles, moving in behind me.

I go to object but he's already snuggling into my back. He is warm even though he has just changed form. I lean back and soak up the heat my body needs. He rolls his hands up and down my arms then slides them down to the tops of my thighs.

'Is this what you call keeping your hands to yourself? Gee, I'd hate to see them roaming.' I chuckle, and he kisses the top of my head releasing a low growl. 'Where are you from?'

'I'm originally from the Outback, near Kings Canyon.'

'I'd expect that area to be flooded with tourists.'

'Our cave is on the far side of the canyon. The terrain is too rough for anyone to venture there. And the Aboriginal people keep tourists away. We have a great bond with them, as do all the elite creatures in Australia. They taught us how to use bush medicine which has been invaluable.'

'You live in a cave? I thought only dragons lived in caves.'

'We own a large castle and share it with the dragons. I choose to live in the cave as I love flying over the tourists camping at night, listening to their stories.'

'Dragons?'

'The majority of the elite are at peace here in Australia. It's Attor who decided to put a wedge between the clans. But the dragons who live with me have gone over to England with Hudson, Drake's father, to help resolve the issue.'

'Oh.' My mind fills with thoughts of Drake and how he died.

I continue creating the orgles until my eyelids close and I fall asleep. I wake when I am being carried up the stairs, my eyes barely opening.

'What are you doing?' I ask Ash, who has me cradled in his arms.

'You're exhausted, beautiful. I'm taking you to bed.'

'No! I have a boyfriend,' I mumble.

'You keep telling me that, but I see how you look at me. I know you loved Drake, who is a gargoyle, so I know I'm in with a chance.'

'No chance in hell, my friend.'

'Hmm, we'll see, beautiful,' he rumbles. 'I'm putting you in your bed, alone.'

I roll my face into his broad chest. I haven't got the energy to argue. He places me gently on the bed. I sink into the soft mattress and feel like I am in heaven. I groan my appreciation as the blankets are pulled up and over me.

Ash kisses my forehead then, after a few seconds, kisses my cheek.

'Thank you,' I whisper, then feel his lips pressing softly onto mine but thankfully, only for a split second. I drift off into a deep sleep.

I toss and turn as a dream takes over my mind, showing me the replay of Lazarus flying away from me.

Two strong hands are on my shoulders, holding me. I fight against them, letting an electric shock surge through me.

'Ouch!'

I spring up in bed. Ash is shaking both his hands. 'Did I hurt you?'

'Just a shock,' he says, rubbing his hands together.

'I'm sorry but what are you doing in my room?'

'I was watching you sleep and then you started to… I thought you were having a nightmare.'

'It was one I should be having in private! You shouldn't be in my room.'

My door bursts open and Jet enters with his chest puffed out and his face full of anger.

'Get out!' he yells. 'Jasmine, are you all right?'

'I had a bad dream, that's all,' I'm quick to say, not wanting him to crush Ash.

'Oh, thank goodness it's you, Jet. If her dragon boyfriend found me in here I'd have my head ripped off.' Ash laughs, sarcasm dripping from his words.

'That's after he made toast out of you,' I add.

'I said get out!' Jet's not impressed with his new relative. 'I am her protector, not you!'

Jet drifts towards me and pulls the bedsheets up to my neck, covering my underwear. I suddenly realise that my t-shirt and jeans have been removed. I gasp and Jet's eyes shoot to mine.

'What's wrong, Jazz?'

'Nothing's wrong.' I scan the room for my clothes.

Ash walks over to a chair in the corner. My clothes have been neatly laid over it. He runs his finger over my t-shirt then smiles at me. I glare back at him, narrowing my eyes. I daren't say a word as Jet is a torpedo about to fire.

'Sweet dreams, gorgeous.' Ash blows me a kiss before leaving.

Jet spins around and squats beside my bed. 'Did he do anything inappropriate?'

'Hell, no. Don't you think I would have zapped him one? He woke me from a nightmare and I shocked him.'

'Well, at least he knows not to tick you off.'

'I'm fine, Jet. Go enjoy the company of a cute gargoyle. I'm sure there's at least one out there who catches your eye.'

'My eyes are focused on protecting you.'

'Oh, bugger off and act your age. Have fun before you get too old, too boring and too grumpy... oops, too late.'

'Hilarious, Aunt Jazz.' He tucks me in tightly by poking the bottom of the sheet under the mattress. 'Sleep well and remember I'm here if you need me.'

'Thank you.' I smile before wriggling further under the sheet. 'Oh, before I forget. I spoke to Sky, and she sends her love and wants you to be happy.' He smiles and nods at me. 'I love you too, Jet.'

'I love you.' He smiles before pulling the door shut. He tries to lock it but when he burst through, he must have broken it. He pops his head back in with a guilty look, 'Sorry about the door handle. I'll fix it after you wake.'

'Never let a door stand in the way.' I chuckle, hearing him do the same as he walks down the stairs. I hear the chatter around the house and force my senses to shut down. I need to sleep. Tomorrow will be a big day. With my pendant in my hand, it takes minutes to drift off.

Chapter Eight

T**HE NOISE OF** chattering guests wakes me in the early hours of the morning. If they keep up this nightly noise, I will have to return to Nogard Hollow so I can get a decent sleep.

I jump up and slip my old jeans and t-shirt back on as most of my clothes are in my truck.

I walk down the stairs and sense all eyes on me. I scan the room and it's a sea of blue glowing eyes.

Malachi joins me as I walk the stairs. 'Morning, Jasmine. They are waiting for you to hand them their orgles.'

That explains why they're all looking at me. 'Oh! I was so exhausted last night I drifted off to sleep before handing them out.'

Ash is waiting at the bottom of the stairs. He is extremely handsome but unfortunately, has the ego to match. He holds out a small bag made from kangaroo leather. 'I kept them safe for you.'

'Thanks.' I take the pouch of orgles from him. I inhale his scent as I walk past and find Corbin staring at me, one eyebrow questioning me. I raise mine as if to say 'whatever'. 'I need to be grounded before handing these out.'

I head towards the door and the sea of gargoyles part for me. It's an eerie feeling but not a threatening one.

I sit cross-legged on the ground and place the pebbles in front of me. Ash walks over and sits beside me, stretching one leg out straight. Using his long index fingernail, he cuts into his leg, forming an inch-long bloody gap.

'What the hell are you doing?'

'Lolana put her orgle inside her leg so it can never be taken from her. I'm doing the same.' He shoves the orgle stone inside.

'I'm going to be sick.' I cough, forcing back the food in my stomach.

'I've got you, beautiful.' Ash pulls the tip of his finger out from the bloody hole in his leg. I shake my head and turn my eyes away.

One by one, the gargoyles sit beside me, grasping my hand until I find their orgle. I sit mesmerised as the miracle unfolds before me over and over again. The excitement on their faces when they change form is one I will remember forever.

I hear one small gargoyle scoff, saying he thinks he looks better as a gargoyle than a human. I have to disagree, as they are all striking to look at. I'm glad Lazarus isn't here because the women are all stunners and I'd be extremely jealous if I heard his heartbeat kick into a different gear.

The banter settles as the sun peeks over the tree-lined creek. They grumble as they change form but not before thanking me.

Ash, still in human form, walks confidently over with the sexiest grin on his face. 'You've made a lot of creatures happy this morning.' He smiles, his blue eyes radiating.

'I hope so. I'm feeling proud.'

'Thank you, Jazz.' He kisses me on the cheek.

'You're welcome but you don't have to kiss me all the time.'

Jet walks between us, giving Ash a sideways look.

'See you tonight, Aunt Jazz.' He kisses me on the cheek then continues on to the castle.

'Jet can kiss you so why can't I?' Ash pouts.

'I am his aunt and you are…' I don't know what to call him.

'I am your friend, Jasmine. I would love to be more, but I respect that you *think* you're in love with a dragon.'

'I am in love with him and by the way, who gave you

permission to remove my clothes last night?' I snap, remembering my state when I woke. 'If I'd told Jet he would have ripped your head off.'

'Your bed sheets were so clean and your clothes were so dirty.' He grinned from ear to ear. 'I promise I didn't look.'

'Never do that again.' But his childish grin makes me smile.

'I won't, even when you're begging me to.'

'Go before my boyfriend arrives. He is on his way and, considering the mood I left him in, I don't think he will want you anywhere near me. And don't say another word, as he can hear you.'

'You are one amazing sorceress if you can hear him coming. The word is out that you're talented, but I know they have underestimated you.'

'Go and sleep, Ash.' I nod my head towards the castle's rooftop.

'See you later, beautiful.' He grabs my forearms and kisses me loudly on the lips.

'You definitely have a death wish. He will fire at you and not think twice about it.' I'm shocked by his actions.

'Dragons don't scare me,' he says over his shoulder as he heads to the castle.

I close my eyes and listen to the sound of Lazarus flying towards me. I walk in his direction, listening to his heartbeat. It's anxious. I keep mine pumping at a steady slow beat but that all goes to pot when I spot him gliding over the top of the trees. He lands a fair distance away from me, which makes me think he doesn't trust himself.

'Don't change form. I want you to carry me back home unless you don't want me there,' I whisper.

He shakes his head and starts the red swirl that appears every time he changes.

'Don't!' I run as fast as I can towards him. He roars and

fires a warning flame, but I ignore it. I want to prove to him that he will never hurt me even if I look like a threat.

He roars again but I keep on running. I hear the scrambling of gargoyles on the roof and stop to see Jet opening his wings wide, warning the others to stay on the roof. I raise my hand and wave to let them know everything is okay. I'm thankful he is keeping everyone away so I can sort this out alone with Lazarus.

I turn back and Lazarus is about to take flight.

'If you leave, never come back,' I threaten, but my heart thuds in disagreement.

He stops and spins around, lowering his head. I set a fast pace in his direction, watching his head to make sure it doesn't rise and that his tail stays low to the ground.

I slow when I am metres away, but I keep moving forward. He keeps still and his heart is beating out of control.

'Please don't leave me again.' My tone is soft and full of pain. 'I need to be with you.'

I reach out and touch his large head and he keeps still. I open my arms and lie my body in-between his eyes. He breathes me in. His eyes pop open wide in full alert, his head lifting before pushing me aside. I look up and he is glaring daggers at me, his stance becoming strong and angered.

'What?

He lifts his head and roars into the air, firing off another flaming shot.

'I don't know what I have done. You need to keep calm.'

He creates the red dusty hot swirl and within a long few seconds, he is standing in human form before me.

'Who have you been with?' He starts to pace back and forth.

'Excuse me?'

'You're dripping with the smell of gargoyle.' He grabs me

in his arms and presses his lips against mine. 'Darn it, Jasmine! You taste like one as well! Who was it? I will rip his head off. Was it Jet?'

'Ew! No, it wasn't Jet. He is my nephew.'

'Who. Was. It?' He slowly paces out his words, forcing each one through his gritted teeth.

'I spent the whole morning with all the gargoyles, making orgles for them. They hugged and kissed me as a thank you.' Then I remember Ash holding me last night and removing my clothes.

He drops his head and inhales me again. 'Do you let them run their hands all over you and kiss you on the lips?'

'No.'

'Think before you speak because you are a terrible liar, Jasmine.'

'I'd prefer to talk about us and why you left me alone in the middle of nowhere.'

'I nearly snapped your head off your shoulders.'

'I know better than to move quickly. It was totally my fault.'

'What if it happens again and I actually… bite you?'

I try to lighten the mood. 'If you actually "bite me" it will be quick and I'll be dead.'

'I can't put you at risk. You shouldn't be anywhere near us dragons.'

'What are you saying?' I feel my heart tightening.

'I don't know what I am saying but I'd prefer you alive and if that means keeping away from us—from me—so be it.'

'My powers are strong, and I can handle you and the others. I can stop you if I need to.'

'You were concentrating on the snake. I had plenty of time to kill you.'

'But you didn't. You stopped and controlled yourself.' I move closer to him and run my hands up and along his arms.

'There are some instincts I can't control. I was on you in a blink and I knew it was you.' He gently pushes me away.

'I was being a cow—teasing and tormenting you. I know I can't push those buttons when you're in dragon form. We can work this out.' My voice quivers. I have a feeling he is about to run.

'I won't risk your life so I can be happy.' He drops his head and starts to walk away.

'Don't do this to us, Lazarus. What about my happiness?'

'You're a beautiful woman and by the smell of you, there's someone at the castle who has your attention.'

'But I don't want him. I want to be with you. Aren't you connected to me?'

His eyes shoot up to mine. 'It's called "inked". Who told you about that?'

'Falcon told me. Are you inked to me? Because I'm connected to you and I'm damned if I'm letting you out of my life.'

He lifts his hand to his chest, covering his heart. 'Yes, you are well and truly inked in my life.'

He removes his hand and I scan his dragon tattoo. My name is written alongside the red dragon. I've never noticed it before. 'See? We're meant to be together.' I smile and walk towards him.

'Stay back. I'm not right for you.' Lazarus moves quickly away, and with a red dusty swirl of particles, he changes form.

'No! Don't leave me! Please, Lazarus!'

He turns and blinks once before spreading his massive wings and taking flight.

'Please, I will do anything you ask. Don't leave me!' I fall to my knees and watch him fly away without turning his head once to see me. I cry hysterically as the creature I love flies out of my life.

I fall to the ground and sob my heart out. I hear

Grandfather and Sky trying to echo but I shut them out. I don't want to be told by anyone that it's better this way. Because it's not!

I cry for what seems hours. My stomach and head ache, while my heart's shattered into a million pieces. I exhaust myself and have no energy to move.

A shadow casts over me and I pray it's Lazarus returning. 'Lazarus?'

'It's Jet.'

'Oh. Jet, he's left me.' I continue to cry.

'I heard. Let me take care of you.'

His hard stone features don't match his soft caring tone. He scoops me up, cradling me in his large arms. He pulls his wings around me, protecting me from something. I don't know what. Maybe the curious eyes of the gargoyles that have no doubt seen the floor show.

I drift off to a fatigued sleep in the safe, secure arms of Jet. I stir when he places me on my bed, pulling back the sheets to slip me underneath. 'Leave my clothes on, please.'

'Why would I remove them?

'Because the sheets are clean and my clothes are not. Ash removed them without asking.'

I hear Jet growl and cuss under his breath. I roll over, not caring for his tantrums, and cry myself back to sleep.

I WAKE TO the angels coming in, carrying a plate of food and drink. 'Morning, Jasmine. You have slept all day and night. We brought you something to eat,' Gabby says, her smile sweet.

I roll over, turning away from them. 'I'm not hungry. Please leave and lock the door behind you.' I sniff and cry myself into another restless slumber.

They return that night, offering me more food, but I refuse

to acknowledge anyone or anything, my mind numb and my body lifeless.

During the night I have several visitors trying to enter the room, but I hold it firmly shut with a point of my index finger. Jet pleads with me to eat and, after an hour of his coaxing, I promise I will eat something.

The angels return with my dinner, leaving it on the side table next to my bed. It smells delicious but when I place it in my mouth I'm nauseated and roll over to cry myself to sleep.

I wake during the night and find my phone on the bedside table with a note from Jet stating I should call my mother for comfort. I dial and, on the second ring, she answers with a knowing voice.

'He needs time to sort out his emotions. You should take this time to sort through yours. I imagine your powers are ricocheting around in your head. Now is a good time to learn how each and every one of them can help you.'

'I wish I'd never tapped into them.' I sniff.

'Do you really wish that, baby girl? I can have them and everything you know erased if that is what you truly want.'

'Why did you give it up?'

'When I met your father, he didn't want any part of this life. Few creatures know, but your father went under a different name before he met me and was known to be one of the strongest sorcerers in Australia. He still goes to great lengths to cover his identity. There is a daily ritual he must do to cover his and my scent from all creatures. He passed a lot of his knowledge onto Paul, who took over being your life's guardian, so we could live a regular life, giving you and Sky the normal lives you deserve.'

'Dad was a…' I stop, knowing everyone in the house can hear me. I cover myself in a dome of silence and continue my conversation. 'You… he never mentioned it.'

'We had no intention of ever returning to that life so there was no reason to talk about it.

'When Grandfather died and Sky disappeared, we had your memory erased, but unfortunately, the memories still appeared in your dreams. We presumed the orgle you wear has something to do with it, but we feared what would happen if we took it from you. It gave you peace.'

'Does Lazarus know what you both are?'

'He recognised me and sensed your father had something irregular floating around him. He asked him on your last visit, but your father told him it's to be left in the past for your safety. Lazarus agreed, not wanting to put you in danger.'

'He never mentioned anything to me. No wonder I find it hard to trust people!'

'If he had said anything to you, he would have lost my and your father's trust. Try to see it from that angle, Jazzy.'

'It doesn't matter anymore. He has left me,' I say, the waterworks starting again.

'I can fly up to be with you. It sounds as if you need your mother.'

'Huh. What are you going to do, grow a set of wings and fly up here?'

'You'd be amazed at what I can do, baby girl.'

'I love you, Mum, but I don't want you or Dad to change your beliefs because I chose this life.'

'Did you choose it, or did it fall upon you?'

'I chose it, Mum.'

'You can always un-choose it.'

'Great English.' I snigger.

'It's good to hear you laugh. Get some rest and call me again soon. I'd like to know what those Europeans are up to even though I'm not practising anymore.'

'I'm a strong sorceress. You don't have to worry.'

'You are stronger than you know. Promise me you'll keep on the positive trail and remove all the negative creatures that surround you.'

'I have only seen the positive light and I promise to keep it that way,' I lie, not wanting to worry her.

'Please keep what I have told you about your father a secret. Creatures will kill to get to him and I worry they will do the same to you if they know there's a connection.'

'I will. Tell Dad I love him.'

'He can hear you and sends his love,' she says, but I had already heard my father's voice in the background.

'I love you too, Mum. And don't change your ways for me. I have a fantastic group of friends and creatures here, all wanting to be my guardians. They wouldn't hesitate to put their lives in danger to protect me.'

'I have heard about Jet, Sky's son. I look forward to the day I meet him. When your Uncle Bill disappeared, I raised her like a daughter, and I think of him as my grandson. Please send him our love and tell him our door is open to him. In human form, of course.' She chuckles.

'I'll let him know. Bye.'

I close my sore red eyes but this time I have the added warmth inside me that only my mother can give.

I picture my father as a master sorcerer and giggle myself to sleep at the silly picture I have of him dressed in a cape, holding a wand. He has always been a soft kind-hearted man. I can't imagine him wielding an anoric at anyone or even raising his voice. The thought lightens my heavy heart.

A warm hand touches my shoulder. I instantly recognise it as a dragon. I spring up in my bed, hoping to see Lazarus, but instead, I see a beautiful woman with long black hair and lime green eyes. We stare at each other until I recognise her scent.

'Hello Jasmine, I am—'

'I know who you are, Kite. I have your scent.' I rub my eyes open.

'I wanted to meet you in this form. I'm still learning to control my dragon form near humans.' She looks down at her fidgeting hands. I'm not sure if it's a look of guilt or nerves.

'Have you ever hurt a human?'

'No! But I've never had one approach me either and Falcon said you are bold enough to do that. I wanted to… be around you and hopefully become friends so if and when the day comes that we meet and I am in dragon form I will be able to control the urge to…'

'Eat my delicious pounding heart?'

'Yes. How did you know?'

'It took Lazarus a while to get used to it.' An unexpected sob escapes my throat.

'I'm sorry for what has happened between you and Lazarus. If it makes you feel any better, he is miserable without you. Falcon tried to calm him but copped a swipe of his tail for his effort.'

'Not that I care, but did he hurt Falcon?'

'He has a gash on his neck, but it will heal.' She smiles. 'Falcon told me that you and he don't see eye to eye. I hope that doesn't affect our friendship. I am hoping to live here permanently and would like to have at least one girlfriend I could talk to.'

'That oversized gecko will never see me as more than the one who killed his father and I will never see him more than someone who kept me hostage, choked and burnt me.' I slip out of bed and her eyes scan my legs.

She drops her eyes back to her fidgeting hands. 'He told me about his father and how he brainwashed him into thinking the gargoyles should be eradicated. He regrets not standing up to him. It wasn't until he saw several gargoyle friends die overseas that made him realise what a big mistake he'd made.'

'It's a little too late, if you ask me.'

'I understand that you're hurt and you don't trust him. But I love him and, from what I saw in Europe, he has earned my trust.'

'It takes more than one kind gesture to gain my trust, but I am happy for you. I judge people on what I see and not who they hang out with.' I give her a reassuring smile. 'Let me have a quick shower and then we can talk more.'

For some odd reason, I want to get to know this woman. Maybe it is because she is a dragon and at this very moment, any dragon will comfort me.

'Of course. I'll be downstairs with the others. The moon is rising early so we are having a get-together of sorts and you should eat something. Your clothes are hanging off you.'

'What others?' My heart jump-starts with the thought that Lazarus is here.

'Hmm, you do need to control that heartbeat, Jasmine.' She shakes her head. '*He* is not here but everyone else is. I have information about the European dragons.'

'Sorry, Lazarus is always telling me to control my beat. I won't be long.' I give her a sympathetic smile before heading for the shower.

As the cool water runs over my head and face, it only takes mere seconds before my tears join in. I miss Lazarus and my aching heart is the dreaded reminder that he no longer wants to be with me.

I walk gingerly down the stairs, my head feeling light, presumably due to lack of food. Malachi is suddenly beside me, scooping one of his arms under mine and around my back to support me.

'Any excuse to hug me, hey, Malachi?' I joke, but I feel embarrassed for being so pathetic. He smiles and winks at me.

We eventually reach the end of the stairs and find Falcon,

Kite, Corbin, Paul and Xandria all sitting in the lounge room.

Falcon is the first to stand. He moves quickly towards me. 'Jasmine, you look awful,' he says, taking over from Malachi and slipping his arm around my waist.

'I can always look to you for an honest appraisal, even when it's not asked for.' My tone is snide.

'He wouldn't want to see you like this,' he whispers.

'He doesn't want to see me at all, Falcon, which I'm sure pleases you.'

He helps sit me in a single lounge chair. 'That's far from what I want. He is wrenching his heart out over you. Believe it or not, I care for him and I don't know why, but I find myself caring for you.'

'I'm not living with you anymore so we don't have to pretend we like each other, you overgrown bat!'

'Jasmine!' Paul says.

'It's all right, Paul. She doesn't mean it. I know where her heart is.' Falcon taps his ear with his index finger. I poke my tongue out at him and he laughs. So do I.

'I'm so sorry Lazarus has left you. Maybe he will find one of his own kind to love,' Xandria says. I notice when she is in human form she doesn't speak in the third person. Thank goodness!

'Jam it, Xandria. I don't want your pity.'

'She was only trying to be nice,' Kite whispers.

'There are two sides that coin, trust me.' I shake my head. 'So what is the reason for this gathering?'

'I have received news that the rebel group of European dragons have ceased attacking and have gone into hiding. There are clans that have withdrawn their support for eradicating the gargoyles and, instead, are banding together to protect them.'

'How many are left in the rebel group?' asks Paul.

'The word is that they are down to twenty dragons and

several sorcerers. They are having trouble tracking the rebels due to the dark sorcerer's blocking spells but the threat of them travelling over here has lessened. I wouldn't say they definitely won't come here, but for now, we are safe.'

'So we are celebrating tonight with a huge feast,' Xandria says.

'Celebrating what, exactly?' I ask. 'That we may be attacked by twenty dragons and a few dark sorcerers instead of a hundred?'

'That we creatures have come together to form our own clan. That gargoyles and dragons can live side-by-side as one, as it has been done for many years. That we are one big family,' Gabby says from behind me.

'Terrific. We're one big happy family.' Throwing my hands in the air, I stand up and head for the bar. 'I need a drink.'

Malachi smiles. 'I have breakfast made for you, Jasmine.'

'Eat it yourself. I'm on a liquid diet.' I lean over the bar and grab a glass and a bottle of champagne.

'You haven't eaten for days. You shouldn't—' Gabby says.

'Don't tell me what I can and can't do. I have a mother and you're not her. I am the strongest here and there's nothing holding me here anymore. You need me in case the dragons attack.'

'We don't need the attitude.' says Falcon.

'Start with me Falcon, please. Bring it on! There's nothing that would make me happier than throwing a few anorics your way. I haven't forgotten how your fingers felt as they strangled my throat closed. How cold and numb my body became while locked in a cave to die, struggling to breathe as my lungs shut down on me. How, every time I open my eyes, I see the hideous markings you so kindly gave me. So please, give me one bloody reason to fire at you!'

'I understand you're hurt but being disrespectful won't bring Sky or Lazarus back.' Falcon stands up and rolls his shoulders back as if he is God Almighty.

Within a blink, I throw a small anoric at him. He moves quickly enough to avoid it, but it punches a mighty hole in the couch.

'You know nothing of how I feel! I look at all of you and I don't trust one of you. You have lied to me or betrayed me. And maybe you shouldn't trust me because right now I don't trust myself.' I pop the cork off the champagne bottle and take an unladylike mouthful. The cold bubbles block my throat which I am thankful for as I am about to burst into a flood of tears. I head for the door.

'Can I join you in a glass?' Kite asks as she follows.

'Whatever.' With a violent wave of my hand, I force the front doors open. I'm shocked at how little effort it takes.

I walk to the creek, my head light and my eyes squinting from the bright sun. I fall to my knees and try to cry but my tears are dry and my mind numb, which leaves my anger raw.

A small warm hand rubs my back then embraces me fully. 'I know my words won't heal your pain so I am happy to sit beside you, hold you and listen to you weep until my words can help,' whispers Kite.

I erupt into tears and she squeezes me tighter. She rocks me for the next hour until I find myself staring into the distance with no emotions to tap into.

'You can let go of me now,' I say, half-dazed.

'Would you like something to eat?'

I lift the warming champagne bottle and fill the glass to the top. 'I'm fine.'

'Then I will join you.' She takes the bottle and fills up her glass to a reasonable level.

'Tide's out,' I tease.

'I'm not a big drinker, especially around a human.'

'Right now, I wish you would take a bite out of me so I wouldn't feel this way.'

'He will come around. Give him time.'

'Falcon is probably your first boyfriend, so what would you know?'

'I was inked to another, but he was killed.' Her tone is mournful.

'Oh shit. I'm sorry, Kite. I never meant to be so heartless.' My heart thuds hard. I wish I could withdraw my words. I reach over to grasp her arm in comfort. 'I know nothing of what you've gone through. It must be bad in Europe for your parents to send you over here.'

'It's scary watching elites I've grown up with suddenly side with King. My dearest friends have turned dark, and on many occasions, tried to turn me.'

'Is that why your parents sent you here?'

'My boyfriend of seven years died before me, at the hand of King. When King kills, his concentration is focused solely on his victim, which gave me time to escape.' She swirls the wine around in her glass. 'I know what you're thinking. Why didn't I stand and fight?'

'I don't judge others, but I thought a dragon's first instinct is to attack?'

'It is but not against King. My boyfriend yelled for me to leave and save myself. If I'd stayed, I would be dead. King is the strongest sorcerer I've known.'

'I didn't mean to offend you before.'

'I know this is not your normal nature. Your heart gives you away.

'When you were verbally attacking Falcon, your heart was screaming out in pain for Lazarus. That is why Falcon didn't retaliate as I'm sure you would have a few singed hairs if he had.'

'He did this to me.' I point to my legs, which are covered in vine-like tattoos.

'I like them.' She smiles. 'And the one on your face is stunning.'

'He was attacking the castle and he burnt me. I was in so much pain.' I shiver as I remember the event.

'I can understand your lack of trust. He has to earn it back and the way he cares for you, he will.'

'He doesn't care for me.'

'You're wrong. He sees Sky in you and he feels the need to protect you.'

'That's all I need—more over-protective creatures.'

'I'm going to give the angels a hand setting up, as the moon is rising early today. Do you want to come back to the castle?'

'I'm a little embarrassed. I need to take some time before I blow a hole in someone.'

'Don't be angry. It's not a good trait for a sorceress or an elite creature. You should also eat if you're thinking of polishing off that bottle.'

'I'm not angry. I know you're right. And thanks for being so sweet. Who knew a dragon could be like that?'

'Who knew?' She laughs over her shoulder as she walks away.

CHAPTER NINE

As I POLISH off my warm champagne, I listen to the hustle and bustle behind me as they set up for the evening's festivities. The temperature starts to cool. I gather the evening is approaching. No one has come near me, which I am grateful for.

I lie on the cooling ground, my head in the dirt, my fingers squashing small ants racing around.

'Hello, gorgeous. It's nice to see you up and about, but your choice for hydrating isn't the best,' Ash says, standing tall and strong over me.

'Go away, Ash. I neither have the strength nor the desire to talk to you,' I murmur through numb lips.

'Nope. I am sitting here until you eat.' He drops to the ground with a plate full of food.

I try to sit up but fail. He places his massive plate of food beside him and lifts me into a sitting position. I feel like a child and am slightly ashamed by my state. I was always a one-pot screamer. 'Could you fit any more food on that plate?'

'I'd push some of it aside to fit your delicious little self on there.'

'Ash, I'm not interested in a relationship. Please, my head is spinning. I can't handle your flirting.' I try to brush my hair from my face and end up slapping myself.

'I know you are a single woman. I am a strong handsome man who can take care of you without hurting you or putting you in danger.' He places a carrot at my lips. I open my mouth and bite down. It crunches and my eyes shoot up to his amazing blue ones.

'One bite from you and I'll have a life-threatening disease

that affects my nervous system. Not to mention you could rip me apart with your strong clawed hands.'

'I don't have rabies. I also control what I put into my mouth, unlike a dragon.' He grins before forcing another carrot to my lips.

'I'm not a rabbit.'

'You're as skinny as one. Here, eat this.' He fills his fork with a slice of roast beef.

'You don't have to babysit me. Go back and enjoy yourself. I'm happy sitting here alone.'

'You're warm-hearted, vibrant and enthusiastic demeanour captivates me. I can't leave.' He sniggers.

'Sarcasm is the lowest form of wit. Anyhow, I have a bone to pick with you.'

'Pick away, beautiful.'

'If you ever remove my clothes without my permission, I will blow two large holes in you. Understand?'

'You have already scalded me for that, and I agree to wait until you ask me to remove your clothes, and you will.' He forces the fork into my mouth, his glowing blue eyes watching me.

I sense Falcon behind me, but I keep my back to him.

'I was checking to see if you wanted something to eat, Jasmine.'

'I'm fine, but another bottle of wine would go down nicely. And before you tell me I've had enough remember what the couch looked like after I blew a hole in it.'

'I remember and I do believe you've had enough, but here.' He hands me a bottle.

I reach up, confused. He is looking down at me. Is he questioning the alcohol or is it because I'm sitting with Ash?

'Don't keep judging me. Kite is trying to convince me to trust you, but every time I glance at my legs it makes it harder.'

'I don't think I've ever apologised for that. I am truly sorry and hope one day soon we can have a friendship like you have with Jet.' He drops his head low and his eyes hood.

'I don't hate you, especially when you're giving me a bottle of wine. But it's always been difficult for me to regain trust in someone.'

'Maybe it's time to try.'

'Maybe,' I murmur before he walks away. 'But who will I tease?' I yell over my shoulder, hearing him chuckle.

'I'm sure you'll find someone,' he whispers, knowing I can hear him.

'Thank you, Falcon.'

Another forkful of food is shoved in front of my mouth. I shake my head, but the fork jiggles up and down.

I hear and smell the creeping of three of my favourite creatures. 'I've already heard you guys. You can't sneak up on me, Kip, Tag and Nelly.'

Ash jumps up and away as I roll on the ground with three oversized dingoes licking and playfully growling at me. I sense Ellie and Rhys close by.

I giggle and push the pups away only for them to jump back on top of me. My face is lacquered with dingo saliva.

'Enough, enough. You guys win.' I laugh, looking up at Ash, who's grinning widely. 'Ellie and Rhys come over. It's fine.'

They walk out from the protection of the trees and Ash gasps.

'Haven't you seen a dingo before?'

'Not this big and I presume they are…'

'Don't ask and I won't lie.'

'I understand,' Ash murmurs. 'We have dingoes at home but not this size.'

'Trust me, there's something in the water here. Nelly, take

your brothers over to the paddock. Blue Boy is over there with another horse. You can play with them but remember not to scare them.' They instantly take off in the horses' direction.

'Ellie and Rhys, you are welcome to join our celebration. There is plenty of food, so please go help yourselves.'

Rhys walks passed and winks several times at me as if to say thank you, but Ellie stops and nuzzles me with her soft wet nose. She whimpers in my ear and caresses my cheek. She is sympathising with me. I kiss her soft furry cheek. We hold eye contact for several long seconds before she follows her husband.

'They seem very fond of you,' Ash says.

'I'm very fond of them.' Hearing the pups play in the paddock with the horses makes me smile. 'They are a part of my family.' I pour the wine into my glass and gulp it, forcing down the sad feelings that are creeping up.

'I'm a part of your family.' He sits behind me, wrapping his large arms around me.

'Ash, you can be my friend and nothing more.'

But his arms slide around my waist. 'Friends can cuddle, can't they?'

'As long as the friend doesn't get the wrong impression.' I refill my glass and scull half of it. It hits my stomach hard. 'I think I need to use the restroom.' I try to get to my knees but fail miserably. My spinning head joins in. I try to move again but I fall back into Ash's arms.

'Hey, beautiful. Let me help you up.' He jumps up and tugs me with him.

My head spins and nausea swamps my gut. I close my eyes and pray I don't throw up the few pieces of food that were force-fed.

I try to step forward but collapse. Ash is quick to save me.

'Oh hell! I'm out of control. I'm pleading for you to get me to my bed before I pass out. Please.' I close my eyes.

'I've got you, Jazz.' He scoops me up into his arms. I tuck my head into his chest and breathe long deep breaths, trying to calm my stomach.

With no effort, he carries me up the staircase and I breathe a sigh of relief when I hear my bedroom door swing open. He sits me gently on a chair beside my bed, making sure I am balancing on my own before releasing me.

I close my eyes and keep the deep breaths flowing in through my nose and out my mouth. Eventually, I start to feel better and slowly open my eyes.

Ash has pulled back the top sheet of the bed and is squatting in front of me, concern etched over his face. 'How are you feeling?'

'Better, thank you. You can leave. I can look after myself from here.' I force a smile.

'Let me help you to your bed.'

'I'd prefer it if you left now.' My tone is stern.

He helps me stand up and pulls me into his strong arms, encasing me. I gape at him and before I can tell him to release his hold his mouth is pressing firmly onto mine.

I push him as hard as I can, turning my face away from his. 'Ash! What the hell? Let me go and leave!'

'We will have a bond like no other. I know down deep you want me as much as I want you.' He leans in for another attempt to kiss me.

'No, stop. I will scream and every creature will burst through that door.'

'I'll stop for now, but I can see it in your stunning blue eyes that you have feelings for me.' He lets go of me and I stagger backwards, jolting my already soggy brain. My head spins and I fall ungracefully towards the ground, blacking out.

I wake with Ash on top of me with his lips inches away

from mine. He pounces on my lips.

I push hard against him, trying to force him away but his strong overpowering body is in control. I thrash my face side to side, avoiding his approaching lips. 'Ash, I don't want you. I'm in love with Lazarus!'

'He has hurt you and walked… well, flown away from you. I will never walk away from you and I can protect you better than anyone else.'

He catches me unaware with a firm commanding kiss. I try to twist my head away from him, but his force is overbearing. He pulls back, giving me time to turn my face sideways. I try to draw on my powers, but they stop dead in my gut and fade away.

'I will crush you if you do that again. Do you understand?' I yell.

'You're not meant to be with a dragon, Jazz.'

'I have never given you any reason to think I was interested in you other than as a friend. Please get off me.' I keep a calm but forceful tone.

'He doesn't want you. I can make you happy. Dragons are unpredictable and constantly lose control. I can guarantee I will never hurt you physically.'

I kick and flap my arms and hands, trying to avoid his advances, but he is too strong.

'I don't want this! I don't want you, Ash! Please, I'm begging you to stop this!'

The door flies off its hinges and a warm gust of air fills the room.

'She said to get off her, gargoyle!' Lazarus' tone rumbles the walls.

Ash is violently whipped from me and tossed aggressively to the floor. I am panting on the bed, my breath stolen by Ash's advances.

'You had your chance, dragon,' Ash spits, jumping to his feet.

His chest is puffed out, his arms contracted and ready to attack. He runs at Lazarus and, with a clash of flesh, they collide, forcing him back several metres. They stop when they hit the wall near my broken bedroom door.

Lazarus swings his clench fist, punching Ash square in the face several times, with one swift hit to his abdomen. Ash staggers back with an angered growl.

'She is mine, gargoyle!' spits Lazarus. I open my mouth to stop them, but my voice is lost.

Lazarus runs at Ash, collecting him in his strong arms, hitting the window. The sound of shattering glass pierces my ears, together with the noise of the brick wall fracturing.

Ash forces Lazarus back with several hard-hitting blows of his own. Lazarus' head whips back. He staggers but is quick to regain his balance, thumping his clenched fist into his hand. He smiles the devil's grin then charges at Ash, hitting the fractured wall with an impact that would move a house. The wall cracks wide open. They disappear out the broken wall, falling to the ground with an almighty crash.

I race to the edge where my window once sat and look at the two rivals. They both stagger to their feet, shaking off the debris from the castle's wall.

People and creatures from the celebration come running from all directions to see what the commotion is about.

'Back away. No one is to interfere. This is between me and the dragon,' Ash says, holding his hand up.

Lazarus changes form and Ash is quick to do the same.

'Stop it, both of you,' I yell, finding my voice.

My head spins and with the added mix of adrenaline, tilts me forward and out the gaping hole they graciously made. I fall helplessly toward the ground, letting out a garbled scream as it rushes towards me. I don't see my life flashing before me or my grandfather's face welcoming me into heaven. I'm disappointed that my ending is not what I had imagined and embarrassed that I will die because I had too much alcohol and fell out my window. Or maybe my welcoming party isn't here because it's not my time to go.

A jolt has me in the talons of a dragon. Déjà vu! It's the same pain I felt when Lazarus caught me. I am being punctured by a set of dragon claws.

I am lowered and dropped a metre from the ground with the dragon landing beside me. I flick my head to my rescuer and am filled with heart-stopping panic. Kite's green eyes are locked on me with her razor-sharp mouth a metre away. I glance out of the corner of my eye to see Ash and Lazarus fighting.

'It's me, Kite,' I murmur, too scared to blink.

She runs her tongue over her sharp teeth and blinks several times. I can't read her, but I hear her breathing in my scent.

'You know my scent, Kite. I'm your friend.'

She growls and opens her mouth wider. I inch my legs into a position that allows me to get out of her way if she attacks. She growls again, rumbling like a thunderstorm about to erupt and then takes a step closer. I draw up any energy and power I can, but it is muffled and floats aimlessly around my stomach. I concentrate on getting it to my hands, but it falters. I glance down at my stomach and see blood soaking my t-shirt.

I quickly glue my eyes to Kite's. I keep them locked even though the earth trembles and the ear-splitting noise of the two fighting creatures is in close proximity. I don't know who is hurt and who isn't but pray that someone is dousing the testosterone-fuelled fight.

'Falcon,' I whisper, barely moving my lips. 'I need your help.'

In a flash, Falcon is standing beside me. He positions

himself slightly in front of me but leaves room for Kite to see.

'Keep still, Jasmine,' he whispers. 'Kite, you can control this. You have Jasmine's scent. You know she is not your enemy. You're confused because she is bleeding. Draw her in again then back away.'

Kite pulls her lips back further and lifts her shoulders high, her tail in the air like a scorpion before it attacks. I hear the dingoes' protective growl as they move beside me. From my peripheral vision, I can see saliva drooling from Rhys' snarling rolled back jaw.

'Falcon?' I'm too scared to breathe.

'I will protect you, but the dingoes need to back away. Kite sees them as a threat. She doesn't understand that they're protecting you. She will take it as an attack against her.'

'The dingoes are harmless.'

'One bite from a dingo's back teeth is the same as getting bitten by ten redback spiders.'

'What?'

Kite rumbles, dripping her tail over her back, lowering it towards us.

'Tell them now, Jasmine,' growls Falcon.

'Rhys, Ellie, you need to step back. Please. For me.'

Rhys' tongue races around his jaw, so I know he has heard me, but it takes a good few seconds before he steps back. Kite relaxes, lowering her dagger tail to the ground.

'Thank you, Kite,' I whisper.

She blinks several times and shakes her head. Her eyes roll over me before she slowly lowers her head. I think she recognises my voice. She takes another step forward and stretches her neck so her nose is touching my shoulder. I freeze stiller than a stone statue and hold my breath as she inhales my scent. She draws a long deep breath. Falcon moves to her side and runs his hand over her polished red scales.

'I'm proud of you, Kite. That was quick thinking, catching Jasmine. Go to the creek and I will join you shortly. I need to help sort out my overzealous brother.'

She nuzzles my stomach and I wince in pain. She must have noticed my torn torso that her long, unclipped claws have pierced.

I keep perfectly still, only moving my lips to talk. 'It's nothing compared with what might have happened if you weren't there to save me. Thank you.' She drifts quietly away from me before taking off in a warm gust of air.

Falcon pivots and lifts me up onto my feet. Rhys and Ellie are back by my side, sniffing my blood-soaked top. I sway for a few seconds until I gain control of my spinning head.

'Are you all right, Jasmine?' Falcon asks, scanning me head to toe then turns his focus to the two creatures ripping each other apart.

'I've lost control over my powers so I can't stop them from fighting. Otherwise, I'm fine.'

'I don't want you anywhere near them. They're too angry and may accidentally hit you. Leave it to me.'

'If you change form, the gargoyles may see it as a threat. Many are still wary of you.'

'I'm not changing form. I'm sure Laz has shown you we are just as quick when in human form. I can get out of their way if need be.'

'Be careful.' I frown to hear these concerned words coming from my mouth.

'Hm. Careful, someone might think you care.' He winks before turning to the two dingoes that are still sniffing me. 'Ellie and Rhys, can you guys watch over Jasmine? I need to stop this fight before it starts a war between the dragons and gargoyles again.'

He doesn't wait for their reply and races off, giving me a

better view of what is occurring. I gasp in horror when I see Ash and Lazarus bleeding, their bodies and wings ripped and broken. The area has large crater-sized holes with broken trees and fences littering the ground. Their massive forms have created a war zone.

I stagger closer but make sure I'm still a safe distance away. Rhys leans up against me, steadying my balance. Ash has several huge gashes, one yawning across his stomach and one running the length of his back. He is barely standing up, his body beaten to a pulp. I can see by the way he carries himself that he has more than half his bones broken.

I know if Lazarus wanted him dead, he would be by now, as he is the stronger of the two. He is punishing him for kissing me.

I flick my eyes to Lazarus. He is stalking Ash in the same attack position Kite used on me and the dingoes moments ago. His killer sphere tail points over his back. His stance is fierce, full of aggression and his eyes are black and locked on Ash. He has one wing folded into his side, broken and bleeding, with several of his red scales ripped raw.

'Stop fighting!' I croak, not recognising my panic-stricken voice.

Lazarus flicks his head and stares at me as if I am his next victim. Is he mad at me? I didn't ask Ash to kiss me. It isn't my fault!

Ash takes advantage of Lazarus' lack of concentration and jumps into the air. He comes down on Lazarus' head with a clenched stone fist and he thumps hard into the ground.

It takes several seconds for Lazarus to acknowledge the blow, giving Ash time to roll under his long neck and bite his sharp teeth into the tender underside of the dragon's neck.

Lazarus roars and pins Ash with his four-pronged foot, rending him helpless. Lazarus curves his long neck like a swan, edging his head so it's a metre away from Ash's face. He bellows out a loud roar, firing a continuing flame but controlling it so it stops a hot inch away. Ash growls into the flame that persistently rolls in front of his face.

Falcon is close, as is Corbin and Jet. They're taking their time to move towards the two angry creatures. They are in human form and one flick of Lazarus' tail or a sideways bump from Ash will kill them instantly. If any of them changed to their true form it could start a war. I'm glad they've let the two fight alone, even though I want it stopped.

My eyes stay glued on Lazarus as he keeps the fire burning in Ash's face, roaring his disapproval. His jagged claws surround Ash's golden soul. If he pushes an inch further, he will be holding it in his claw.

Ash succumbs to defeat. His body goes limp underneath Lazarus' grasp and his growl diminishes. Or maybe he has lost his will to fight further, but whichever it is, I am happy it's finished.

'I love you, Lazarus. Only you.' I pray he releases Ash from his clawed hold after hearing my confession.

He closes his mouth, extinguishing his threatening flame. Lazarus licks his lips before backing off and away from Ash. He backs a good distance away then turns to look at me. His eyes soften and return to their original lime green colour. He inhales a deep breath; his large belly expanding on the intake before he exhales with a sigh. He looks beaten—his body limp like a sad wet dog. He has taken quite a pounding.

Ash rises and races towards Lazarus, whose focus is still on me. Jet and Corbin jump at him, bringing him to the ground and creating a tunnelling torpedo into the already broken soil.

Lazarus spins around in attack mode. Falcon stands fearless and solid in front of him with both arms held up and his fingers spread wide apart. Lazarus snorts loudly then slowly lowers his head to rest his flared nostrils against Falcon's chest.

'Don't be the dragon that is blamed for starting the war in Australia. She loves *you*, brother, so relax.'

Lazarus slowly drops his tail and, with a deep breath, relaxes his tense body.

Lysander steps onto ground zero and yells loud enough to wake the dead. 'That is enough from both of you!'

Everyone halts, freezing where they stand or lie. The silence is deafening; even the birds have stopped chirping. The only noise is the breathless panting of two creatures and the men who are restraining them.

'Sort your differences out in human form so you are equals and use your voices not your fists.' He throws his clenched hands onto his hips, his eyes flicking back and forth between them. His glowing blue eyes are narrow and piercing into both of them, radiating disgust and anger. 'This is how a war starts and I refuse to let jealousy over one woman be the cause of it. The clans in Australia pride ourselves on the way we respect one another. It was only Attor's twisted and greedy idea of eradicating us gargoyles that tore our families apart.'

Lysander turns so he can confront Ash face-on. Corbin and Jet are still pinning him down, each wrapped tightly around one of his large gargoyle arms. 'Ash, you are a guest here and should respect those who live here, no matter what race they are. Go inside the castle and heal and I will deal with you in a minute. Gabby will tend to your wounds.'

Gabby obediently heads off towards the castle's front door.

'Lazarus, this is your home, but you must respect our rules as we respect yours at Nogard Hollow. Malachi will be more than happy to tend to your wounds if you wish. To everyone else, I will not allow any creature to disrespect another. Not on my land and not in this country. The generations before us kept the peace for hundreds of years and we owe it to them, and to ourselves, to follow in their peaceful footsteps.

'All I ask for is respect between creatures. We have nothing if we don't have one another. There have been too many deaths including Sky... the love of my life.' He hesitates with his voice quivering, revealing the emotion bubbling inside. 'Death is final, guys. I don't wish this heart-wrenching sorrow I feel every day, every minute, every darn second, on anyone. That is why I am thumping down hard on you all.' His eyes flutter as he rolls back his shoulders and returns to his dominating pose.

'Please return to the celebration and forget this unfortunate and disgraceful incident. But do remember that a prerequisite of being here, and a part of this family, is you must respect all creatures. There is no room for racism!'

The guests return to the festivities, leaving the site littered with wounded warriors.

'Did none of you hear me?' Lysander yells at the rest of us, making me jump. Ash stands up with Jet and Corbin hanging off his tree-trunk arms. They let go, dropping a short distance to the ground.

Ash growls and lowers his head but not before flicking his eyes to mine. 'I apologise for my actions, Jasmine. I never meant to go that far.' He slowly walks towards Gabby.

Jet and Corbin dust themselves off and when Ash disappears inside, they burst into laughter.

'High five, bro,' Jet says, holding up his fisted hand in the air.

'Teamwork, bro.' Corbin hits his knuckles against Jet's. 'He's built like semi-trailer and we *so* brought him down while in human form.'

'We were awesome.'

Falcon drops his head to speak quietly into Lazarus' ear, then flicks his eyes to mine, giving me a short sharp nod. He walks towards the creek, and I gather he's going to seek out Kite. He passes the two others on his way.

'High five me, bro.' Corbin holds his fist in the air, waiting for Falcon to punch it.

Falcon walks over and stares at Corbin, shaking his head.

'Oi! Don't leave me hanging,' he says with a pout.

Falcon sniggers then punches his fist into Corbin's.

'Not that you did anything special. Laz was already subdued. We, on the other hand, took down the almighty Ash.' He and Jet keep bragging all the way over to the other guests.

Rhys and Ellie nudge me and whimper.

'I'm fine, guys. Go over with the others. I need to speak to Lazarus.' They hesitate until I kiss their furry heads. 'Thank you for standing by me. And when were you going to tell me about your deadly rear teeth?'

Ellie blinks and whimpers. I believe she's talking and gather it's about my wounds.

'I'll head in to see Gabby soon. I don't think the wounds are deep.'

My eyes flick over to a sombre and hurt dragon. I move towards him and he takes several steps back, but I keep my steady speed until I am beside him. I reach up and run my hand along his neck until I am staring into his cat-slit eyes. 'Your wounds look bad.'

He blinks and I listen to his heart beating. It's slow and fatigued.

'If you need to leave to heal, I understand, but I would prefer it if you'd change form so I can take care of you.' He shows no sign of hearing me. 'I have been miserable without you and by the way you dismantled my bedroom door and my window and my wall, I take it you have missed me.'

He keeps his head low and breathes calmly.

'Damn it, Lazarus! Speak to me. Change form, please!'

He inhales a deep weary breath and steps back. The warmth of the swirling air radiates my body. I close my eyes tightly, as my head is still playing havoc with me. I don't want to look at anything that goes around in circles yet.

I peek when his hot hand touches my arm. He is black and purple with bruises and there's blood covering one side of his torso. I circle around him. His back has severe lacerations and his throat a large gash which is dripping with fresh blood. I gather that is where Ash sunk his teeth into him when I distracted him.

I stand in front of him, staring up into his green eyes. I hint a smile, curving the corners of my lips, but his face stays expressionless.

'Talk. Tell me what you're thinking,' I eventually say.

'Whenever I am around, you get hurt. You fell from two stories high due to my stupidity and I didn't even know until Falcon told me.'

'No, I fell because I haven't eaten for three days. That was because I'm miserable without you. And maybe because I drank too much wine.'

He drops his eyes to my stomach and gasps. 'And you're injured again.' He growls and lifts my t-shirt.

I grab the hem and pull it back down. My stomach is still nauseated and full of the magic I couldn't release. The sight of my own blood may topple me over. 'You yelled at Ash, telling him I was yours, but you say you're no good for me. If you don't want me and you won't let him have me, who can I love? Make up your mind, Lazarus!'

'I don't want you with a gargoyle!'

'And I don't want a gargoyle, I want you. Stop torturing both of us. I know you love me.' I pray I am correct. I lift my hand to cup his cheek and he leans his face into it. My heart sings when I feel his warm skin.

His eyes shoot to mine and we are locked in a loving hold. 'You are right, I love you,' he admits as if he is in great pain.

'Thank you.' I roll onto the tips of my toes and kiss him on his rosy red lips. He kisses me back and slips his good arm around my waist, pulling me into him. I wince when his torso moves against my punctured stomach and his brow creases. 'Oh, I'm sorry, babe.'

'Let me take care of you. I am happy to go back to Nogard Hollow if that makes you feel better.'

'I don't have the strength.'

'My room has had a few renovations. I can always use Sky's vacant room. Lysander has kept it exactly the same way she left it. Under the circumstances, I'm sure he won't mind.'

'I suppose.'

'If it makes you uncomfortable being under the same roof as Ash, I will sleep outside with you.'

'No, you're injured, and your wounds need attention.'

'As do yours, stubborn dragon.'

We walk hand in hand into the castle. Gabby is tending to Ash, who has changed into human form before he goes into stone sleep to repair further. The two men glare at each other, but no words are spoken.

'Malachi will come to your room with the healing lotions,' Gabby says. Lazarus' hand tightens in mine; his jealousy still lies just under that leather surface.

'Thank you but could you come up when you have finished with Ash? I need you to help me with my wounds.' I hold eye contact with Gabby. She nods, understanding my unspoken words.

'How bad are your wounds, Jazz?' Ash asks.

'She's fine, no thanks to you and your groping hands!' Lazarus answers before I can.

'I didn't ask you, dragon,' he retorts.

'This wouldn't have happened if you'd stopped when I asked, Ash. Both of you need to respect the rules of this house and live in peace. I will have my full powers back tomorrow and will use them to subdue either of you. It will be more than a few broken bones or a torn wing you will have to worry about if I get annoyed,' I say.

I hear Lazarus snigger under his breath.

'I am talking to you as well,' I snap, halting his hidden chuckle.

We bathe before Malachi enters with his amazing healing cream, stitching up our wounds, much to Lazarus' dislike.

I remove my t-shirt, cupping my breasts with my hands so Malachi can reach the areas that need attending too. Lazarus huffs every second that Malachi has his hands on me, breathing hot air down his neck while the angel gently and calmly stitches my punctured torso. Lazarus relaxes when I slip a clean t-shirt back on.

Malachi lacquers Lazarus' wounds in large amounts of green cream, taking special care to cover the stitched wounds to prevent infection. Then he moves towards me with the cream in his hand, but Lazarus snatches it from his angelic fingers and shows Malachi the door. He closes it behind the angel and flicks the deadbolt. Then he turns and gives me a sheepishly cheeky grin.

'You do know that everyone who lives in this castle can break through that door if they wish?' I smile.

'They can also hear us, so do your thing, babe, and give us privacy.'

I lift my arm, grabbing my imaginary colourful crayon and draw the rainbow that shelters me from any creatures' inquisitive ears. I'm relieved that my powers have returned and will take note that alcohol and lack of food interferes with them.

Lazarus smiles a cheeky grin, his eyes glistening as he moves towards me like he is stalking me. I see his dragon characteristics in his human form so often and I love it.

I smile and step back, hitting the base of the bed, stopping me still. His grin grows wider and his eyes grow narrower. He has his prey exactly where he wants it. I am trapped but definitely not helpless; I love playing his little games.

I flick my eyes to see if I can jump out of his reach to make his chase harder and the game a little more interesting, but when my eyes return, he is an inch away from me, smiling as if he has just caught his victim. I'm glad he caught me as I'd hate to pull a stitch out trying to run.

'No one can hear us,' I whisper.

'Your heart sounds lip-licking delicious, babe.' He leans forward so my lips feel the heat from his. I lift my face so there's less than a centimetre between us.

'But first things first.' He winks and pulls away, waving the healing cream in the air. 'I don't want you to get an infection.'

My heart flutters and bounces recklessly in my chest. Lazarus sniggers under his breath and smirks widely. He grabs the hem of my t-shirt and gently lifts it up my torso. I raise my arms, instantly feeling the pull against my newly-sewn stitches. He lifts my shirt over my head and tosses it to the chair. I cup my breasts and keep my eyes locked on his.

He dips his index finger into the cream and gently dabs it on my wounds. It numbs them instantly. He squats so he can see them better. He leans forward and places several soft kisses on my stomach. My heart somersaults.

'Control, babe,' he murmurs against my skin, sending a rush of adrenaline through me.

'I want you to know what you do to me so if you ever leave me again it will hurt you as much as it does me.'

'My heart broke with every breath I took. I would fly to the forest, just close enough to hear you. I died over and over listening to you weep.' He wraps his arms around my hips, pulling the side of his face hard into my stomach.

'I never sensed you.'

'You rely on your emotions too much and it interferes with your senses, just like when you don't control your juicy little heartbeat. Keep a clear head and know what is going on around you. You didn't hear me or sense me when I was downstairs before I pulled that gargoyle off you.'

'His name is Ash, but I don't want to think about anyone else but us right now. Have you finished applying the healing cream? I have something on my mind I'd like to do.'

He slithers up my body, his bare chest battered and bruised, but firm against mine. His questioning lime green eyes are illuminating mine. Oh boy, he is one handsome devil!

'You might not want to talk about him, but I do.'

'What do you want to know?'

'Why was he in your bedroom?'

'I drank too much and he helped me to my room. I told him I had a boyfriend. Since you weren't around, he kept pursuing me. It got out of hand.'

'It got more than out of hand.'

'I'm sure he now knows where he stands.'

He narrows his eyes and softly growls. He loosens his grip, walks around the back of me and continues to apply the cream. 'You're a mess, babe.'

'Would you like a mirror, Laz? You're a bigger mess.'

'Hmm, I like the way you shorten my name.' He whips around in front of me. He tosses the cream on the floor and wraps his strong arms around me. He searches between my eyes and I question him by raising an eyebrow. 'What was I thinking, leaving you?'

'Never leave me again.'

He lunges at my lips, kissing me, but it's short-lived. 'I can still taste that bloody gargoyle.'

'Then you're not kissing me hard enough.' I push my chest

against his. My hands grab either side of his face, holding him firmly to my aching lips. He runs his hands over my numb back, kissing me as if it's our last kiss.

He lifts me onto the bed and, being as gentle as he can, lies me down. He stares into my eyes, in search of my soul. I raise my hand so I can touch the tattoo on his chest. There are two dragons which form a yin and yang symbol, with my name engraved over the yin. I am inked on his heart and soul.

'I balance you and you balance me. Maybe I should get one tattooed over my heart with your name on it.'

'After today, you will have added to your markings and I don't think I'd contain my anger if someone was touching your chest with a vibrating needle. I might accidentally break his neck,' he says, flicking his eyebrows.

'Since you won't let anyone else touch me, and I so desperately want to be touched…'

He lies beside me, pulling me into him. His mouth moulds to mine as he kisses me hard. My inquisitive fingers seek out his strong biceps and contracting back. His hold is firm, my pain is gone, and my mind is thinking only of him.

A melody of our love sings in my ears as our heartbeats tick in time. He runs his large warm hand down my leg, hitching it up so I am wrapped around him.

We are all arms, legs, mouths, tongues and lips. Our breathing is erratic and our blood fills with heated adrenaline.

I'm floating in heaven with a man who can steal my last breath away. Who can, with one casual look, stop my heart. I have found the 'yang' in my life and the purpose for me to live. He is inked on my heart, my soul and my being. I now know the true meaning of love.

CHAPTER TEN

WALKING INTO THE kitchen, I find Ash cooking beside the angels with Lysander sitting at the table.

'Morning,' I murmur, testing the water to see if it's still boiling after yesterday's fight.

'Morning Jazz, Lazarus,' the angels say in harmonic unison.

Lysander nods and smiles at both of us. Lazarus sits beside Lysander and mumbles something I don't quite catch.

'Morning, gorgeous,' Ash says, walking over to kiss me on the cheek.

Lazarus growls. 'Really, gargoyle? You want to try me again? Next time I won't just rough you up. I will rip your concrete head off your boulder shoulders!'

'I've kissed her every morning and more than once a day. Are you jealous, dragon? I can kiss you to if you wish, with my lead fist!'

Lazarus flings his chair back, glaring. 'Bring it!'

'Enough!' Lysander snaps, slamming his large fists on the table. 'We had a gathering yesterday of elite creatures who came to form a family of one. You two disgraced yourselves by fighting. If you can't be civil, I will remove both of you from this castle.'

Silence falls upon us all and it takes the boiling of water to make someone move. 'Coffee, anyone?' Gabby purrs in her angelic voice.

'Please,' I answer, reaching for several cups.

'Jasmine, I want you to spend time with Jet as he is having a few problems adapting,' Lysander says, giving me a short, sharp nod.

Jet must be trying to tap into his sorcery side, which we are keeping a secret from the guests.

'Of course. First thing after breakfast.' I smile, filling a cup with coffee and handing it to Lazarus.

'And you two are going to sort out your differences. Even if it takes all day and all night. I refuse to have any animosity in this castle,' Lysander says, staring at Ash and Lazarus. 'And Ash, what you did to Jasmine is unacceptable. A dragon, gargoyle, elite creature or man should never use their strength to bully or overpower a woman! It's beyond pathetic and it will not be tolerated. Do you understand?'

Neither of the men say a word but both hang their heads.

'I'll take the silence as a yes or I should I help you both pack your bags?'

'Fine,' Lazarus says, plonking back into his chair.

'I couldn't think of anything else that would make me happier than spending the day with a dragon,' Ash says snidely.

'Good. Now that is settled, how can I help cook breakfast?' I say in a lighter tone.

'All done, gorgeous. Sit your pretty little self down and let me serve you,' Ash says. I know it's to get a rise out of Lazarus.

I walk over to stand behind Lazarus and place my hands on his shoulders. I lean to him and kiss the top of his head. 'I love you.'

I feel his shoulders drop and his tension release.

Breakfast is delicious and goes down without anything being broken or thrown. I hunt Jet out and we head to the creek, stopping on the way to see Sky's resting place.

'How are you holding up?' Jet asks.

'I'm sore but good. Malachi's bush medicine heals open wounds quickly, instantly numbing the pain.

'I hear you're having trouble handling your powers. How can I help?'

'I can draw the earth's energy up my body, but it stops in the pit of my gut and I lose it. I'm even having trouble with my telepathic waves.'

'That's probably my fault. I have blocked it since Sky died. I promise to open up that channel again. Here, let me teach you what your mother once taught me.'

I show him how to draw up the energy from the earth and how being grounded will be his best friend. I tell him he needs to block out Drake's voice and how to practice each sense separately until he masters them perfectly.

Ash and Lazarus are off in the distance, far enough for Ash to not hear us, but close enough for me to hear them both. They are snapping and speaking snidely to each other and don't seem to be getting anywhere. Their egos are bigger than their heads which they continue to bump against each other.

Jet and I spend hours concentrating on the small but fun task of choosing a pebble or twig and hovering it off the ground with the point of a finger. I laugh when I remember how Sky taught me how to lift a cow off the ground, its little legs running in mid-air, until I placed it down and then it took off running. Jet sees the humour in it and laughs along with me.

'Those two are still at each other,' Jet says, nodding in the direction of Ash and Lazarus.

'As soon as my wounds heal, I will return to Nogard Hollow. Laz is too jealous and has a short fuse. And from what I know of Ash, he will pull his strings every second he can.'

'Must be nice to have two creatures fighting over you.' Jet nudges me.

'I care for Ash, but my heart belongs to Laz. He is my universe.'

'I hope there's enough love for me.' Jet reaches over to hold my hand.

'You are my true family and a part of my soul and heart. I can't function without you. So of course I love you, silly man, um… gargoyle-come-sorcerer.' I squeeze his hand and give him a warm smile. 'Hey, you want to have a bit of fun?'

'Always.' His smile lights up his face.

I draw on my earthly energy and point to a small rock. I hold it in the air before flicking it all the way over to where the two boys are arguing. It hits Lazarus on the shoulder, and he spins and glares at Ash, releasing a small puff of smoke.

'Pick your target.' I giggle. He bursts into laughter then copies me by flicking one at Ash's shoulder. He cusses and blames Lazarus. We roll on the ground in fits of laughter.

'Let's do it together,' Jets says, through his tears.

We pick up another rock each and hold them in the air side by side.

'On the count of three, let's aim for their heads.' Jet sniggers. 'One, two, fire!'

We flick our fingers and the rocks fly towards our unexpected victims. Crack! We hit our targets and both spin around and glare at us. We are rolling on our backs laughing, holding our bellies, gasping for air.

I hear Lazarus growl. I spring up and yell loud enough for both of them to hear. 'Start playing nice, you two.'

Lazarus shakes his head, rubbing where I hit him. I hear them both chuckle and pray it has broken the ice between them.

'You have done exceptionally well for your first lesson,' I say to Jet. 'Your target practice gets an A+.'

'Thank you, Aunt Jazz. It was more entertaining than I thought it would be.' He chuckles. 'But I need to leave. There's someone who wants to talk to you.'

'Well done, Jet. I sense her too.'

He leans over and kisses my cheek before walking away

and passing Kite, who comes towards me with caution.

'Hi, Kite,' I shout, hearing her footsteps quicken.

'Hi, Jazz, I didn't want to interrupt you and Jet, but I need to talk to you.' She sits beside me.

'What's up?'

'I am so sorry for hurting you. I never meant—'

I hold up my hand then grasp hers in mine. 'I would be flat as a pancake and you'd have been scraping me off the ground if you hadn't snatched me up. You did exceptionally well meeting your first human.'

Her eyes drop to our hands. 'It's not my first meeting, Jazz.'

'Oh?'

'I've told no one except my brother, who was with me at the time. I've only met one human and I killed him. He was a dark sorcerer.'

'Oh! Well, I'll consider myself lucky.' My voice is nervous.

'Falcon has been helping me work on my emotions and my need to kill. I know I won't touch you as I've locked your smell away in a positive area of my brain. It's hard to explain, but it's like I have a jar filled with scents that drive me crazy—kangaroo, possum, snake and my favourite—crocodile.' She licks her lips. 'Then there's an empty jar I hope to fill with scents which are good for my nose but not my taste buds. Does that make sense?'

'Definitely, and anytime you want to come over and get a good old nostril full of my scent, go for it.' I laugh and she joins in. 'Sniff away, baby!'

'Am I forgiven for squeezing you like a sponge?'

'There is nothing to forgive. Will you accept my thanks for saving me?'

'That's what friends do.' She wraps me tightly in her arms.

Her strength pulls on my stitches, but I bite my tongue. I don't want her to feel guilty again. 'Yes, that is what friends do.'

'I need to ask your permission for something.' She pulls back with a serious gaze.

'Ask away.'

'My family are travelling over here and I have asked Falcon if they can stay at Nogard Hollow. He said I need to ask your permission first.'

'It's not my house, it's his.'

'Apparently, it's Lazarus' and, since he is inked to you, I need your permission and his'.'

'Have you asked Laz?'

'Yes, but he said it is up to you.'

'Well, I suppose there's enough room. How many are there in your family?'

'My father is staying behind to help our relatives keep the peace. My mother, sister and brother want to start over in a country that doesn't discriminate between elite creatures.'

'Were any of them running with the rebels?'

'My brother was, but when he realised what was happening was wrong, he came home to us and is eager to leave Europe to start over again.'

'Please don't tell me he is good-looking and jealous?'

'He is very charming, as is my sister.' She giggles. 'My mother is quiet and keeps to herself. She loves to clean and fuss around a house and, no offence, but Nogard needs a little TLC.'

'Tell me about it! It gives me the creeps but that's probably because I was held captive there.' I shake my head.

'What?'

'It's a long story.'

'I've got time if you have.' She settles into a more comfortable position, her face etched with intrigue.

THE NEXT FEW days are a great time of healing and learning. Jet establishes a good grasp on his newfound powers and Ash and Lazarus speak more than two words to each other. They make snide comments and it reminds me of the banter that Drake and Lazarus once had. It makes me smile even though I can see it niggling at Lysander.

Kite's family arrives at Nogard Hollow and Falcon, Kite, Lazarus and I leave to welcome them.

Kite introduces us to her mother, Malinda, who is exactly as I imagined—a sweet, timid lady, who had, before we arrived home, opened all the windows to let fresh clean air flow through the house. She has a calm aroma encircling her.

She then introduces us to her sister, Bell. Bell lunges at me, wrapping her arms around my neck, inhaling my scent without any shame. I watch as she does the same to Lazarus, listening to his heartbeat, which, fortunately for his sake, keeps the same slow tick. He winks at me, knowing that I am listening. Maybe the dragon's jealousy is rubbing off on me.

Lastly, she introduces us to her brother, Ethan. He is charming and good-looking, as she described, but I notice his eyes are not lime green, they're a dark hazel. He has a quieter approach than his sister and shakes my hand, then politely inhales my scent. I smile to let him know I've heard him, and he gives me a knowing nod.

As we show them around the property, I take in their scents, with Ethan's being the only one that stings my nose. After showing Malinda the vegetable garden, she heads off with a basket, filling it to the brim with fresh fruit and veggies. She locks herself away in the massive kitchen to concentrate on cooking us a lavish meal.

After dinner, we relax in the lounge room with a refreshing glass of old-fashioned lemonade Malinda had made.

'Tell me about what's happening over in Europe,' I say, directing my question to Ethan.

'I believe you met Attor,' he says, and I nod, flicking my eyes to Falcon, whose eyes are locked on me. 'He was under King's rule but wanted to have his own kingdom of creatures, one that would fight for him without question. His aim was to take control of King's followers and then kill him.'

'I've heard King is unbeatable.'

'No one's unbeatable,' says Falcon. 'Everyone has their kryptonite.'

'I'm unsure of what powers he holds and pray I will never find out,' says Ethan, 'I'd recommend you don't attempt to either.'

'Didn't you run with the rebels?' I say, hearing Lazarus gasp a breath before glaring at Falcon.

Falcon shrugs his shoulders. 'It's the first I'm hearing it.'

'I did but it's in my past where I'd like to keep it,' says Ethan.

'Is there anything you can tell us that can help us prepare for an attack?' Lazarus leans forward in his chair, getting in Ethan's personal space.

'I was a scout for Attor, which I did only to stay alive. If an elite didn't join Attor, he killed them. Nothing was ever discussed in front of me. I'm sorry, I don't have any information that is of value to you.'

Kite stands up with the jug of lemonade and refills everyone's glass. 'That's in Ethan's past. He came here to leave that all behind. He wants a fresh start, just like we do.'

'But Kite, you weren't running with the rebels. He was,' says Lazarus. 'You must understand our concern. The protection of the Australian elites is our responsibility.'

Malinda leans forward in her seat. 'You have my word that my son no longer runs with the rebels. He would never lie to his mother.' She looks at her son and he nods. 'And I know Aldore will vouch for my word.' She looks at me and smiles.

'I don't know Aldore,' I say. She blinks several times before dropping her smile and her head.

'I do,' says Lazarus. 'As much as I believe you're telling the truth, Malinda, I need to verify this with Aldore. It will take some time, so I ask that Ethan be with one of the Australian elites at all times.'

'I agree,' says Falcon. 'If you're not feeding with me or Lazarus, I ask you to stay in the confines of Nogard Hollow.'

'I apologise that the welcome mat has been rolled back in, but we must protect what is ours,' I say.

'Of course. I don't want my arrival to upset anyone,' says Ethan.

'I believe I speak on behalf of my family when I say how grateful we are. Allowing us to join the Nogard Hollow clan is a true blessing,' says Malinda, placing her hand on Kite's. They smile at each other.

'Enough about me, tell us about this beautiful country we're in. Is Elyograg Castle close by?' Ethan's smile is fake and I sense it doesn't come from his heart.

'Close enough,' says Lazarus.

'I'd love to see it! Is that where the gargoyles reside?'

'Oh, they are fantastic creatures and so much stronger than the ones back home,' gushes Kite. 'Jasmine created orgles for them so they can change form. She is an amazing sorceress.'

Lazarus' eyes lock with mine and narrow. As much as I enjoy Kite's company, I need to keep my powers hidden. She means no harm but bragging about my powers to the wrong person can get me into trouble. I'm glad she hasn't mentioned Jet and pray she doesn't know he's a hybrid.

'We've heard of Jasmine and how she took down Attor,' says Malinda. 'You're a hero in Europe.'

'It was a team effort. My powers are very limited; the way I want them to stay.'

'The word is that you are the strongest sorceress here. Surely you took Attor's powers after you killed him,' says Ethan. Falcon shifts in his seat, visibly uncomfortable about the conversation we are having about killing his father.

'As you said earlier, Ethan, it's in my past, where I'd like to keep it. An elite and their powers are only revealed when the need arises. Surely you know the law of the elite,' I say.

Ethan bow's his head as if in defeat.

Lazarus turns the conversation to where and what they feed on in Australia, while Falcon sits quietly, staring down at the floor as if in his own world. I wonder if he's thinking of his father and how I pierced his heart.

I'm curious as to how much Kite knows of my powers and what she has already re-laid to her family. My trust issues will always leave me wary of strangers; a trait that will probably one day be my downfall.

THE NEXT FEW weeks fly by. Getting to know Kite's family is a joy. I introduced her sister, Bell, to Jet. They seem to have hit it off well and sneak off together whenever they can. I warn Jet to keep his powers a secret and he agrees to do so.

'Malinda, it's been a joy having you here and taking over the role of cleaning and cooking the evening meal,' I say, watching her slice a carcass with a large butcher knife. 'The house smells so clean and you've brightened it up.'

'I was taught to cook by a sorceress many years ago. And even though we hunt and have no need to eat this small meal, I enjoyed cooking for her.'

'I hope it's not a polite gesture on my behalf.'

'It isn't, because I love it and it occupies my mind, as I

miss my husband. And it is because I can never repay you for allowing us to join your clan.'

'Your skill around the house is thanks enough.'

'You're very fond of Kite.'

'Kite's and my friendship is as close as the one I had growing up with Kelly, my best friend back in Melbourne. We giggle like young teenagers at silly things.' I laugh thinking about her. 'Poor Ethan is over us giggling and is constantly rolling his eyes at us.'

'She thinks the world of you.' Malinda smiles warmly.

Paul walks into the kitchen and kisses Malinda on the cheek. 'Hm. What's for dinner?'

'Stir-fry veggies and…'

'Steak!' says Paul, picking up a slab of meat. He picks up a carrot and takes a bite.

'Come on, you, let's leave Malinda to do what she's good at,' I say, pulling at his arm.

'She's better than good… not that I'm saying you're a bad cook, Jazz. But…'

'Let's go before I change my mind and leave you here to wash the dishes.' I shake my head.

We jump into the truck and head to the back of Nogard Hollow, putting the cave between us and them. I know it blocks out most of what we are doing.

'I want to try and join our powers again,' says Paul.

'Last time we did that you got hurt.'

'I've been practising drawing deeper, using the Earth's energy to stay grounded. I reckon I've got it mastered.'

'You're a sucker for punishment but I'll try again.'

I stand beside Paul, holding his hand.

'Okay, start to draw your anoric up through your body and I'll do the same,' he says.

I draw the Earth's energy up through my feet and let it fester there. 'How's it going?'

'Good.' He opens his free hand to show me a small anoric. 'Why haven't you got one?'

'I'm drawing slower, so I don't hurt you.'

'Go for it! I'm grounded deeper than the roots of a tree.'

I draw the Earth's energy up through my body and down my arm. As it reaches my elbow, Paul flies to the side. I've shocked him again but this time he only flew a short distance away.

'Ouch!'

'I'm sorry. I did it as slowly as I could.'

'Maybe your powers are too strong for me, but it might be an idea to try it with Laz. You are inked to him so there may be a chance you can join your powers.'

'It will be one big explosion if we do. And if we don't and I shock him, I may lose an arm.'

'Laz is wound tight.' He stands and brushes off the loose dirt. 'Maybe we can practice moving objects. It'll be safer for me if we do.'

'Sure. I've got another hour before I need to see Kite. I spend an hour each day with her in dragon form, becoming accustomed to me as a human.'

We spend the next hour lifting large broken trees and boulders; throwing them around as if they were tennis balls.

When we arrive back, Kite is sitting near the corrals in dragon form. She's showing me she can be near the horses without being tempted to eat them. I laugh when I see the drool dripping from her lips. She must have been sitting there a while.

Paul excuses himself and heads inside. He trusts the dragons in Australia but doesn't tempt fate when it comes to the new members of our clan.

'Afternoon, Kite. Have I told you how much I enjoy this part of the day?' She winks.

I move slowly towards her with my hands open wide,

showing her that I'm no threat. I place my hands under her nose. 'Breathe me in.' She does, long and slow. 'Good girl.'

Once she has my scent locked away, I walk down her neck, running my hand over her leathery skin. I make sure I keep contact with her so she doesn't bump me. 'Your skin is beautiful and soft. You must be moisturising it.'

She snorts a laugh, blowing a mouthful of smoke.

'I'm going to climb up your leg then onto your back. Are you happy with that?' She blinks once, which we've agreed is yes.

I rub the area I'm about to stand on. I slowly climb up her leg, grabbing hold of her scales to pull up. I wiggle away from her neck and sit in front of her wings. 'Did you want to try to fly with me?'

Lazarus bursts out of the front of the house and stands in front of Kite. 'Like hell she's taking you flying. I know you're friends, but I'm the only one you fly with.'

'Party pooper,' I say. Kite blows a lungful of smoke over him.

He shakes his head. 'I meant it, Jasmine!'

'Okay. Can she walk around with me on her back?'

'Why can't you be happy with just sitting there? It's not as though she's going to be taking humans for rides.'

'What if there's a need for her to carry Paul or one of the gargoyles?'

'She has claws for that.'

'Lazarus! You're being ridiculous, but I'll let you win this one.'

'I'm the alpha of this clan! I should win everything.'

'Yes, dear.'

He gives me a sideways look, unimpressed that I have dismissed him. He walks away shaking his head. I keep my mouth shut as I can't do a silencing spell while sitting on top of Kite. She might not appreciate it.

I continue to tug at her scales and slide down her side. She opens her wing. I run my fingers over it, knowing it makes her laugh. I duck when she draws it in, laughs, then spreads it out for more.

The only part of her I don't trust is her tail. The memory of Drake being speared by one is still fresh in my mind.

After our dragon/human bonding time is over, Kite takes off for an extra helping of deer. She says I make her work up an appetite.

Without fail, Ethan is waiting close by to talk to me. His conversations with me always end in him questioning my powers and how he heard that I was 'the ultimate sorceress'. I laugh, saying that Xandria, the local fairy, has more power than I do. He eyes me warily and I know he is not interested in me other than finding out what powers I possess.

He tests me by throwing an apple or an object at me, waiting to see if I will obliterate it or react in any magical way. Lazarus catches most of them, moving like a flash of light, otherwise, I let them hit me. It is sometimes an effort to not throw something back just to shut him up, but I keep my secret sealed.

I ride out to see my dingo family and let the kids ride Blue Boy. Corbin kindly allows me to take his horse for them as well. He has become attached to the young pups, as has all our clan.

Attaching his reins to the back of my saddle, I quickly head out. I hear their excited squeals from several miles away, making me grin all the way there. They are in human form and are squabbling over who is riding who first.

I break three twigs, making them different sizes and line them up level in my hand, hiding the unlevel bottoms in my closed palm. They each pull a twig out, and the shortest twig goes last. Nelly pulls the short stick but is happy to hang off me. She jumps onto my back, wrapping her small arms around my neck while kissing and tickling me.

I giggle at the thought that Lazarus always orders me to shower after I have been with the pups as he says I sink like a feral dog. I constantly remind him that they are not dogs.

Rhys and Ellie are in dingo form and are lying lazily under the shade of the trees. I wave and they acknowledge me with a warm-sounding howl.

Kip and Tag have ridden along the creek towards Elyograg Castle. I told them to ride one way for fifteen minutes then ride back.

It has been twenty minutes and Nelly hasn't stopped talking and I wonder when she will come up for a breath of air. Her love for me shows on her sweet, tender face, always smiling and hugging me when possible.

We hold hands, swinging back and forth. 'I miss you when you're not around. Seeing you one day a week isn't enough,' says Nelly.

'I miss you as well. You know how much I love you, don't you?' She purrs like a kitten and nearly does a backflip whenever I say those three little words.

I enjoy spending time with this side of my family. I am at peace but exhilarated at the same time, and my soul fills with a loving energy.

'Nelly, how about I organise a girls' sleepover?' I watch her face as she smiles with confusion.

'Yes, please. But what is a girls' sleepover?'

'That's when us girls have a night together, with no boys around. We watch movies and eat chocolate and cake and drink lemonade or champagne. Then we sleep in a big bed together, giggling and laughing until we can't keep our eyes open.'

'I don't know what movies, chocolate and cakes are, but it sounds fun.' She smiles, jumping up on the spot.

'It's very yummy food, and a movie is something so amazing you won't believe your sweet hazel eyes. I will talk to your mother before I leave, as she might want to join in. The more girls there are the better it is.'

'Oh, it sounds so fun! You are my best friend, Jazz.' She squeezes me tightly.

I hear the familiar sound of a dragon's wings in the air and inhale to collect its scent. It's Ethan and I wonder why he has headed out to this area. The dragon hunting grounds are in the opposite direction and he agreed to always be with one of the elite.

'Take cover, Nelly, just in case he's hunting and mistakes you for dinner.'

He lands gracefully a short distance away and Nelly takes off, hiding in the tall grass. I hear her change form and spot her tan furry coat lying low beside a clump of shrubs. I wink at her and she winks back.

Ethan walks towards me in a calm posture so I keep my hands relaxed, feeling no threat.

'You're in the wrong area for hunting.' I point to the area behind him. 'You should be miles away in that direction and with one of the elite.'

I'm glad I found you alone. I need to speak with you,' I hear Ethan echo.

I take note not to blink or register I can hear him.

I know you can hear me, Jasmine. Don't make me change form to prove it because it won't be pleasant if you make me use my powers unnecessarily.'

'What the hell!' I spit, shocked at his small threat.

I have an important proposal for you. I need you to listen carefully.'

'Do I now?' I say out loud, not using my telepathy.

'*Yes, if you want to live.*'

I close my fists and draw up the earth's energy through my body to create my anorics. If he threatens me again, I will send a warning blast at his feet.

'How are you telepathic?'

'*As you know, when you kill another creature you can, if you wish, draw on its powers. I have killed several sorcerers, one which had the skill of telepathy.*'

I keep my face blank, not showing the shock and horror of what I am hearing. He is blatantly telling me he has killed more than one human.

'What is your proposal, Ethan?'

'*The rebels are about to land in Australia. I have been here scanning the area to set up a training ground. If you were to join us in our plight, it would lessen the amount of blood that's shed.*'

'Are you telling me you have been lying the whole time about being connected to the rebels in Europe?'

'*You are the only one standing in our way. If the others don't join us, we can take them down.*' I notice he is moving closer.

'Do your mother and sisters agree with what you are doing?' I'm shocked and hurt that I've been tricked by all of them. Especially Kite, who was supposed to be my friend.

'*They know I was a rebel, but I convinced them I was no longer against the gargoyles. Except for my father, who you know has stayed back in Europe. He is now head of the rebels since you took Attor's life. He rules under the great sorcerer, King.*'

'Let me get this straight. Your father is the leader of the rebels and you came here to find somewhere to train them. And your mother and sisters have no idea what you two are up to. Am I correct?' I feel my heart kick-start a speedy beat.

'*You're a very bright woman, Jasmine. With your powers, we will be unstoppable. You can train our sorcerers and Falcon can teach our dragons the talented skills his father taught him.'*

'Is Falcon in on this?'

'Not yet, but I don't think he will be hard to convince.' He has drawn closer and is less than ten dangerous metres away from me. My hands are hot from the anorics spinning in them and I fear if I throw them, I might receive the aftershock from the blast.

His revelation has thrown me off guard. I need to waste time so I can think of a quick and safe way to escape.

'I'm confused as to what you want me to do.'

'You are a smart woman. I'm sure I don't have to spell it out for you.' His hot breath coats me, which means he's too close. I lock my eyes to his mouth in anticipation of a flame shooting from it at any moment. I will burn to a crisp in a blink of an eye if he bellows at me.

'You are absolutely deluded if you think I would join the rebels or hurt any member of my family. I will devour each and every rebel if they step one scaly foot in this magnificent country and if that includes your deceitful father, so be it.' I slowly take a large step backwards.

'If I have to kill you, I will, and gladly take your powers.' He stretches up on his solid legs, making him look an extra three metres taller.

'You are a disgrace to your mother and your sisters. Kite has so much faith in you.'

I keep my eyes locked on his razor-sharp mouth, waiting for any movement so I can release my anorics. I don't want to be the one who makes the first move.

But keeping my eyes on his dangerous mouth leaves him wide open to use his most dangerous tool, his tail. And before I know it, he has whipped it over the top of his back and stabs it directly at me. A scorpion attack!

With a flash of a furry golden coat and a cry that will haunt me forever, I see Nelly being violently pierced by Ethan's razor-blade tail. She has put herself between me and Ethan, receiving the impaling that was meant for me.

He withdraws his tail and she drops lifeless to the ground.

I scream and throw my anorics, protecting my Nelly from any further attacks. It hits Ethan head-on and he staggers back. He regains his stance and I throw several more, making him fall to the ground with two gaping holes in his side.

I scream to the gods above and draw on every colour I can, including the darkest of dark. All around me stones, rocks, boulders and any loose object are held in the air by my fury. I release a banshee scream and pelt them at the murderer in front of me.

He roars in pain, but I keep pounding him with anorics one after another, after another. They are filling my hands quicker than I can throw them, releasing a grenade-like explosion when they hit him.

He soon drops his long neck to the ground, defeated. I hear his heart slow, but I keep throwing like I am swimming in a race of a lifetime. I scream, letting out the frustrated anger I have inside as I watch pieces of dragon splatter the ground and shoot off across the grasses, colouring them a magnificent candy-apple-red.

'Stop, Jasmine. He is dead.' Rhys touches my shoulder. The contact makes me jump and I blink. 'Look at your hands.'

My hands are black. I spit on them and rub them against my clothes, trying to wash away the darkness. After a few long seconds, they return to the right colour, but they are covered in thick red blood. My clothes are also soaked red; I am covered head to toe in dragon blood and guts.

I look over to where Ethan lies. It looks like a bomber has dumped its load on him. I scan the surrounding land and stop when I see Ellie huddled and crying over Nelly's motionless body.

'No!' I run over, skidding on my knees in the dirt beside them. Ellie has lifted Nelly into her arms and is rocking back and forth, crying. Nelly is struggling for breath, gurgling on the blood that fills her small sweet lungs. She coughs and blood spurts out of her mouth, splashing onto Ellie's face. She doesn't flinch. She just keeps rocking her baby girl.

'Nelly, I'm so sorry. I love you, sweet girl,' I cry.

Nelly's blood is quickly covering her mother's body and the ground I kneel in. Ellie's tears race down her blood-covered face, leaving clean streaks through the blood.

Nelly's small body shudders as she gasps for breath, her mouth and tongue gulping. I'm unsure if she's trying to breathe or speak. The shuddering slows, then stops, as does her rattling gasps. I listen to her small heartbeat and hear her last dying thud as her blood stops pumping. Her eyes glaze over and Ellie howls a cry only a grief-stricken mother can.

My throat contracts, not allowing me to speak and I can barely breathe. I wrap my arms around both of them and rock back and forth to Ellie's howling sobs.

The two boys are cantering back on the horses. I jump up and try to stop them from seeing their dead sister but they both spring off the horses' backs and run over. They scream when they see her and howl a deafening cry.

Rhys embraces his family as they howl out their pain. I sit with my blood-soaked arms wrapped around my legs, rocking for what seems hours while listening to their broken hearts. Listening to their howls of pain, huddled together, makes me feel like I am intruding on something that is only meant for the dingoes.

Dazed, I collect the horses. Pulling my drained body into the saddle, I head off with my emotions, senses and mind numb. My eyes are open but my mind closed. There's a pair of strong imaginary hands wringing out my heart, forcing the tears to race down my shocked face.

I find myself at Elyograg Castle with Jet pulling me from Blue Boy's back. I don't remember riding there and when I look into his face, I see his lips moving but I can't hear a word.

He carries me into the house and I see Corbin, who is also talking, but I am oblivious to what he is saying. He takes off out the door when Jet places me on the lounge room couch. I curl up into a ball and stare at my hands. A warm blanket is placed over me, but the rest is unclear. It's like my head is underwater and everything is muffled. My mind, my hearing and my sight are all a great distance away.

I am scooped up and carried. Where and by whom I don't know and don't care. I am the cause of Nelly's death. My mind recalls her heart-wrenching scream as Ethan viciously killed her. I scream out and the arms holding me pull me in tightly. I blink and look up to see Lazarus, eyes wide and staring at me. I am still wrapped in the blanket when he lays me on a bed.

He unravels the blanket and gasps. 'Are you hurt, babe?'

'I am fine. It's dragon blood and bits.' I can't look at him in the eye. I feel guilty for killing a dragon but not for killing Ethan. 'I killed Ethan.'

He frowns but I am too weak to work out his thoughts. I have obliterated a dragon into millions of pieces and parts of him are stuck to my skin and clothes.

'I saw his remains and heard the cries from the dingoes. I presume one or more of them died.' His tone is soft.

'Did you hear what I said, Lazarus? I killed a dragon! You should hate me for that!' I pull the blanket back over me.

'I know you wouldn't kill anyone unless you or your family was under threat.'

'He was dead, and I kept on firing at him. I couldn't and didn't want to stop. My hands were black with hate and anger. I was drawing on my dark side and I enjoyed it.'

'Shh, keep your voice down. Between both of us, we will deal with it.' He runs his fingers over my forehead.

'You don't understand. Ethan's remains are spread over a kilometre of bush and if it wasn't for Rhys, I'd still be there firing at his bloody remains.' A sob escapes before I burst into tears. 'Nelly is dead because of me. Damn it! Damn you bloody dragons!'

I hit him in the chest with my clenched fists. He draws me to him, trying to control my flailing arms. I scream out as Nelly's last cry reverberates in my ears again.

Lazarus' strong arms contain mine, pulling me in and cradling me on his lap. I sob a hiccupping cry until I am too weak to do so. He rocks me, combing his warm fingers through my blood-soaked hair. His hot breath warms me and encourages my limbs to relax.

'Do you think differently of me now?' I ask, after a lengthy silence.

'You killed Attor and it made no difference. So no, I love you more than you can imagine.' He affirms his words by kissing my temple with his warm lips. 'Let me get you in the shower and when you're clean, we can talk more.'

'Are you frightened I will do the same to you?'

'Oh, babe, where are you getting all these silly questions? I'm the one with the jealousy and anger issues. You have and will never frighten me. Please let me get you into the shower.' He stands up with me still cradled in his strong arms.

'I need to speak to Lysander and Jet,' I say, holding eye contact.

'After your shower.'

'No, now!' I snap.

He frowns, his brows pulling tightly together. He releases them and forces a grin. 'All right. I will run and get them.' He places me on the bed and zips out the door only to return seconds later. 'They are on their way.' He leans against the wall closest to me with his arms folded across his chest, his eyes scrutinising me.

There is a small knock on the door before it opens. Jet and Lysander enter.

'Ethan is a rebel. His father is a leader under King's law. They're on their way here to eradicate all the gargoyles and set up a training facility for dragons.' I hope they're keeping up with me.

'What about his mother and sisters?' Jet asks.

'They know nothing of Ethan and his father's plans. But after being tricked by Ethan, I trust none of them. I'm sorry, Jet, but you must be wary of Bell, no matter how much you care for her.'

'Let's keep the focus on what happened. Explain exactly what went down,' Lysander asks, moving to stand in front of me.

I explain how Ethan approached me and asked me to join the rebels and their plans to take over Australia. I cry when I describe how brave Nelly was to throw herself in the path of his murderous tail.

My eyes shoot over to Lazarus. I know his greatest fear is accidentally hurting me with his tail. His eyes drop to the ground and his head lowers. I cut the story short, saying I killed Ethan with my powers, keeping the finer details between Lazarus and me.

I hear a bellowing roar and sense several sets of dragon wings coming our way.

'It's Ethan's family.' I gasp, swallowing hard. 'They're coming for me!'

'There is a strong westerly wind. Ethan's scent would have reached Nogard Hollow. We need to explain what happened before they attack,' Lazarus says, unfolding his arms, ready to leave.

'Stay here with Jasmine and get her clean. Jet and I will and explain what happened. If they see her with Ethan's remains dripping off her, they may retaliate. I can only pray that Falcon and Corbin are with them,' Lysander orders.

Lazarus sniffs. 'Both Falcon and Corbin are with them. Remember, they would have flown over the remains, and trust me, it's not a pleasant sight. I flew over it to get here.'

'Clean her up!' Lysander shouts over his shoulder as he follows Jet out the door.

'Come on, babe, get in the shower.'

He escorts me in and turns on the shower. I remove my blood-soaked clothes, letting them drop to the floor. I step into the shower and let the water cascade over me. It turns blood-red and I fall to the base of the shower, crying.

Lazarus jumps in, clothed, and holds me in his arms. 'It was him or you.' He pushes my drenched hair from my face. 'It's called survival, and you did the right thing.'

'But Nelly is dead!'

'She's a devastating casualty of war.' He reaches for the shampoo and pours a large amount into the palm of his hand and trails it over my head. He massages my hair, getting a lather that would wash ten heads.

'Were Sky, Grandfather and Drake casualties? Where does it stop?'

'Unfortunately, yes, and there will probably be more. I can't predict the future, but you need to understand that this is the way we live. Humans kill humans for no reason or they do it accidentally, and so do elite creatures. It's life.' He leans me forward under the shower rose, letting the shampoo wash from my hair.

'I thought if I lived in the Outback I could escape being hurt.'

'If that is what you truly want, I will leave with you today. We can go right now and put this life behind us. There is an enormous Outback out there. Most of it has never been touched. We can start our life together without another living soul.' His voice is sincere and I believe he would leave his clan and this way of life to make me happy.

He lathers the sponge and slowly washes my body clean of Ethan's remains. After several applications, he turns off the shower and wraps me in a large fluffy towel. He rubs his warm hands up and down my body, drying me with his heat.

He leaves and returns quickly with a pair of shorts and a t-shirt from Sky's closet.

'Your jeans are soaking wet,' I point out.

'With the heat my body expels they will be dry in no time.'

I smile but my heart is still breaking. The sound of shouting echoes through the castle.

We head downstairs. I'm greeted with a dozen sets of eyes glaring up at me. I stop midway on the staircase, hesitating until I'm sure I will not be attacked.

'I'm so sorry, Jazz,' cries Kite. 'I love my brother and will grieve his loss, but he wronged you and lied to us, as my father has done. You must believe us when we say we never knew he was still with the rebels.'

I say nothing and continue to scan the faces of all who are there.

'Jasmine, are you hurt?' Falcon says breaking the silence.

'She's fine,' Lazarus answers. 'Is everyone up to speed with what has happened and what is going to happen?'

'Yes, and the dragons are standing by us,' Jet replies.

'I can't trust them,' I murmur.

'We have little choice,' Lysander says.

'Yes, we do. You have me and they don't know how powerful I am and to be truthful, nor do you.' I feel everyone's eyes on me.

'I understand you don't trust us and I don't blame you,

Jasmine. I won't fight my husband, but I will fight any dragon that threatens the way we live here. The peace we feel amongst you is something I will fight for. In Europe, we lost too many clan members. Most of them were my direct family,' Malinda says, staring up at me. 'My daughters feel the same way.'

'I killed your son. How can you stand beside me and not against me?' I take several steps down the long staircase.

'As Kite has said, we will mourn Ethan, but now we need to fight for what is right and the life we want. Kite has a unique and strong bond with Falcon, as Bell does with Jet. We consider this our home and we will do everything to protect it.'

'I'm sorry but I have lost all trust in dragons. Not all, but most of you,' I correct, hearing Lazarus inhale a sharp breath. 'If Lysander and Jet trust you, that's up to them, but keep your distance from me. If I feel threatened by you, I can't promise I won't retaliate. I hope you understand and I apologise if I offend you.'

'Jasmine?' Kite gasps. I look into her eyes and they quickly fill with tears. My harsh words have come crashing down on her sweet soul but, right at this moment, I have no will to soothe her.

'Give her time, Kite,' Lazarus says as if I wasn't in the room.

He places his hand on the small of my back and guides me down the last few stairs.

'They have landed and will be here in the next four hours,' Corbin says, his eyes closed as he listens for more information. 'There is a minimum of twenty dragons and several sorcerers.'

'Lysander, you and Jet need to refuel before they come. The dragons will be at the forefront. You gargoyles can use the castle as protection,' Lazarus says.

'Like hell! I'm not hiding behind a castle wall,' yells Ash from the top of the stairs. 'I will be right beside you, Lazarus, kicking some mean dragon butt!'

'Ash, you should be in stone sleep. You will need all the energy you've got.' I say.

'I love how you worry about me, gorgeous, but I'm looking forward to breaking a few dragons' necks.' He chuckles, rubbing his large gargoyle hands together.

'She's right, Ash. You need to refuel. I will need you at your best if we are to bring down twenty dragons. Just don't get confused which ones are on our side.' Lazarus nods.

'It would be great if you could put a bell around your neck so I don't kill the wrong dragon.' He smiles at Lazarus before heading up to the roof.

Lazarus shakes his head.

'Count us in,' Lolana says, standing in gargoyle form with Demona.

'All you gargoyles should be resting! Lysander?'

'Jasmine is right. If the rebels are four hours away that means they'll get here close to dusk. It gives us enough time to be at our best. If the plan changes come and tell me, Laz,' Lysander says, placing his hand on Lazarus' shoulder before heading upstairs.

The gargoyles disappear to the roof and the dragons stand around the lounge room planning their counterattack. I sneak out, heading for Blue Boy. If I get to the rebels early, surprising them, I can kill their leader. It may make them think twice about attacking my family.

I reach Blue Boy and slip on his bridle.

'Jasmine, where are you going?' Kite asks, standing in front of me.

'I want to get Blue away from any danger.' I fumble with the leather straps of the bridle.

'You are a terrible lair.'

'So I've been told. But if I surprise the rebels, I can take out a few of them, and then the attack won't be so severe. Or they

may turn back. It also gives the gargoyles more time to refuel.'
I throw my leg over Blue Boy's bare back.

'Lazarus!' she yells and I glare hard at her.

In a split second, Lazarus has me whipped off the horse's back and in his arms. He slowly slides me down his body.

'She was about to—'

'I know exactly what she was stupidly about to do. I heard every stupid word. Give me a minute alone with her please, Kite,' he says through gritted teeth.

'You said "stupid" twice,' I snap.

'Because you are being absolutely stupid!'

'I can't let you fight. I can't lose you!'

'Oh, babe, I won't be going anywhere. Stop thinking you can take on the world. There are sorcerers coming and we know nothing of their powers.'

'I know they're not as strong as me. Ethan told me that before I...' I gasp at the memory.

'I don't believe I am saying this because I don't want you anywhere near the fighting, but we will do this together. You and I, we are a team in love and life and we will fight together.'

'When I said I didn't trust dragons, you know I didn't mean you or Corbin.'

'I know but hearing it still twinged at my heartstrings. I explained to Corbin that he was excluded from your comment, which relieved him. As hurt as you may be, you should be careful how you say things. We dragons get offended easily.'

'You're right, I never meant to hurt either of you. Funnily enough, I believe I can trust Falcon, but I will never say it to his face. That would be just too nice.'

He kisses me hard and passionately, desperate to show me how much he cares. I return the kiss with as much passion.

He pulls back, his lime-green eyes locking with mine.

'I must be the luckiest creature alive to love you.' He looks at my lips. 'Your lips are so swollen and rosy from crying.' His grip tightens as he presses his hot mouth to mine.

We are lost in our own little world for a very short time, but one I will remember. I am desperately in love with this man and I will do everything in my power to protect him.

CHAPTER ELEVEN

THE WAITING GAME is nerve-wracking. The dragons, who are in human form, are pacing the lounge room at a fast pace, stopping now and then to sniff the air and listen. I pick at my fingernails impatiently, expecting the rebels any minute.

Several loud howls break the deathly silence.

'They're at Nogard Hollow and are now heading our way. We need to get into position,' Corbin yells.

Lazarus is gone in a flash and returns in less than a heartbeat.

'I've alerted the gargoyles,' he says. 'Let's go, and remember to keep clear of Jasmine.' He nods to Malinda, Kite and Bell, then turns to look at me. 'Stay close to me, do you understand?'

'I do and I trust you.'

He grabs my hand and tugs me out the door of the castle. Flashes and red swirls fill the air as Falcon and Corbin change form. The other three pass me and, within seconds, change form.

'I love you so don't do anything silly.' Lazarus kisses me quickly.

'Ditto!' I force myself to contain my emotions.

He changes form and, in seconds, he is kneeling for me to climb up. He nuzzles his nose under my bottom and flicks me onto his back. I quickly settle so he can take off with the others.

In one mighty downward thrust of his wings, we're elevated into the air. With several large thrusts, he is beside Corbin.

'I trust you with my life, Corbin,' I yell and he growls and blinks at me. 'You are like a brother.' He roars, and it has a good vibration to it. I smile and he blinks again.

I rub between Lazarus' shoulders then lean down and open my arms to hold what I can of him. 'I love you,' I whisper. He rumbles and it rattles through his body.

The dragons land with the castle still in close proximity. Corbin took Blue Boy and his horses around the back so they are out of harm's way. I look back at the castle and they are well hidden.

I slide down Lazarus and watch as the dragons spread out. They are in an attack stance so I need to be wary of their sharp spear tails. They are all here for one reason and that is to kill.

Kite walks past, sniffing me, giving me a small nudge to show she is in control around me.

'Stay safe, Kite.' I wish I could say more but her brother's betrayal is fresh in my mind.

She blinks and moves to the far side of Lazarus. He and Falcon stand either side of me.

The roar of the rebels echoes across the land like a pack of hungry lions. I swallow hard and close my eyes before echoing to my loved ones. As I picture them, I feel my powers decrease.

'We will fight beside you, Jasmine. You are so powerful that there's enough energy for us to do so,' Grandfather echoes. I open my eyes, and on either side of me is a ghostly outline of my grandfather and Sky. I embrace them both, but I don't know how they appeared.

'You drew on us to be here, so here we are. Try not to work it out now. We have a rebellion to bring down,' Grandfather says.

Falcon rumbles in his large vibrant body. Sky walks to his side and places her hand on his front leg.

'I have missed you as well, Falcon. Take care, my friend,' Sky says and then returns to my side.

'Your powers are divided between the three of us. If you become

weak, draw us back in, and you will have your full powers back. Do you understand, Jazzy?' Grandfather says.

'Yes. I love you both.' I try to focus on what is in front of me.

'We know. We hear you every day. Now let's kick some rebel butt.' He laughs, reaching over to hold my hand. Sky does the same and I feel my powers increase.

Paul runs past, briefly stopping to acknowledge Grandfather, 'G'day, old mate. I feel a lot better now I know you're here.'

'Stay sharp, Paul, and take care, my friend.'

The impact on my nerves is enormous when I see the sky filled with large red dragons with flames billowing out of their mouths. The sound scatters the wildlife below.

Malinda takes off, flying towards them. She wants to see if she can talk her husband down. But by the greeting she's given, I presume he declines her offer. She dodges a warning flame, scurrying out of the way of the pack.

Grandfather and Sky release my hands and I instantly feel the drain. Digging my feet into the earth, I roll my shoulders back and open my hands as wide as I can. Ash startles me by moving his large gargoyle frame in front of us. I sense the other gargoyles as they spread out behind the dragons. Jet and Lysander move so they are standing in between Sky and me. Lysander's glowing blue eyes smile and wink at Sky.

'Hello, my love,' Sky says sweetly, and I hear a soft warm rumble come from Lysander's chest.

I force back my feelings and draw up a bubbling pair of anorics through my body, as do Grandfather and Sky. I concentrate on drawing bright colours and leaving the dark ones to simmer. I know I can draw on them if I need to.

Several of the gargoyles are gliding above and heading straight for the dragons. Out of the corner of my eye, I see a large wedge-tailed eagle. It's my guardian angel, gliding above me, circling and screeching loudly.

'Hello, my friend. Keep your distance,' I whisper, before dropping my eyes back to the enemy.

The dragons take off with a gust of air that blows me back several feet. The sky is filled with bright red dragons and bursts of orange flames.

I set my sights on one dragon who is fighting with Kite. I take a steady aim and fire at it, hitting it square in the gut. It flails and quickly glides to the ground. Several gargoyles take off, heading for where it lands, completing my kill.

Grandfather and Sky are doing the same. Some anorics are connecting and some are not.

A dragon lands close by and two humans clamber down from his back. One is a female and one male.

'That's Kyle and Tania! They are dark sorcerers. Watch out, they play dirty,' Sky yells.

I nod and reduce the distance between them and me. Sky and Grandfather follow behind me. They continue to throw anorics at the dragons above so I can concentrate on the sorcerers. I can feel every anoric they throw drawing up through my body, slowly draining me.

I run at the two sorcerers who are standing hand in hand. I throw directly at them and hit them both solidly in their chests. They fall backwards lifeless. Yes!

'No way, that was too easy. It's a trick,' Sky shouts.

I spin around and the same two sorcerers stand hand in hand behind me. The female has already released an anoric, which is heading straight for me. In less than a blink, I draw back the energy I've been sharing with Sky and Grandfather and they disappear from sight.

My guardian eagle is in front of me, wings spread wide, protecting me from the oncoming anoric. It's hit it in the back, forcing it to collide with me, pushing us backwards onto the ground.

I look into the eyes of the eagle and recognise its warm comforting stare. It has the eyes of someone I know, someone I love, but I can't connect the two.

'Thank you, my guardian angel. I owe you my life,' I whisper. Its eyes close and its wings, which are covering my entire body, go limp.

A bright purple colour flashes between us before a hot surge floods my body. I'm receiving the creature's power. In an instant, I feel the courage and strength to fight on.

I wiggle out from under the eagle to find the two sorcerers heading towards me. I shoot to my feet and draw up from the earth every colour I can see. Stones and rocks lift from the ground, my hands filling with black anorics the size of basketballs.

I scream and throw them towards my two enemies, creating a large hole in the male's torso, killing him instantly. I miss the female. She leans over the male's dead body and draws in his powers.

I take advantage of the distraction and throw another at her, hitting her hard in the shoulder and ripping her arm from its pit.

She falls to the ground and I race over to her. 'Why do you have to kill another creature? Why do you fight for King?'

I look up in time to see an aggressive dragon bearing down on me, its mouth wide and razor-sharp. I drop and roll, avoiding its mouth and large talons. Its tail slaps the ground beside me, the impact making my body jump off the ground.

The sorceress slowly staggers to her feet, brewing up an evil batch in her open palm. 'There is one greater than you, Jasmine.' She smirks.

I create a barrier over me; a power Paul recently showed me. As I finish, her anoric crashes against its exterior.

'Maybe, but it's not you! I was going to let you live, witch, but now you've just ticked me off.' I fire off my anorics and hit her face-on.

I spin around to see who my next victim is. The ground's littered with wounded gargoyles and dragons. My heart pounds uncontrollably as I scan the sky for Lazarus. I spot him fighting a large dragon.

I hear the loud growl of a gargoyle and see Jet on the back of a dragon, ripping its wings to shreds. His powerful blade claws and razor-sharp jaw make light work of it and the dragon arrows towards the ground.

Jet glides off its back before it hits the unforgiving earth. He pounds it with large anoric boulders as he glides above it, rendering it helpless.

I wonder how he can draw anorics when he's not grounded. He is a true mixture of gargoyle and sorcerer. He stands over the dead dragon and I pray he's not drawing in its powers.

Lolana has been badly injured. Paul is shielding her from any further attacks.

Without warning, I am scooped up in the arms of a gargoyle. Ash's quick move gets me out of the direct line of an oncoming dragon.

'Stay focused,' he growls at me, setting me down then turning to confront the dragon.

Lazarus lands with the large dragon still in pursuit of him. I run as fast as my legs will carry me. I draw up the devil himself, feeling the dark energy fill me. I throw one after another like I did when I killed Ethan.

The dragon fires at me and I feel it burn but I keep running and throwing. My hands are cold as if I am holding ice blocks and in my peripheral vision, I see they are as black as the ace of spades.

I can't stop even though the dragon's heartbeat is fading.

I keep on throwing. I want this creature dead, especially as it was trying to kill Lazarus.

With two outstretched hands, I raise his limp body into the air. I drop it down hard, splattering its blood over any nearby creature. I lift it again and listen for its beat; there's none. I drop it hard. I want it deader than dead!

Its head is last to hit the ground with an almighty thud. Its tongue hangs out of its bloody mouth, its eyes lifeless and open.

I lift it again but a cool hand on my shoulder stills me. 'Jasmine, it's over. Don't become one of them.' Jet's voice is gruff but soft.

'Too late!' I drop the dead dragon to the ground with an almighty thud. The air becomes quiet and the sky a royal blue. All I can hear is the rapid beating of my heart and my breath whistling past my teeth. I'm beyond exhausted and use the little energy I have to stand. There is not a dragon in the sky, but the ground is littered with death.

In dragon form, Lazarus walks cautiously towards me, keeping his eyes locked on my hands. I glance at them and they are frozen black. I open them to show him they are empty.

'I am sorry,' I whisper. He has seen my dark side and I'm ashamed.

'Let me take you back to the castle. You don't need to be here for the clean-up,' Ash says, picking me up in his large gargoyle arms.

'I should help,' I mutter, but I'm exhausted and my body collapses.

'We'll collect our families' golden souls and burn the remains, together with the dragons. There is nothing you can do.' He places his cool lips to my forehead and gently kisses me.

'There is an eagle that was killed. Please give it a separate burial. I have a connection to it.'

He wraps his large wings around me and carries me into

the castle. As soon as he leaves, I race to the roof where I can witness my family at work cleaning up the bloody site.

As far as I can see there is a haze of red. Even the tall gum trees are littered with the colour. There are no high fives or hitting fisted knuckles. This is not a victory any of us are proud of.

Lazarus is standing where the large eagle fell. I close my eyes and concentrate on the warm purple energy I received form it when it died. Its warm eyes mysteriously match the loving colour of my mother's. I see clearly into its soul and feel the love that only my mother would give.

'No!' I pant, trying to control the sudden urge to vomit when I realise who the eagle is. I race down the stairs and out the doors of the castle. I scream and run like I am being chased by the devil, heading towards the lifeless eagle.

Lazarus charges for me, catching me in his solid arms.

'Let me go! Let me go!' I kick and scream at him.

'You don't want to see her, Jasmine. Please.'

But I keep kicking and fighting to get out of his hold. He wraps his arms around me tightly, holding me firmly to his body. My body goes limp, my head falling backwards, and I sob hysterically.

Lysander wraps my mother's body in a blanket then cradles her in his large arms. He walks over but I can't see her clearly through my tears.

'I'm sorry, Jasmine.' Lysander's tone is distraught. 'We will bury your mother alongside Sky.'

'No!' I feel my heart pounding up through my throat. My body surges with an earthly power I can't control. The build-up is so intense I feel like I am suffocating.

An almighty electric shock releases internally, then nothing.

I WAKE WARM and cosy in Sky's bed with Lazarus gazing at me. 'Hey, babe, how do you feel?'

'My mother. Was it a dream?'

'I'm sorry, babe. She has been laid to rest beside Sky. Paul has left to tell your father.'

'I should be the one to tell him.' My eyes fill with fresh tears.

'You're not in any state to do anything.' Lazarus forces a smile to his lips. He runs his bandaged hands over my forehead.

'You're hurt!' I spring up. His arms and hands are bandaged and his bare chest is badly burnt. 'Who did this to you?'

'It doesn't matter. I will heal in time.'

'How many of our family are gone?'

'Lolana was hurt but is healing as we speak. Six of the gargoyle relatives died.'

'Ash, Jet, Lysander, Corbin, Falcon, Demona…?'

'They have a few bumps and bruises but will heal in time. A few of the rebels escaped but we are keeping tabs on their whereabouts. I don't think this war is over but at least this fight is for now.' He leans close and kisses my temple. 'My concern is you.'

'Did you kill the mongrel that burnt you?'

'Enough about me. Do you think you're ready to visit your mother's grave?'

I nod before bursting into a flood of tears. He draws the blankets back and I slide my legs out. My markings are darker than I have ever seen them and now there's a purple vine running up the middle of my left leg. It's my mother's energy; her loving soul is embedded in me.

I smile and remember how often I saw the eagle flying over me. I now realise it was my mother watching over me. She used her powers even though she said she didn't. Maybe she was protecting my father and me by keeping it a secret.

The castle is dark with only a few candles lighting up the area where people are sitting. The mumbling stops when I come down the stairs.

Jet stands the instant he sees me, as does Ash. They meet me at the bottom of the stairs and Jet is the first to hug me. His hold his firm as he presses his lips to the top of my head.

'I'm sorry for your loss, Aunt Jazz.' His tone is full of sorrow.

I nod and force a small smile, as my words are lodged firmly in my throat. He releases me and another set of arms encase me. Ash has me in a big bear hug, lifting me off my feet.

'You did well today. Your mother would have been proud of you. I'm proud of you, especially since you did my job for me and singed Lazarus.' He sniggers.

I spin around and with shocked eyes, stare Lazarus directly in the face. 'Did I do that to you?' My breath chokes me.

'Oh sheesh, Laz. I thought she knew. I didn't mean to upset—'

'Shut it, Ash!' Lazarus says, holding up his bandaged hand.

I take off, running for the front door. I make it out, but only just. Lazarus has me caught in his burnt arms. The arms I burnt!

'You are right. We're no good for each other. If you don't kill me, I will kill you!'

'Shh, you're emotional and I'm not leaving you so stop trying to run away. I'm too quick for you anyway,' he says, talking into my hair.

'How did I do this to you?' I wrap my arms around him, fresh tears rolling down my cheeks.

'It was my own fault. I felt you building up and thought it was going to be like the little shocks you give me when… well, when we are kissing. But this felt stronger and you exploded and sent an electrical current that would light up the caves at Nogard Hollow.'

'Holy hell, look at what I have done to you.' I step back to see his chest peeling and bubbled. He drops his head. 'You can't look me in the eye. And why would you want to after you saw me lose control, killing and devouring more than one dragon?'

'Oh, babe, I can do more than look at you in the eye. These burns are nothing. I will heal quickly. We are connected in here.' He places his hand over my heart. 'Our souls are connected. You can't get rid of me even if you try to. We need to stop running away from each other, instead run to each other in times of need.'

'I would never hurt you on purpose.' I cup his face in my hands.

'And I am madly in love with you.' He leans in and presses his lips on mine for a soft, gentle kiss.

I spend the majority of the night sitting beside my mother's and cousin's graves. The tranquillity of the night is shattered by the howling cries of the dingoes. They're mourning the loss of little Nelly. I feel dehydrated from crying.

Lazarus wants to take me home to Nogard Hollow, but I'm scared of the reaction I may receive after what I did. I was told that the large dragon I pounded into the ground was Kite and Bell's father; Malinda's husband. I may put a spell on my bedroom door preventing anyone from entering, just as a precaution.

Lazarus is waiting outside the house when I drive over. I wanted to bring most of my private belongings, not that I own that much. His smile reassures me that all is well in the dragon household.

I nervously enter to find everyone sitting in the lounge room in human form. Falcon is the first to approach me with his arms open wide, welcoming me into his hold. 'Welcome home. How are you feeling?'

'Fine, thanks. How are you?'

'We're getting there,' he says, holding his grin firm. His body is black and blue with bruises.

'Jasmine,' says Kite, standing beside me quicker than I could hear. 'I miss you.' She opens her arms, nodding as if to ask permission to hug me. I nod and smile and we embrace as best friends do.

Corbin and Bell both embrace me before running off together, heading out to meet Lolana and Jet. I smile, knowing they are keenly awaiting their arrival.

Malinda stands and nods but keeps her distance. 'It's good to see you, Jasmine. Forgive me for not embracing you but I need more time to digest what has happened.'

'I am so sorry for… If I had known it was your husband…'

'You would have done exactly the same, as you should when someone is trying to kill your loved one,' she says, smiling at Lazarus. 'I don't blame you and I'm not angry or going to take revenge. I just need time to mourn the death of my son and husband as you do your mother, Drake, Sky and Nelly.'

'I understand.' I drop my eyes to my twiddling hands. I hear her leave, change form and head down to the cave.

I turn to see Lazarus' hands filled with my bags, nodding at me to follow him to my bedroom.

'Before you leave, I wanted to talk to you,' Falcon says, grasping my arm.

'Sure.' I smile.

'I want things between us to be comfortable. I suppose I'm asking if you would consider us having a friendship of sorts.'

'I already consider you as my friend, Falcon. We both love and care for the same people and I believe we have both learnt a hard lesson in life.' I give him a sympathetic smile before reaching up to kiss him on the cheek.

'All right, enough of that!' Lazarus says sternly.

Both Falcon and I shake our heads before I follow Lazarus. 'I trust you, Falcon.' I whisper over my shoulder and I hear his lips curve into a huge smile.

Lazarus walks me into a different bedroom. 'Whose room is this?'

'This is our new room—yours and mine.'

It's decorated similar to the last bedroom but its larger, with views as far as the eye can see.

'Why the change of bedroom?'

'I know you find it hard to relax here, so I wanted to start fresh, with a room that has no memories.'

'Hmm, I'd like to make some new memories right now.'

In a blink, he has me in his arms. 'Jazz,' he whistles through his teeth.

'You need to stop moving around so quickly. You make my head spin.'

He nuzzles into my neck and runs his warm lips along my collarbone, his breath warming me inside and out.

'That's what all the girls say.'

'Is that so, dragon?' I pretend to snap. 'Remember who you're talking to and what I can do.'

'Oh, babe, what am I going to do with your jealous tendencies?'

'I have one thing in mind.' I nip his earlobe. He growls and I quickly cover us in a privacy spell before he throws me on the soft feather bed.

Lazarus rolls out of bed and kisses my forehead before heading for the bathroom. Minutes later, he comes out smiling.

'This room also has a large free-standing bath. I've got the tub filling for you with some essential oils Xandria picked up for me.'

'A bath?'

'I was going to show you it before, but you magically lured me to the bed.'

'Are you complaining, dragon?'

'Hm, never, witch.' He pulls back the bedsheet and holds his hand out for me. I place my hand in his and he tugs me hard, making me fly into his heated arms. 'Damn you're beautiful.'

'You're not too bad yourself.' I reach up and kiss his divine lips.

My mind wanders and Lazarus pulls back with a questioning brow. 'If my mother could change form, and since I have inherited her powers, I should be able to do the same.'

'She was known as a shapeshifter and yes, you will inherit it. What you can shift into no one will know until it happens. I'd wait until you can speak with your grandfather as he could also shift, not that he did it often.

'You may have always been able to shift due to her blood running through you. You will need someone to guide you through the changes, as it's different for me, as I am first a dragon and second a human.'

'And what a handsome human you make.'

Lazarus walks me backwards, never loosening his strong grip around my waist. He stops when we are in the bathroom and spins me around. He has small tea light candles sitting in colourful glass jars spotted all around the room. It smells heavenly, which shocks me as I would have thought Xandria would buy something I would despise just to annoy me. 'You did this just for me?'

'Yes, because I am crazy about you.' He pulls me back into his embrace, my back to his front.

'Are you sure you're not soaking in oils then sprinkling me with salt and pepper so you can eat me?'

'As much as your beating heart excites my taste buds and a

few other areas, I don't want to eat you.' He smiles against my skin. 'I want to *devour* you.' He growls and playfully bites my neck, sending a warm adrenaline rush through my veins. 'Hm, you are delicious.'

Rolling my head back on the rim of the bath, I close my eyes and inhale the aroma of the essential oils. I'm quick to drift into a calm and relaxed state, the only noise being the flicker of the candles.

'Did Xandria choose well?'

'Yes, Xandria. You chose very well.' I smile, keeping my eyes tightly closed. I hear her move next to my head and sit on the bath's edge, splashing her feet into the water. 'I don't mean to be rude, but I am trying to relax.'

'Xandria knows, but she has a secret.'

'If it doesn't have anything to do with me, I don't want to know.'

'Oh, but it does. Is your privacy screen still up?'

'Yes, it should be.' I open my eyes, curious as to what information she has. 'What is your secret?'

'Did you get a surprise when you saw Xandria in human form?'

'Yes, I did, but what is the secret?' I'm annoyed she is interrupting my blissful bath.

'Jasmine is so impatient.' She huffs. 'Someone special to you will take you on a date.'

'I presume you mean Lazarus.'

'Yes. But there's more to the secret.'

'And?'

'There is a question you must answer. You must dig deep into your heart and soul to find the answer. Look at Xandria, as she will give you a clue. What does Xandria remind you of?' She is standing up and in her hands is one long-stemmed single flower. Her two hands hold it in front of her, belly-high. She walks the rim of the bath, stuttering her walk.

'Xandria, can you speak plain English and tell me what the darn question is and why is it such a bloody secret?'

She throws the flower into the bathwater, placing her small hands on her petite hips. 'You have offended Xandria so she will not tell you any more. All she wants is to be your friend, human, but you snarl at her and hurt her feelings.'

'I'm sorry, Xandria, but you never get to the point and your stories lead me into trouble.'

'This was not a story; it was the truth. You will have to wait to find out the secret because Xandria is leaving.' She flutters her wings and flies off, slipping under the door.

I shake my head, confused, and roll my head back to enjoy the bath my favourite dragon has set up for me.

I must have dozed off when a gentle tap on the door wakes me. The water in the bath has cooled and several candles have gone out.

'Babe, are you still in the bath?' Lazarus questions through the door.

'Yes, I'm getting out now.'

'Malinda has cooked dinner, even though we dragons have already eaten.'

'I'm not hungry. I was going to slip back into bed and was hoping you'd join me.'

'She has gone out of her way to cook. It would be nice if you pretended to enjoy it.'

'I suppose I could eat a little something.' I sigh.

'Thank you, babe.' I hear his smile through the door.

'Xandria visited me and told me I was going on a date. I presume the gentleman taking me is you.' I wrap a warm towel around me.

The door flings open and Lazarus stands tall in front of

me. 'I am the only man you are ever going on date with.' His eyes are glowing. 'What else did our precious little tattle-tale say?'

'Nothing I could understand. Why, do you have a secret?'

'Maybe I do, maybe I don't. You, my delicious-smelling baby, will have to wait. I will take you somewhere special tomorrow for a picnic lunch.' He sneaks slowly towards me. 'I hear that's what humans do on dates.' He leans over and kisses the tip of my nose.

I pout, as I was hoping he would kiss me.

'If I kiss you, we will be late for dinner and everyone is waiting.'

'Let them wait.' I walk my two hands around his taut waist.

I WAKE EXCITED that I am going on a date with Lazarus. He has been busy all morning in the kitchen with Malinda. I can smell freshly roasted chicken and baked bread. My mouth waters with anticipation.

He was going to fly me to the undisclosed picnic area, but he changed his mind. He wants to spend time talking in the car as he thinks I will have plenty of things to talk about on the way back. I'm intrigued.

He packs the picnic and we head out, driving for over three hours. It would've only taken us a third of the time if we flew. He pulls the truck up alongside the river. As I step out, I can hear running water. I listen further and realise it's a waterfall.

I carry a blanket and Lazarus the picnic basket. There is a stunning twenty-metre-tall waterfall. Dropping our gear and stripping to our underwear, we walk into the cool water.

Lazarus confidently swims over to and under the fall. I watch as he comes out of the surging water and shakes the droplets from his dark hair. His eyes are illuminated against the backdrop of the waterfall, making my heart skip a beat at his handsome beauty.

I dive in and swim over to him and together we head under the fall. We swim until my fingers and toes are wrinkly.

We devour the picnic and I notice Lazarus is nervous and jumpy. I turn my emotions off and use my senses to listen out for any danger. I know he would have had the area checked out before he brought me here. He would never put me in danger if the rebels were close by. There is nothing I can sense, so his jittery behaviour is uncalled for and makes me question his mood.

I lie down and soak up the hot sun rays when he pulls out a small box, placing it on my stomach.

'What's this?'

'A gift. Open it.' His gaze is guarded.

I grab the small box and sit up. I flip it open and see the most spectacular ring. It is silver in colour and exactly the kind of ring Lazarus would give. The stunning design has a dragon wrapping around the finger with the tail and mouth coming together on top. In the dragon's open mouth sits a glistening red ruby and in its curled tail is a striking white diamond.

'Oh, Laz! It is stunning!'

'Do you like it?' He smiles but still seems a little nervous. His body heats to boiling point, radiating to mine.

'Who wouldn't?'

He removes the ring from the box and takes my left hand in his. My heart is beating wildly, and suddenly, like a light switch being turned on, I realise what Xandria was trying to tell me. Lazarus was the one who had a question to ask me and she was giving me a clue by pretending to hold a wedding bouquet. My eyes grow wide, anxious and excited, anticipating his words.

'I love you with every breath I take. You are my reason for living and why I wake each day happy to be alive. You are my world, you are the love of my life and it would make me a very ecstatic dragon if you will marry me.'

'I… I…'

'Jasmine?' His tone is slightly alarmed.

'Yes, of course I will marry you. I'm trying to think of something as beautiful to say as you just did, but I'm too excited. Yes, yes and yes!'

He sighs loudly, showing his relief, and eagerly slides the dragon ring onto my ring finger. The ruby sparkles in the sunlight as the diamond reflects into my eye.

'You are the love *of* my life. And I would be an ecstatic little witch to be your wife.' I smile and kiss his waiting lips. 'You are my reason for living but you are not my world, you are my universe, and without you, I would no longer be able to breathe. We are inked!

'I remember the first day I saw you. I ran my eyes over your naked chest and handsome features wondering if I had received a knock to my head as you were one very good-looking man. And when you kissed me for the first time I nearly passed out. I can still feel the adrenaline rush that flooded my body. It made me weak at the knees.' I smile cheekily. 'I thought I knew what it was like to be in love, but I was wrong. It wasn't until I fell in love with you that I knew. Every atom in my body sings and dances when I touch and kiss you. And when we make love… oh boy, I explode!'

'I know, babe. I've felt it and have a few scars to prove it.' He chuckles.

'I believe a kiss is nature's clever way of telling us there are no more words to express our feelings, as a loving kiss speaks louder than words.' I lock my eyes onto his emerald green ones. He leans in and presses his hot rosy lips to mine, allowing nature to do the talking.